"But first, I do believe it is customary to seal our engagement with a kiss?"

Before she could think to respond, he lowered his head.

Whatever fears had been simmering in her brain were forgotten at the feel of his lips on hers. How was it possible, she thought in the one corner of her brain still capable of coherency, that something could feel firm and soft all at once?

Then he tilted his head, deepening the kiss as his arms came about her, dragging her against the hard length of his body. The last of her mental faculties disappeared into the ether and her body came alive. Perhaps, just perhaps, being married to this man might not be so bad after all.

Praise for Christina Britton and Her Novels

"First-rate Regency fun!"
—Grace Burrowes, *New York Times* bestselling author

"This is a knockout."
—*Publishers Weekly* on *A Duke Worth Fighting For*, starred review

"Moving and heartfelt."
—*Kirkus Reviews* on *Someday My Duke Will Come*

"Swoonworthy romance."
—*Publishers Weekly* on *Someday My Duke Will Come*

"Christina Britton proves she has mastered the craft of engaging Regency romance."
—*Shelf Awareness* on *Someday My Duke Will Come*

"Readers will be hooked."
—*Publishers Weekly* on *A Good Duke Is Hard to Find*, starred review

"This was my first book by Christina Britton. It won't be my last."
—TheRomanceDish.com on *A Good Duke Is Hard to Find*

Some Dukes Have All the Luck

CHRISTINA BRITTON

FOREVER

NEW YORK BOSTON

Copyright © 2022 by Christina Silverio

Cover art by Judy York. Cover design by Daniela Medina. Cover photography © Rick Gomez Photography. Cover copyright © 2022 by Hachette Book Group, Inc.

Forever
Hachette Book Group
1290 Avenue of the Americas, New York, NY 10104
read-forever.com
twitter.com/readforeverpub

First Edition: November 2022

Forever is an imprint of Grand Central Publishing. The Forever name and logo are trademarks of Hachette Book Group, Inc.

The publisher is not responsible for websites (or their content) that are not owned by the publisher.

The Hachette Speakers Bureau provides a wide range of authors for speaking events. To find out more, go to www.hachettespeakersbureau.com or call (866) 376-6591.

ISBNs: 9781538710401 (mass market), 9781538710418 (ebook)

Printed in the United States of America

OPM

10 9 8 7 6 5 4 3 2 1

ATTENTION CORPORATIONS AND ORGANIZATIONS:

Most Hachette Book Group books are available at quantity discounts with bulk purchase for educational, business, or sales promotional use. For information, please call or write:

Special Markets Department, Hachette Book Group
1290 Avenue of the Americas, New York, NY 10104
Telephone: 1-800-222-6747 Fax: 1-800-477-5925

*Dedicated with love to Gerry O'Hara.
I can never thank you enough for
nurturing the dreams I confided in you
when I was a teenager and just trying
out my writing wings. Your
encouragement helped me to fly.*

Acknowledgments

I am so very grateful to my readers for welcoming the Isle and its romantic misfits into your hearts. Because of you, I get to write more stories set on my beloved Synne. You all mean the world to me.

Thank you to my fabulous agent Kim Lionetti, my amazing editor Madeleine Colavita, and everyone at Grand Central Forever for working so enthusiastically on my books, including Ambriah, Dana, Luria, and so many more. And thank you to my Forever sisters, Bethany Bennett, Samara Parish, Emily Sullivan, and Kate Pembrooke, for your amazing support. I'm so blessed to work with you all.

Thank you to the friends and family who have supported me. A special thanks to Jayci Lee for always being there for me to bounce ideas off of and for always showering me with love no matter if I'm crying in despair or shouting with happiness. And thank you to Cathy, for being such a fabulous cheerleader when I need it most, and for reading through a (very) rough first draft of this book and giving me just the encouragement I needed to finish it.

And, of course, a huge thank you to my husband and children, for dealing with my angst and stress and always making certain I have what I need to write, whether it's supplies or privacy or emotional support—even if I *still* haven't put a sword with a secret compartment in the hilt in one of my stories. I love you so much.

Author's Note

SOME DUKES HAVE ALL THE LUCK contains content that may distress some readers. For content warnings, please visit my website:

http://christinabritton.com/bookshelf/content-warnings/

Affectionately Yours,
Christina Britton

Some Dukes Have
All the Luck

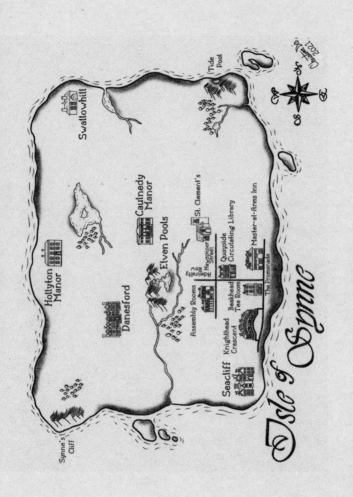

Isle of Synne

Swallowhill

Tide Pool

Cautnedy Manor

Elven Pools

St. Clement's

Hollyton Manor

Haypgier Street

Quayside Circulating Library

Adelaide Row

Master-at-Arms Inn

Danesford

Assembly Rooms

Beakhead Tea Room

The Promenade

Knighthead Crescent

Seacliff

Synne's Cliff

Chaldon 2021

Chapter 1

London, June 1820

W hat the hell is *she* doing here?"

Ash Hawkins, Duke of Buckley, cast a glance in his partner's direction before returning his attention to the deed in his hand, another nobleman's family treasure sacrificed to the gambling gods. Hope was a fickle mistress, and Ash had benefited from misplaced optimism on more occasions than he could count. This time was no exception, if the property laid out in the deed was any indication.

"I'm certain whatever female has entered these sin-filled halls has every right to be here," he murmured, though it was more from habit now than anything else. Augustus Beecher was not known for his charm, after all, and no amount of correction was going to stop him from having his say. His passionate, abrasive nature, so different from Ash's own cold control, had worked to their benefit, and so Ash could not begrudge him his constant state of pique. Ash himself was just as tenacious and determined as his partner was, but where he had developed rudimentary social skills to infiltrate the ranks of nobles, Beecher was the brawn behind the scenes, using his intense ruthlessness to their advantage. With one owner from the highest echelons of society and the other from the deepest bowels of Seven Dials, the partnership was ideal, having turned their faltering gaming hell into one of the premiere gambling clubs in London.

That was not to say Ash didn't think Beecher wasn't a blustering blowhard most of the time. Especially in moments like these when the man, not one to couch his words on a good day, refused to be ignored.

"This particular female is an exception," he said darkly. "Even you with your progressive thinking will agree." He turned away from the wall of windows to glare at Ash. "I thought we agreed your wards were not to set foot in Brimstone."

Ash's head snapped up. "My wards?" he barked, lurching to his feet and striding to where Beecher stood looking down on the gaming floor. "They're here?"

"One is," his partner replied in his deep rasp, pointing his lit cheroot toward the long line of tables that stretched across the floor. "The serious one."

But even without Beecher pointing her out, Ash would have seen Regina. The girl stood out from the ostentatiously dressed lords and ladies who clambered for places at his tables, her simple gray gown at odds with the garish riches about her. Frustration mounted in him. Damnation, he had told her, he had told *all* of them, that Brimstone was no place for them. Not only were they much too young, but this place was too dangerous, too immoral. And he had vowed to protect his wards, a promise he had made to the woman who had for all intents and purposes been their grandmother, and it was a vow he would not break.

Yet there was Regina, the eldest of the lot at just sixteen, striding through the throng as if she were doing something as innocuous as walking the halls of her beloved British Museum. Just then an inebriated gentleman grabbed her arm, swinging her about. Before Ash could react, Regina lifted one dainty foot and slammed her heel down on the man's instep.

Beecher's rough laugh, so little used, rumbled through the spacious wood-paneled office as the man who had dared to lay a hand on Regina, hopping about on one foot, howled in pain below. "I don't like your wards being here one bit," Beecher said. "But damn if that isn't the funniest thing I've seen in a long while."

Ash shot him an acidic glare. "I'm so glad a young girl being accosted brings you amusement," he bit out before striding from the room, slamming the door behind him. With each step he took down the narrow stairs, his agitation grew. Regina had better have a damn good reason for disobeying him.

He threw open the door to the gaming floor, and there stood a flushed but furious Regina. Before he could drag her away from prying eyes, however, she spoke, proving to him that she actually *did* have a good reason for being at Brimstone. A very good reason indeed.

"Eliza and Nelly have run away."

* * *

A week later and that simple sentence still had the ability to rock the very foundation of Ash's world.

He paced his office at Brimstone, a path he had walked almost constantly since hearing of his two younger wards' flights from home. It was a wonder that he hadn't worn a rut straight down to the floor beneath.

"Dammit, Beecher," he growled. "What good are your connections if you cannot utilize them to locate two young girls?"

"My informants are used to tracking people, not spawns of Satan," his partner grumbled, the leather of his chair creaking as he shifted.

"If I wasn't in complete agreement," Ash drawled, stopping in his tracks and shooting the other man a glare, "I would punch you in your blasted mouth for that insult."

Beecher snorted. "As if you could get a punch in."

Despite himself, a bark of laughter broke free from Ash's lips. But he quickly sobered. Beecher knew all too well that Ash had not raised his hand to another soul since shortly after his mother's death, when he'd nearly killed his father in his rage.

He made his way to the seat across from his partner, sinking heavily into it. "Plenty have before me, if the shape of your face is any indication," he shot back, determined to forget the constant burden of being his father's son, holding on to the moment of levity so he might get his head back on straight. Or as straight as possible under the circumstances. Which was not very straight at all.

"Touché," Beecher murmured, his mouth crooking up at one corner as he rubbed the bridge of his nose, which had seen more than one punishing break in its day.

All too soon, however, the lighter mood passed. Beecher took a deep draught of his whiskey, scrubbing his blunt fingernails over his closely shorn hair. For the first time Ash noticed just how ragged and unkempt the man looked—or, rather, more unkempt than usual. And no wonder, for he'd put in an incredible amount of effort over the past sennight in attempting to help Ash locate his wards. Ash felt a pang of guilt for snapping at his friend; as much as Beecher swore that the girls were the bane of his existence, he had been nearly as frantic to locate them as Ash himself had been. He pressed his lips tight. Guilt was nothing new to him; he may as well add this particular remorse to the ever-present— and ever-growing—pile that he was constantly buried under.

Even so, he could not let his unfeeling rudeness slide. "I'm sorry, Beecher," he said gruffly. Suddenly weary beyond belief, he leaned his head back and ran a hand over his eyes. "I shouldn't have taken my anger out on you."

Beecher grunted. "You've a reason, I daresay. And don't think I'm not beating myself up over it as well. I've never come across anything like this before. I've got every one of my informants searching, and they haven't come up with a damn thing. I don't understand it. How do two slips of girls disappear without a single trace?"

The panic that had clung to Ash since he'd first learned of the girls' disappearance wrapped its tentacles around his neck, squeezing hard. It had kept him up every night since, with horrible visions of his wards hurt, frightened, or worse. He had tried so damn hard to give them good lives, to protect them. And he was failing them.

Which only made him remember his previous failings. Memories surfaced, of when he'd returned home that final time to find his mother bruised and ill. And the same torturous question that always accompanied it rose up as well: How many times had she suffered through such things without him knowing? It was a question that branded him with guilt, damning him.

The years had passed, his father finally in his grave, and Ash had begun to hope that maybe, just maybe, he might put that nightmarish time behind him and claw his way free of the pit of despair that had constantly tried to suck him down. But the specter of that man was never far, the memory of his cruelties painting Ash with broad, vicious strokes. And then the girls had come under his care, and he realized he would never be able to break free of the past.

He had done what he could, giving them the best of everything: nurses and maids and nannies, tutors and governesses, an opulent home to live in and plenty of food to fill their bellies. And each year that passed saw them testing boundaries and rebelling until he was hard-pressed to know what to do to keep his vow to protect them.

As if to mock him, the door to his office was suddenly thrown wide, and there stood Regina. Once more in Brimstone, the place he had forbidden her from entering.

"Your Grace. Mr. Beecher," she said in her cold way, looking from him to his partner before striding into the room. Today she wore breeches and a loose white shirt with a jacket, her rich sable hair tucked up under a hat. No doubt an outfit she had wheedled from one of the stable lads if the roughness of the material was any indication.

"Regina," he growled, lurching to his feet. "I told you to never come here. And what the devil are you wearing?"

"Whatever I please," she shot back. "And I would not have to come here if you visited the town house on occasion."

Again that guilt, so bitter he thought he'd choke on it. As Beecher, mumbling something incoherent, fled the room as if the hounds of hell were on his heels— the traitor—Ash faced the girl. "If you had sent a note, I would have come to you immediately," he replied, even as his heart fractured for her. Behind the constant chill that she wore like armor was a pain so deep he feared he would never be able to heal it.

"Well, I am here, and so we may as well discuss what I came for." With that she held a slim leather-bound journal out to him.

Shock tore through his body at the sight of the book, at once so familiar and so painful. He stared at it, unable to tear his eyes away. "Where did you get that?" he rasped.

"In Eliza's room."

His eyes snapped to meet hers. "But we searched every damn inch of her room."

Regina's lips twisted, at once faintly mocking and agonized. "Eliza is much cleverer than most people give her credit for. I located this hidden behind a loose base-board beneath her bed."

Which was much more telling than Regina probably meant for it to be. It revealed that she had been searching, possibly nonstop, since her sisters' disappearance a week ago. He saw then the fear in her eyes, desperately concealed. She was worried for the two girls.

It shouldn't be a surprise. They were sisters, after all, and had suffered through the same heartaches and upheavals. Yet Regina had never been as close to the younger girls as they were with each other. It was a distance that had only grown more pronounced over the past years, most notably as Regina matured into a young woman. If one were to look in from the outside, they might assume there was no love between Regina and her siblings, which he saw now was not the least bit true.

But that did not explain why she had come all this way, disobeying his explicit instructions, to bring him this when a note would have sufficed.

She must have seen the confusion and frustration in his eyes, for she moved closer to him, thrusting the journal at his chest, forcing him to grab hold of it. "I think this book is the clue to where Eliza and Nelly have run off to."

He frowned, looking down at the worn green cover and the gilt letters embossed in the corner, tarnished now with age. *M. Caulnedy*. Mary Caulnedy, his mother's maiden name. How many times had she read to him from her journal, stories of her childhood, a time in her life when she had been happy. Before she had married the duke and become a duchess, and suffered more heartache and degradation than any one person should.

Later, after his father's last cruel beating—God knew how many there had been before that fateful day—he had spirited his mother away and taken her back to the home of her youth, a property that had been left to her and that had, a short time later upon her own death mere days after their arrival, been passed on to Ash. He could still hear the faint sounds of the ocean and seabirds, the smell of brine and life on the breeze, the sun warm on his face as he'd carried his mother, thin and frail and a shadow of the woman she had been, out onto the terrace to see that last sunset before her eyes closed forever.

"Caulnedy Manor," he whispered.

"They must have gone there," Regina said. "Why else would she have stolen your mother's journal and hidden it in her room?"

"But how did she even know about it? I told none of you."

"Like I said," she replied quietly, "Eliza is clever, as well as very curious."

Which was an understatement if there ever was one. He could very well picture his ward digging through his things, locating the journal, reading from it as if it were a book of fairy tales and not one of his most private, precious possessions. For a moment he berated himself for leaving it where she could have access to it. It had been years since he had lived at the Mayfair town house with the girls, preferring to stay in his apartments at Brimstone, a place where constant work allowed him to forget for a short time the sins staining his soul, as well as to protect his wards from being polluted by them. But he had left most of his things at the town house as a way somehow to stay connected to those girls, even if he couldn't reach them emotionally.

Spinning about, he quickly deposited the journal in a drawer in his desk, locking it tight before turning back to Regina. "Thank you for bringing this to my attention," he said, his mind already whirling with what he had to do to prepare for the journey ahead. "I'll leave for the Isle of Synne at first light and bring the girls back home."

He thought that would be the end of it; Regina had done what she'd come to do; surely she would leave now.

But she didn't. Instead, she planted her feet wide, as if preparing for a blow, and said, her chin set mutinously, "If you think you're going without me, you're deluded."

Ash, in the process of seating himself behind the desk to write the necessary notes before his departure, scowled at her. "You are not going with me. Your place is here, with your new governess." Who had been difficult enough to secure, considering his wards' propensity for terrorizing everyone he hired on.

"The governess is gone," Regina pronounced bluntly.

Ash stood slowly, raising himself to his full, formidable height. "What do you mean, *she is gone*?"

She didn't answer. But Ash could very well guess what had happened. The girls had made it a kind of game to see how quickly they could run off each person hired on to watch over them. He'd had to search far and wide for this last one; there were not many willing to take on the monumental task of teaching the Duke of Buckley's wild wards. Damnation, where the hell was he going to find another governess?

But that was neither here nor there. He tamped down on his frustration, leveling a furious glare on Regina. "Regardless, you will remain here, in London."

But Regina wasn't the least bit fazed. She raised her head higher and narrowed her eyes. "You will take me with you, or when you return to London you shall not find me."

He was still trying to figure how to respond to that blatant attempt at emotional blackmail when she did the one thing that would sway him.

Her voice dropped to the smallest whisper, showing a vulnerability he had never witnessed in her before. "They are my sisters."

His heart wrenched in his chest, his every argument decimated in the face of her pain. There was no doubt in his mind that Regina would do exactly as she threatened if he did not comply with her demand. And even if he took the chance that she would not, he could not possibly leave her here alone, anxious over her sisters' fates. He had to take her with him.

"Very well," he replied softly. "Be ready at first light."

The pathetic relief that flashed through her dark eyes was so brief he very nearly didn't see it. But it was powerful enough to bring tears to his eyes as, with a firm nod, she spun about and raced from the room.

The Isle of Synne. He had not thought of that place

in longer than he could remember. He'd been a different person then, not even a man, afraid and uncertain but with a raw determination that had driven him to flee home, to try to save the one person he could. And even in that he had failed.

So many years trying to make up for his failings, atoning for his father's sins. Sins that stained Ash's soul as surely as those horrible crimson stains on his mother's snowy white handkerchiefs. He clenched his back teeth together, the force of it making his jaw ache, shooting pain into his temples. A question clung to him then, a ghoul grasping onto his back, digging in its claws: Once he found Eliza and Nelly, how could he hope to protect them if they were determined to run again? How could he keep them safe and see to his business at the same time? And how could he protect them from the same shame that polluted him?

As he wrote a quick letter to his solicitor, hurriedly sprinkling it with sand to dry the ink before grabbing up a blank sheet to start on the next, he determined to focus on one problem at a time. Mayhap, by the time he located them, he might find the answers he needed.

Chapter 2

Isle of Synne

*S*he was late.

Miss Bronwyn Pickering pushed open the door to the Quayside Circulating Library and hurried to the rich blue curtain that graced the back wall, her sturdy boot heels clicking sharply on the gleaming wood floor. It had taken every bit of her talents for persuasion—which were regrettably lacking as it was—to convince her parents to allow her to come to today's meeting. She pressed her lips tight, waving distractedly to the two younger Athwart girls as they saw to several of their patrons. She did not know what she would do without her weekly visits to the Quayside to meet with her friends, the one thing she looked forward to most in this world beside her studies of the local arthropods. Something which her parents had already forbid her from doing in their attempts for force her to find a husband.

A husband. She shuddered involuntarily as she pushed

the curtain aside and hurried down the narrow hall beyond. The one time she had actually wanted a man to propose, he had merely been playing with her affections in order to teach her social-climbing parents a lesson. A lesson Bronwyn had been paying for ever since.

She paused for a moment just outside the small back office, absently rubbing her fist over the dull ache in her chest at the thought of that man and that time and the heartache it had caused before. Taking a deep breath and rearranging her features to a calm she did not feel, she put her hand on the latch. "I'm so sorry," she said as she opened the door, ducking inside. She cast an apologetic look about the circle of women as she hastily removed her bonnet and deposited it on a side table. "I came as quickly as I was able."

"Oh, Bronwyn," Miss Honoria Gadfeld, the vicar's eldest daughter, murmured, her brows drawn together in worry. "Are they threatening to forbid you coming to our meetings as well?"

"They are." She tried for a brave smile as she hung her bag on a hook, being careful not to disturb the glass jar within. But her lip, the traitorous thing, decided in that moment to wobble tellingly.

As one, the women jumped to their feet and rushed her. In an instant Bronwyn was enveloped in hugs, exclamations of shock and frustration ringing in her ears. *This* was why she needed the Oddments, she thought as she allowed herself, for just a moment, to lean on these people she had come to love so very much.

It hadn't always been like this, of course. She'd not always had this support, this unfailing enthusiasm bolstering her up on even her darkest days. Having grown up without a single friend, she had been cast like an unsuspecting lure into London society in advance of her debut. But instead of earning her a place in the *ton* as her parents had hoped, it had only managed to invite devastation and near ruin—as well as a heartbreak that even now sent lurching pain through her chest. That horrible event had forced her parents to flee with her and take up residence in the seaside resort off the northeast coast of England, the Isle of Synne. And through it all, Bronwyn had struggled mightily. Her *uniqueness*, as her mother was wont to say in an attempt to justify why her unfashionable, strange daughter was such a failure at anything remotely social, had made finding friends a difficulty, if not an utter impossibility.

Until the Oddments. The self-labeled group of women had come to her rescue when she had been at her lowest and desperate for someone who understood her. She would be forever grateful to them.

And now she was in danger of losing even them.

"I cannot believe they could be so cruel," Miss Katrina Denby exclaimed a bit breathlessly as she wrestled her massive dog, incongruously christened Mouse, out of the center of the throng—a ridiculous sight, indeed. She could have easily ridden the creature, as diminutive and delicate as she was. But the beast would not be denied his greeting. Bronwyn, for the sake of her skirts, and because she adored the creature despite—or mayhap because of—his determination to like anyone and everyone who came into his orbit, scratched Mouse behind his ear. He groaned in ecstasy before allowing himself to be dragged away, what appeared to be a grin spread across his massive black-and-white spotted face.

"Surely there is something we can do to help." Miss Seraphina Athwart, oldest Athwart sister and the proprietress of the Quayside, pushed a lock of fiery red hair out of her face and guided Bronwyn to the low brocade settee that held place of honor on one side of the small but welcoming office that doubled as a parlor of sorts. She quickly went to work, rearranging cushions, filling a teacup just as Bronwyn liked it, her manners brisk and capable, just like the woman herself. "Your parents cannot be completely unreasonable."

"You know as well as I that they most certainly can," Bronwyn replied quietly as she settled into her seat. "And besides, you've already done all you can do. My parents will not listen to reason, I'm afraid. Each day that passes and I am not married to a title, they grow more difficult. There is no amount of persuasion that will make them change their minds now." She reached into the pocket in her skirts, extracting a nut and passing it to Phineas, Seraphina's parrot, who perched on the back of the settee.

"We're a' Jock Taimson's bairns," the creature squawked in its thick brogue before it took to breaking through the hard shell with its wickedly sharp beak.

Miss Adelaide Peacham, owner of the Beakhead Tea Room, kind and busy and constantly smelling of all things sweet, passed Bronwyn a plate piled high with biscuits. "What shall you do?" she asked, concern puckering her dark brows.

Bronwyn shrugged as she took a biscuit, an indifferent

action that in no way reflected the turmoil within her. "There is nothing much I *can* do," she replied, fighting panic and the feeling of being buried alive that had overtaken her since the confrontation with her parents that morning. "I have no money of my own, nothing at my disposal to claim independence." She did not even have privacy in her own home any longer. But she could not inform her friends of that particular wound, not yet. It was still too raw, too frightening.

She glanced quickly at her bag hanging on the wall, as if to make certain the items ensconced safely within were still secure. She had been forced to pack up the beetles, what she was certain was a new species she had discovered here on Synne, as well as the research she had compiled over the past years, to bring with her for the short trip to the Quayside. There was no doubt in her mind that her parents would search her rooms while she was gone and would dispose of anything they thought improper for a lady to possess, namely the insects that she had made her life's work. Already all of the mounted specimens she had collected, as well as the great majority of her scientific equipment and supplies, had been consigned to the rubbish heap.

Again that pain in her chest, though this time not muted with age. No, this was fresh, and no doubt would stay sharp for some time. She would not soon forget her panic when she'd returned home not two days ago to find all her carefully curated equipment and specimens gone. And then the despair that had filled her when she'd been informed that all those things, each one precious to her, had been thrown out. And not just thrown out, but methodically destroyed, each piece smashed so it might never see use again. It seemed that the moment she had reached the advanced age of four and twenty and without a single marital prospect, a kind of fever had come over her parents. As if that particular number had a magical effect on all their fears and wishes for her, expanding them tenfold.

She pressed her lips tight against the grief as she looked once more to that precious bag, now holding the entirety of her research. But she could not allow her compiled data and illustrations and the living creatures in her care to be destroyed. Not before she completed her paper and sent it off to the Royal Society.

For a moment the fire in her belly sputtered. She had tried time and again to build up the nerve to send the blasted thing off to that most notable journal, so she might finally be acknowledged for her contribution to the scientific world. Yet each time she thought her work might be ready, she lost her nerve entirely. All this time she had bolstered herself on the belief that if she could just get the blasted thing included in their periodical, her parents would finally be forced to acknowledge that she was worth more than who she could marry and how many children she could whelp. That her mind was much more important than her womb.

But all too soon the poisonous question whispered through her mind: What if she failed? What if they refused to print her piece, and her work was dismissed? Just as she had been dismissed all her life. It would be devastating, forcing her to concede that her parents had been right about her all along.

And so she had waited, and waited, thinking if she could just rewrite it one more time, do more thorough research, create more detailed illustrations, she was certain to succeed. But all the while she was left in a kind of limbo of uncertainty and self-loathing. And now, with most of her research destroyed and the recent and suffocating restrictions placed on her, it seemed she would never be able to break free of that horrible limbo, no matter how she might wish it otherwise.

But this was not the time for mulling over just how much worse her already limited independence had become. "Enough of this," she said bracingly. "I have fought hard for this afternoon and would enjoy this time with you all." With that she bit into the treat she still held. And promptly forgot everything else as the saltiness of the butter, alongside the sweet floral hints of lavender with just the faintest touch of citrus, hit her tongue. She closed her eyes in appreciation. "Adelaide," she said with a sigh, "these are wonderful."

Her friend smiled, dark eyes bright with pleasure. "Do you think so? It's a new recipe, and I wasn't certain I'd gotten the balance right."

Honoria rolled her eyes heavenward, seeming to seek guidance from a higher source. "As if anything you bake isn't deliciously decadent," she scoffed in her blunt but affectionate way. "Which is why I've had to let my gowns out once already this year." She laughed and then, her expression transforming in an instant, turned to Bronwyn with a stern glare. "But don't think you're getting out of talking about your parents' latest atrocity. We cannot stand for this. It's not your fault that the

Duke of Carlisle didn't make you an offer last year. The man fell in love with another!"

Bronwyn took a deep breath, her good mood vanishing; she should have guessed that Honoria, tenacious as a terrier, would not let it go. She sent Seraphina a beseeching glance. Blessedly, her fiery-haired friend was as quick as ever.

"There's been talk coming through the Quayside of someone taking residence at Caulnedy Manor," she said, giving Honoria a sly sideways look. As Honoria predictably perked up at that bit of gossip, her previous passionate subject forgotten for the moment, Seraphina turned to Adelaide, who watched the whole interaction with wide, bemused eyes. "Adelaide, I wouldn't doubt if the same information has gone through the Beakhead; your tearoom is usually the epicenter of all the latest news on Synne, after all."

Adelaide bit back a smile before, adopting a more serious mien, she nodded sagely. "Yes, you're so very right. I *have* heard news pertaining to a commotion going on at Caulnedy. I admit I'm shocked. Caulnedy has been empty for so long, I wasn't certain it would ever see life again."

"Oh! Yes, I had forgotten." Bronwyn sat forward and adjusted her spectacles, vastly relieved at the change of subject. "I've met them."

The news of someone taking up residence at Caulnedy would have been the perfect diversion even without Bronwyn adding to it: there was nothing Honoria liked more than a juicy bit of gossip, something her vicar father had been hard-pressed to cure her of. But Bronwyn's addition, so unexpected because of her preference to abstain from most social interactions, was enough to stun them all into silence.

Finally, Honoria spoke. "And you're just telling us now?" she demanded, hazel eyes wide with outrage and curiosity.

"Goodness, Bronwyn, who are they?" Katrina, ever energetic, fairly bounced in her seat. Mouse, seated on the floor at her feet, tilted his head backward to gaze at her, massive tongue lolling.

Unable to understand why such a thing might interest anyone, much less to this degree, Bronwyn was nevertheless clever enough to know that she shouldn't look a gift horse in the mouth.

"They are two young girls," she replied. "Perhaps ten and thirteen? Or something similar; I'm horrible at guessing ages."

She smiled, thinking that would be the end of it. But no, they all continued staring, waiting. For what? She scoured her mind for what information they might want.

"Er, their names are Miss Eliza and Miss Nelly Hargrove."

"And?" This from Seraphina, who, to Bronwyn's surprise, was just as eager as the others to learn about the newcomers. Seraphina was, after all, the most level-headed of their group, the one who loudly denounced society, who refused to look at the gossip rags, though she was forced to provide them for her patrons at the Quayside.

But Bronwyn, wholly unused to talking at length

about anything other than her beloved insects, was at a loss. "And...they have brown hair?"

This time Adelaide was the one to roll her eyes, another unexpected occurrence, for she was the epitome of patience. "There must be something else you've learned about them. Where are they from?"

"Did you meet their parents?"

"How long will they stay?"

Unprepared for the volley of questions, Bronwyn lurched back against the settee. Phineas squawked with a "Noo jist haud on!" and flapped his wings at the sudden trespass into his space. The breeze created by his moment of pique set the loose curls at Bronwyn's temple dancing about.

"I didn't learn much," she mumbled, face hot. "You know me; I'm no good at that sort of thing."

Which they all did know, very well. Honoria, no doubt feeling she had been robbed of this particular bit of Synne news, grumbled and sat back in her chair. The rest were thankfully much kinder in their reactions.

"How did you meet them?" Adelaide asked, taking a sip of her tea, her eyes bright with curiosity.

"You recall the spot where I discovered that new species of beetle? The meadow below Caulnedy?" At their collective nods, Bronwyn continued. "Several days ago, when I was supposed to be visiting with the modiste, I managed to sneak out to visit the meadow for a bit. The Hargrove girls spotted me while they were out walking and asked what I was about. They were not at all squeamish," she finished almost proudly. It was rare, after all, that she found anyone who had the same affinity as she for insects. Or, at least, anyone who did not turn and run the other way when she showed them a specimen. Which was why the live specimens she was currently in possession of were well on the other side of the room.

"Hargrove." Seraphina took a bite of a small finger sandwich, chewing thoughtfully. "I don't recall hearing of any family by that name owning the property. But then, my sisters and I have not been here all that long." A cloud passed over her face, as it did whenever her past was touched on. It was something she refused to discuss, even among the Oddments.

But she quickly rallied. Looking to Honoria, she tilted her head in curiosity. "When did your father arrive on Synne to take over the vicarage?"

Seemingly mollified, Honoria pursed her lips in thought. "About ten years now. But there has not been anyone at Caulnedy in all that time." She turned to Adelaide and snatched a biscuit from the plate on the low tea table. "You've been on the Isle longer than any of us, as you came here when you were just a girl. Do you recall hearing anything of Caulnedy or its owners?"

"Not a thing. My Aunt Bea would have known, having been born here," she said, referring to her great-aunt, who had owned the Beakhead before her and taken an orphaned Adelaide in when she was a child. "But she never mentioned anything about it to me."

"I am sorry for not learning more," Bronwyn said quietly, feeling as if she had somehow failed her friends but not quite understanding how. Which was always the way of things with her, it seemed. She felt one step behind everyone else, even with these people she loved so well. The realization was lowering indeed, that she might never fully have a place in this world.

Blessedly the others, while not completely understanding her, never failed to ease her mind.

"Nonsense," Seraphina said in that bracing way she had that sounded dismissive and abrupt though Bronwyn knew held affection in it. "You have given us more information than we previously had. And," she continued, a smile in her voice as she leaned close to whisper in Bronwyn's ear, "you have succeeded in helping me distract Honoria."

"There must be someone on Synne who might remember the original family," Honoria mused, oblivious of the whispered words being said about her. She snatched another biscuit off the quickly dwindling mound. This time, however, she passed it to Mouse, who had been closely watching her the whole while, a long string of drool hanging from his jowls. He happily inhaled it without chewing.

"Oh, Honoria," Katrina fretted, grabbing at Mouse's collar as he dove for the rest of the delicacies that dared to sit uneaten on the plate, "I do wish you wouldn't feed him scraps. He's hard enough to control around food as it is."

"Poppycock," Honoria countered. "He deserves it, don't you, you adorable lummox?" She scratched Mouse behind the ear, earning her a deep sigh and a huge head in her lap as the dog leaned in for his massage.

"Honoria is right," Adelaide said, her voice contemplative. "There has to be someone on the Isle who remembers."

"Would someone please mark the date and time that dear Adelaide admitted I was correct in anything," Honoria drawled with a grin.

"Cheeky," Adelaide said with a chuckle. "But truly, who better to ask than the reigning matriarch of the Isle and your own employer, Katrina?"

"Oh, yes!" Katrina said, her pixie face lighting up with understanding, delicate blond curls bouncing in her excitement. "If anyone knows anything about Synne, it is Lady Tesh. I'll ask her when I return to Seacliff."

They all burst into talk at once, their excitement restored. Bronwyn, for her part, sat silently, passing Phineas more of the nuts she had brought specifically for him from her pocket, her mind wandering back to those two young girls. They had seemed cheerful enough, and eager to learn about her scientific studies. Even better, she had liked them immensely, so much so that she had promised them she would return. Of course, she silently mused, disheartened, first she had to wait for another occasion where she might sneak off. And those were now few and far between, as her parents were becoming increasingly strict about any endeavor, no matter how mundane, they deemed *unladylike* in their increasingly focused attempts at finding her a titled husband.

Perhaps, though, they might allow her to call on the girls in a social manner. For under the young girls' cheerfulness, Bronwyn had recognized a loneliness that she had felt much too often herself in her youth, and that still plagued her as an adult.

The tea had just been drunk and the food finished when the door to the small office opened a crack. Miss

Elspeth Athwart, Seraphina's youngest sister, poked her auburn head, a perfect match in hue to her elder sister's, into the room. "Seraphina, the latest edition of the *Gaia Review and Repository* has arrived, and there is already a crowd of people waiting for their copies," she said, a bright smile lighting her round face. "That serial by S. L. Keys is incredible; people cannot get enough of it."

Seraphina looked at the clock above the mantel with a start. "Goodness, is that the time? Forgive me, Elspeth dear. I'm afraid I completely lost track. I'll be there right away." She stood, patting her chignon and shaking out her skirts. Phineas, never far from his mistress, took off from his perch and flew to land on Seraphina's shoulder. She reached up to absently scratch the bird's neck while turning to the rest of the group.

"It has been a joy as usual, ladies. Until next week."

Suddenly she turned to Bronwyn, laying a comforting hand on her arm. "Don't fret. We won't let them take these meetings away from you."

As their small party, chattering like magpies, stood and collected their things, Bronwyn swallowed down tears. She had managed, for a short time, to forget her parents' increasingly cruel efforts and restrictive measures to force her to marry. They had never been easy to deal with, her mother's tenuous connection to a baronet and her father's extensive finances making them feel superior to those who were previously of their class. But there was no escaping it, for Bronwyn, as they had long stated, was their one chance to truly insert themselves into the nobility, a position they felt was rightfully theirs. And the older she became, the less likely they were to see that dream realized—no matter it wasn't a dream Bronwyn shared. Now that she had not only lost the chance at a literal duke the year before, but had then also gone through an entire summer season on Synne, as well as a twenty-fourth birthday, without a single whiff of interest, they were becoming desperate. And Bronwyn, by extension, was being made to suffer.

Securing her bonnet back on her short curls, she gathered up her bag, all too aware of the familiar ache in her chest. It was a common occurrence whenever their weekly meetings adjourned, though now it had increased to a painful degree. What if this was her last meeting with her friends? What power did Seraphina, or any of them, have in changing her parents' minds?

Saying her farewells, Bronwyn made her way through the crowded Quayside and to Admiralty Row beyond. So engrossed was she in attempting to control her self-pitying thoughts that she quite forgot to make certain the walkway was clear before stepping out onto it.

A young boy went flying by in a blur of brown. Blessedly he was able to veer off course and just managed to keep from sending her to the pavement. Unfortunately, his course correction came an instant too late. He knocked her bag from her shoulder. It landed on the pavement with a clatter, its contents spilling out in a jumble at her feet.

"Your pardon, Miss Pickering!" he called over his shoulder, not breaking pace for even a moment.

Bronwyn let out a frustrated growl as she dropped to her knees, desperate to gather up her precious research, as well as the glass jar, which by some miracle hadn't shattered in the collision. "William Juniper, you're lucky you're fast," she yelled after the boy.

His delighted laugh trailed back to her as he rounded the corner. She hardly heard it, however, for the gasp of dismay that burst from her lips to find that the bit of muslin she'd tied about the lip of the jar had come loose. And her beetles were nowhere to be seen.

"No," she mumbled, her eyes scanning the ground with increased desperation. "No, no, no." Had she kneeled on them? Had they been crushed? They were so small, so delicate. She lurched back onto her posterior, her skirts billowing about her in a dark blue mass. Just when she thought all hope was lost she finally spied them, the shimmering green of their elytra catching her eye, glinting up at her from her dress like two brilliant jewels.

She didn't have time to breathe a sigh of relief, however, before a deep voice sounded in her ear. "Stay still, miss, and I shall remove them from your person." And then a large hand was reaching for her skirts—rather, she noted in horror, it was reaching for the beetles in an effort to swat them away.

"Don't you dare!" she cried, slapping at his hand. The man pulled back, no doubt stunned by her use of brute force. But she truly couldn't have cared less for his wounded pride. Turning her full attention to the insects, she took up the jar and gently nudged them within, securing the muslin back in place with a bit of twine, giving it an extra firm tug for good measure. Then, gathering up her scattered notebooks and drawings in her bag, she scrambled to her feet, holding the jar close to her chest while dusting off her skirts with her free hand. The scare of the moment before was rapidly transforming into outrage that her specimens had nearly been damaged. It was with that soured attitude that she turned to the man who had dared to swat at her beloved beetles, a sharp retort rising to her lips. It died a swift and complete death, however, at the sight of him.

Dangerous was the first word that popped into her head. Not that there was anything threatening about him. His clothing was expertly tailored and of fine quality even to her undiscerning eye, his entire person neat and orderly.

And yet there was something about him that made every nerve in her body come alive. There was nothing remotely soft or pampered about him. His shoulders were broad and filled out his dark blue wool coat with impressive breadth. His buckskin breeches, too, left little to the imagination.

But it was his face that had her mouth going dry. His jaw was sharp and shadowed with stubble, his brows a dark, heavy slash, his hair thick and long, the inky waves curling over his collar. His eyes, however, captivated her more than any other aspect of his person.

Captivated? She frowned. Strange word to think in that moment. Perhaps *alarmed* would be more apt. Whatever word she used, however, the effect on her was undeniable. His eyes were a strange, pale brown, almost amber in color, and they were piercing, seeming to see straight to the heart of her.

"Miss?"

And his voice. Goodness, it was delicious, deep and smooth and making her think of the lowing of the wind just before a storm, luring you in, though you knew the danger that surely followed it.

"Miss? Are you all right?"

She blinked, her face flaming hot. Goodness, had she been standing there staring at him all this time? "Er, yes. So sorry."

He tilted his head, his eyes never leaving her face. Once more she felt herself sinking into stupidity but was helpless against the pull of it.

Not without some effort she dragged herself from the brink of doing something utterly ridiculous, like batting her lashes, or even *simpering*, for goodness' sake. As her senses came back to her, however, so did her recollection of his actions from a minute ago.

Furious once more, she glared up at him. No easy thing; the man was ridiculously tall and broad as a boxer, after all. "What did you think you were about," she snapped, "nearly killing my beetles?"

He blinked. "*Your* beetles?"

"Yes, my beetles. They came from my bag, didn't they?"

Instead of looking thoroughly chastised, he merely raised one black brow, his gaze intense on her face. Which, of course, sent her mind packing once more.

Suddenly a dark-haired young woman sidled up to his side, a small sack clutched to her chest.

"I'm ready," she said, turning suspicious eyes on Bronwyn.

"Of course." He turned back to Bronwyn. "Miss,"

he murmured. Then, touching a finger to his brim, he guided the young woman to a nearby carriage.

Bronwyn watched mutely as he helped the girl into the conveyance, trying to understand the sensations churning in her belly: bitterness and warmth and ice cold all at once. A strange mixture, that. And not at all a welcome one, if the way her stomach pitched and rolled was any indication.

When the man, about to vault up into the carriage behind the girl, turned her way, his intense eyes settling on her, Bronwyn was finally able to move. Gasping, spinning about, she hurried down Admiralty Row to The Promenade and home. It was not until she was nearly to Knighthead Crescent, however, that she realized she hadn't even gotten the stranger's name. She tamped down on the peculiar surge of loss that reared up at that and hurried up to her parents' fashionable front stoop. He was nothing to her, after all. No doubt she would never see him again.

Chapter 3

He wanted to see her again.

Ash frowned as the thought crept through his mind, hardly aware of the thickly wooded area the carriage entered as he and Regina made their way ever closer to Caulnedy Manor. It was not the first time he had thought of the young woman since he'd left her standing on the pavement. No doubt it would not be the last. Not a mystery, really. It had been the most bizarre encounter he'd had in a good long while, especially with the lady's peculiar protectiveness over a couple of insects, of all things.

And that had not been the only remarkable thing about her. For a bewildering moment he'd felt bewitched, as if she had put him under a spell. Perhaps she was a fay being; with those large turquoise eyes magnified by her delicate spectacles, the short mop of curls atop her head, and her slender, diminutive form, she could very well be one of those mystical creatures.

Whatever it was, he could only be grateful for the distraction. Returning to the Isle of Synne brought up emotions he had thought long buried.

They rounded a turn, and Caulnedy Manor came into view. He sucked in his breath at the sight of it, a place he hadn't laid eyes on since he was a boy, yet it was eerily familiar for how often he'd dreamed of it. As he stared at the sprawling red brick house, it felt like a knife was lancing his chest open, laying him bare to all the hope and desperation and despair he'd experienced in the short time he'd carved out here.

As if she sensed his turmoil, Regina shifted in her seat. She had been silent for the majority of their four-day trip, speaking only when necessary, keeping her nose buried deep in one of the myriad books she'd packed for the journey.

She wasn't reading her book now. Instead, she sat forward, peering out the carriage window at the house, a kind of aching hope in her wide eyes. She clutched a small package to her chest, the bundle of sweets she had insisted they stop for on Synne's main thoroughfare before completing their journey. A gift to sisters who would no doubt resent being found out.

"Do you think they're here? And do you think they're well?"

Her voice was barely a whisper above the rumble of the wheels on the road and the rhythmic clipping of the horses' hooves and jangle of the tack. But Ash heard the worry in it. It was the same worry that had been plaguing him for nearly a fortnight now.

"I'm certain they are, on both counts," he answered quietly. Hoping beyond hope it was true.

They turned into the circular front drive, and within moments the carriage rocked to a halt before the manor steps. Ash, strung tight as a bow now that the moment was here, threw open the carriage door before the driver could reach it, vaulting to the ground. It took every ounce of self-control not to hurry to the front door and pound away at the hapless oak. Instead, he turned and helped Regina down, guiding her up the steps and ringing the bell with what he thought was impressive restraint. The sound of it was muffled as it echoed through the house, then faded away, replaced with a silence so loud he thought he would scream. Finally, after what seemed an eternity, footsteps. And not the shuffling ancient footsteps of Mrs. Wheeler, the woman who had been housekeeper here when he had come seeking refuge for him and his mother and who was still alive and well and watching over Caulnedy. No, these were quick and eager, like a puppy scrambling across tile. Suddenly the door was flung wide. And there stood Nelly, the excitement on her face quickly transforming to dismay.

"What are you doing here?"

Ash, fighting the surge of joy and relief that his youngest ward was safe and well, held on to the waning residue of his outrage with both hands. Scowling, he pushed into the house, glaring down at her. "What do you think? Looking for you."

Before she could reply—and he was certain it wasn't going to be a declaration of thanks, if the mutinous look in her eyes was any indication—a familiar voice sounded from the landing. "Who is it, Nelly? Has Miss Pickering come to call as we asked her to?"

The next moment Eliza, the middle sister, skipped down the stairs and into view. She froze when she saw him. "Damn," she muttered.

"Damn, indeed," he growled.

Letting loose a sigh, as if she were being mightily inconvenienced, she descended the stairs with maddening slowness. "I thought we had well and truly hidden our tracks. How did Mr. Beecher discover our direction?"

"It wasn't Beecher." Reaching into his pocket, he held up his mother's slim journal.

The glare Eliza shot Regina's way was so hot with fury Ash wouldn't have been surprised if columns of fire shot from her eyes. "How could you?" she hissed, stomping forward to stand nose to nose with her elder sister.

Regina narrowed her eyes dangerously. "How could I? Are you truly serious? You ran off without—" She cut herself off with a click of teeth before, taking a deep breath, she continued in a more neutral tone. "You must have known His Grace would stop at nothing to find you. It was only a matter of time before he discovered the book himself."

"I would think His Grace would be happy that he was rid of us," Eliza snapped. "And that you would be as well."

"Enough," Ash bit out. "Eliza, Nelly, your ill-advised adventure ends here and now. You shall pack your things and return to London with us at once."

The chaos that ensued was deafening. The two younger girls set up a screeching racket loud enough

to wake the dead, Regina's shouted reprimands only
making the din worse. He drew in a deep breath, the
better to gain the volume needed to be heard over them,
when a stooped figure pushed into their midst.

"Goodness me," the woman exclaimed, stopping all
arguments in their tracks. "What in the world is going
on?" She turned her gaze on Ash, her milky blue eyes
magnified by spectacles as thick as the bottom of a
bottle. They narrowed at first, as if she were mightily confused by his presence, before widening almost
comically in stunned recognition. Except Ash was in no
mood to laugh. In fact, he rather thought he was the
closest he had been to tears since his mother's death.

"Master Ash," the woman said in hushed disbelief.
"Is it truly you?"

Ash swallowed hard. "Hello, Mrs. Wheeler."

And then she did the thing he least expected: she
shuffled forward and embraced him.

Ash could only stand there frozen, caught between
joy and grief and utter confusion. His wards must have
been equally confused, for they stared, mouths opened
wide in shock.

Finally the housekeeper released him, stepping back
and brushing a tear from her deeply lined cheek.

"Goodness me," she said, "but I never thought you
would return."

"I never intended to," Ash muttered more to himself.

Mrs. Wheeler, not hearing him, continued. "Especially after that lovely note you sent on with the girls.
It was so nice of you to send them here for an extended
holiday."

No doubt they had forged this letter from him. He shot the younger girls a dark glare. They, however, looked utterly unrepentant.

"But this is lovely," Mrs. Wheeler prattled on, patting his arm. "It will be nice to have some life back in the house. Though the majority of the rooms are still shut up, and there are just a few servants in residence, I'm certain we can have rooms made up in a thrice. Mayhap," she continued to mutter thoughtfully as she began to shuffle away, "I'll send Mr. Wheeler into town to hire on some new staff. I'm certain there are some sweet girls on the Isle who would be happy for the work."

"Mrs. Wheeler," Ash called out, desperate to rein her in. He was quickly losing what little control he had here; if he didn't stop her now there was no telling what scheme his wards might get into their heads—or what further mischief they might get up to. "Mrs. Wheeler, you are mistaken. We aren't staying; in fact, we are leaving immediately."

The woman, however, seemed once more not to hear him. She continued muttering to herself, shuffling along at a surprisingly quick pace for all she looked as if she would keel over on the spot. He began striding after her, determined to shut down whatever thoughts she had of them staying on at Caulnedy.

The two younger girls, however, saw what he was about and rushed past him, hurrying to Mrs. Wheeler and linking arms with her, one on each side.

"Let us help you, Mrs. Wheeler," Eliza said with exaggerated sweetness, her voice carrying, no doubt to prevent the old woman from hearing any more of what

Ash might have to say on the matter. "We would love to be of assistance. Wouldn't we, Nelly."

"Oh, yes!" Nelly joined in enthusiastically. "Anything we can do to help you, Mrs. Wheeler."

Ash, flummoxed that he could have so quickly lost all ground in the situation, growled and made to go after them. He would stop this nonsense here and now.

A tentative hand on his coat sleeve, however, halted him in his tracks.

He looked down to see Regina peering up at him. She was biting her lip, looking as uncertain as he had ever seen her.

"Perhaps we can stay, just for a couple of days."

He gaped down at her. "You would have me reward such behavior?"

"Not reward, no. It's just…" She paused, tense. Then, like a damn bursting, the words poured out of her. "I hardly remember what life is like outside London. And the Isle is so beautiful. Couldn't we stay, just for a short while?"

Ash was struck mute by the impassioned plea. Regina had always remained closed off, restrained. This was the first time since he had known her that he felt he could actually see to the heart of her. And he saw that beneath the armored shell she had created as a way to survive the great upheavals her life had taken, there was still a young girl whose childhood had been cut short.

He swallowed hard at the lump in his throat. "Very well, Regina. We can stay. But only for a few days," he warned, even as his heart leapt at the happiness that saturated her face.

"Of course," she replied, breathless, a small smile lifting her lips. "Thank you, Your Grace." And then she was off, picking up her skirts and sprinting after her sisters and Mrs. Wheeler.

And as Ash, left alone, looked about the front hall, which was painfully familiar to him and which he had hoped never to set foot in again, he wondered what the hell he had gotten himself into.

* * *

It did not take even an hour before that particular question was answered.

"Nelly, Eliza," he barked as the two girls hurried through the upstairs hallway, each carting a piece of furniture on their backs. "Put those chairs down at once."

The only indication they heard him was Eliza's mocking voice as they made their precarious way down the stairs. "'Put those chairs down at once.'"

Nelly's giggle trailed up to him as they descended to the ground floor and out of view.

Ash heaved a sigh, running a hand over his face. Good God, he was exhausted. He had barely gotten settled into his room before the chaos had begun. How was it that two young girls could have so much energy? Were they vampires, draining the life force from him to use for their own nefarious purposes? It certainly felt like it. No wonder they had gone through so many nannies and governesses over the years.

But he had better see what they were up to. For all he knew they were going to break down the chairs and create a bonfire to summon evil spirits. And while he had no qualms if they *were* practicing supernatural arts, he already had enough demons in the form of three young girls in the house, thank you very much.

Eliza and Nelly were easy enough to find. All he had to do was follow the shrieks. That, and the trail of debris. What, he wondered with increasing unease as he sidestepped a pillow, could they be up to?

Whatever he could have imagined, however, it was nothing compared to actual fact. Turning the corner into what he recalled was the dining room, he was struck mute at the sight of what could only be described as a blanket fort.

The table had been extended to its full length, the dining chairs pulled out, several more added to the forest of them to form a long oval. Sheets and blankets and furniture coverings were draped across a good portion of it all, creating a tent of sorts. Beneath were strewn yet more blankets, as well as myriad pillows and couch cushions.

But it was the sight atop the table that his eyes snagged on. Eliza, taking the chair her sister had been carting downstairs, was propping it under the sheets to give them more height.

"What the blazes is going on here?" he demanded.

He half expected them to give a guilty start. They did nothing of the sort, instead looking at him with wide grins.

"Isn't it glorious?" Nelly asked, bouncing on her toes as she surveyed their handiwork.

"We never managed to make something like this back

in London," Eliza added. Done adjusting the placement of the chair, she stood back on the tabletop and placed her fists on her hips. For a moment Ash's heart stuttered as her small heel came precariously close to the edge. "Yes, that is perfect. Nelly, pass me up the next chair, will you? I think if we place them just right, we can reach the ceiling."

"She will do nothing of the sort," Ash pronounced. Striding forward, he gripped a protesting Eliza about the waist and plucked her from the table, depositing her on the floor.

"What are you doing?" she demanded, glaring up at him.

"Stopping you from breaking your neck," he replied tightly. "Now, clean this all up. I'll not have you giving Mrs. Wheeler more work."

"We won't clean it up," Nelly declared, stomping her foot, her small, pointed chin jutting out mutinously. "It's beautiful."

"We worked too hard on it," Eliza chimed in, her eyes snapping fire at him. She stepped next to Nelly, clasping her hand. A united front against their big, bad guardian.

If they only knew. His rush of anger was gone in an instant, only a weary sadness in its place. "Clean it up," he repeated as he turned and strode from the room.

"Or what, Your Grace?" Eliza taunted to his retreating back. "Will you kick us out into the streets? I know you must have been aching to do just that for five years, the three orphans you were saddled with and never wanted."

Guilt, that hot knife that was constantly buried in his heart, plunged in deeper. It was true, he had never wanted them, had never wanted to know that there had been much more he had been unaware of besides his mother's abuse.

Little did they know they had become the most precious things in his life, a last link to that mother he had lost much too early. With effort he kept his face devoid of emotion as he turned back to them.

They looked like two avenging angels, glaring at him with ferocious fire, as if they would be more than happy to smite him on the spot.

He took a deep breath and said, with as much firmness as he was able to muster, "Or I shall cut this ill-conceived *holiday* short and return you to London. Immediately."

"We shan't ever return to London," Nelly cried, her face turning red as a strawberry. "We like it here. We want to live here."

"You cannot live here," he gritted. "Your place is in London. Near me."

"Why?" Eliza demanded. "You don't care about us anyway."

And with that they turned back to their fort, acting as if he were not even there.

Heart aching, he could only watch them as they busied themselves adjusting fabric, strengthening the supports. Only this time they worked in silence, the heart gone out of their game. Because of him.

Without another word he strode from the room. Why could he never do right by them? He had tried so damned hard, making certain they had a roof over their heads, seeing they were fed and clothed and cared for. Yet he never failed to muck things up. They would never understand that he had no choice but to keep his distance from them. For in doing so, in making certain they never came to care for him as he did for them, he was doing the only thing he could to keep them from feeling the same devastating bone-deep shame that ate away at his own soul.

Chapter 4

*T*he next day saw Bronwyn, seated in a miserable mass across from her maid in her parents' fashionable barouche, pulling into the sweeping front drive of Caulnedy Manor for her promised visit with the Hargrove girls, the glass jar of beetles secure in her lap. This trip, however, was not only a social call. No, the arthropods had been discovered the night before, and Bronwyn had been ordered to return the *disgusting beasts*, as her mother so eloquently put it, back where they came from.

She supposed she should be grateful her father hadn't smashed the insects on the spot. Only Bronwyn's incredible effort had managed to save these tansy beetles to live another day. Though, she thought bleakly, gazing down at the glistening green creatures, any further research she might do on the insects was now well and truly over.

The house, tucked as it was near the Elven Pools at the center of the Isle, isolated by a densely wooded area, was not located on any main roads and therefore went forgotten by most of the residents of Synne. Even Bronwyn, who was used to tromping over hills and valleys in search of her beloved insects, and lately spending as much time as she could eke out in the meadow near the Elven Pools, had never had cause to catch view of the house. As she looked up at the dark brick facade, however, she wondered how anything so beautiful could be so completely hidden from the world.

Bronwyn had always been of a scientific mind. Facts and figures had always been the basis for everything in her life. Even when she was a child, instead of delighting in fairy tales and magical realms and make-believe, she had gravitated toward books on flora and fauna and explanations of the natural world.

Now, however, as the driver helped her down, she felt as if she had been transported to some enchanted glen. Though Caulnedy was a sprawling building, two stories tall, with peaked gables and a veritable forest of chimneys that reached for the sky, it had an air of intimacy that drew one in. It had sat empty for years, yet it had obviously been well cared for. The mullioned windows gleamed in the dappled sunlight, the front steps were swept clean, the hedges neatly trimmed, and flowers bloomed in a riot of colors. Who, she wondered, could own such a place and not reside here year-round? It was a veritable paradise.

Before she could reach the front door to ring the bell, it was thrown wide, and the Misses Eliza and Nelly

Hargrove tumbled out, rushing toward her with squeals of glee.

"You have come!" Miss Nelly exclaimed, rushing forward, throwing her arms about Bronwyn's middle.

Bronwyn, wholly unused to being embraced, didn't quite know what to do. In the end she settled on patting the young girl's shoulder awkwardly.

"Nelly, you'll scare her off," the elder girl reprimanded, quickly ruining the effect by taking hold of Bronwyn's hand and squeezing it. "We really are happy you've come. We feared you would not."

"But you must come in," Miss Nelly said, releasing Bronwyn's waist and grinning up at her. "We can have tea and sandwiches and sit and talk like real ladies."

"No we can't, you ninny," her sister scolded. "We haven't a cook."

"I assure you," Bronwyn hurried to say, not certain what the protocol was for this sort of thing but desperate to mend whatever damage she seemed to have done by coming here when they were so obviously understaffed, "I don't need anything of the sort."

"There, you see?" Miss Eliza said. "Miss Pickering has no need of something so formal." Suddenly the girl spied the jar in Bronwyn's arms. "Oh! You have brought the beetles back. Aren't they the sweetest, tiniest things? Have you come to return them to the meadow?"

A lump formed in Bronwyn's throat at that, and she cradled the jar tighter. "I have," she answered quietly. "I'll just run them out quickly and then we may have our visit."

"Oh, but we would love to join you," Miss Nelly said,

pushing a rogue light brown curl out of her face as she peered up at Bronwyn. "Let us go out to the meadow instead of heading inside. We can spend your entire visit there, and you can tell us all about the insects we find."

"That's a splendid idea," Miss Eliza chimed in. "We were never allowed to do anything of the sort in London."

"Do say we can all go, Miss Pickering."

She should refuse. Her parents had pointedly forbidden her from spending more than a few minutes in the meadow, and only to specifically return the beetles. She cast a covert glance at her maid, who stood stiff and unapproving near the carriage. There was also the matter of that woman's loyalty to the elder Pickerings. No doubt it was she who had alerted Bronwyn's parents to the presence of insects in their house.

But as she looked into the eager faces of the Hargrove girls, she felt her own excitement grow. How could she possibly refuse their request? She was a guest here, after all. And wasn't it the proper thing to do to heed her hosts' wishes on this matter?

Well, she truly didn't know about what was proper or not. Nor did she care. All she knew was she couldn't pass up this chance to visit the meadow and indulge in one final bit of research.

She smiled. "That sounds wonderful."

* * *

Ash had spent a good portion of the morning riding across Synne's rolling hills, hiking through the woods, anything to get him out of Caulnedy and the memories it held for him. The place, as big as it was, closed him in until all he could see was the pain in his mother's eyes, her labored breathing, the pale cast of her skin beneath both old and fresh bruises.

Eventually, however, he had to return to that house, to face not only the memories but also his wards. Something he was not eager to do after their quarrel the day before and their coldness to him since.

What he did not expect when he walked through the back door, however, was Regina rushing up to him. Nor did he expect the words that came out of her mouth, words that left him cold with panic once more.

"Eliza and Nelly have left."

Dammit, not again. He heaved a weary sigh, running a hand through his hair. "What the hell do you mean, they have left? Have they run away again? Because so help me—"

"Oh! No. They merely walked out with a woman who came calling. At least," she mused, her dark brows drawing together in the middle, "I assume they were just taking a walk. The woman left her maid here, and her carriage is still in the front drive."

But Ash was already tugging his gloves back on. "Which way did they go?"

Regina looked suddenly hesitant. She was still smarting from yesterday, when her sisters not only pointedly ignored her for the whole night but also immediately dumped into the fire grate the treats she had offered to keep the peace. "I shouldn't have come to you with this," she said, backing away. "I'm certain it's nothing."

"Regina," he barked.

The girl flinched at his harsh tone, her eyes once again suspicious and resentful as they gazed up at him. Guilt flooded him, but he could not back down. They all had to learn boundaries.

Even so, he gentled his voice when he spoke again. "Which way did they go?"

"To the west," she answered, her voice devoid of emotion.

Fighting the urge to curse that he had once again mucked things up with her, he nodded in thanks and hurried from the house. Not for the first time he wondered despondently how he was going to continue to care for girls who had no wish to be cared for.

What he needed was a constant caregiver for them, someone who could keep the girls in line and mind them. Another governess? A companion? No, he had tried those, and had failed each time.

A wife?

The idea made his steps falter just as he reached the stables. Where the hell had that come from? He had never in his life considered marrying. What need had he for a wife? He had no interest in carrying on the family name, would not wish to burden the next generation with the shame and cruelty that came with the bloodline. That particular albatross had followed him all his life, the reputation of his father, and his father before him, and the generations before that, coloring every interaction and polluting everything that might have been good. The world would certainly be a better place if the dukedom died out, if the sins that had attached themselves to it like barnacles died out as well.

Yet here was just such a thought slinking through his brain. And, to his surprise, it had merit. He could take a wife, and have someone in his life who could take control of the day-to-day workings of his family and home while he continued his work at Brimstone.

Again the thought intruded that with marriage came the possibility of children. And children quite often received an inheritance they never wanted.

For a moment he recalled the whispers and beatings when he was a boy away at school, the cruel reminders of the legacy the Buckley title brought with it. He had fought for all he was worth against such a cursed birthright, certain that if he just tried hard enough, he could break free from it. Until one fateful day, in a fit of rage, he had nearly beaten his father to death, proving that it was not something he could ever escape.

Even so, with all of these warnings clanging about in his head, there was something infinitely more important than the possibility of future children, wasn't there? For his wards needed someone who could care for them, someone who was there for them without the need to be paid. Someone who could give them the love and affection that he wanted to but never could, for all he was trying to protect them from the truth. And so a wife for him, and a mother figure for them, really was the ideal plan. He saddled his horse and mounted, urging the animal out of the stable yard and after his wayward wards. The only question now was how he would find this paragon of womanhood who was willing and able to take control of three stubborn girls?

* * *

Bronwyn leaned closer to the feathery greenery, taking care not to move too swiftly, and gingerly lifted a leaf. Her heart pounded as she spied the now familiar shimmer of the tansy beetle hidden beneath. And not just one, but two of the compact insects. She leaned closer for a better look.

"Oh, Miss Pickering, there they are."

Miss Nelly's voice was hushed with awe, her eyes wide as Bronwyn glanced over her shoulder at her. Both girls were crouched in the dry grass beside her, their heads bent close together, expressions of intense curiosity on their faces.

It still had the power to shock her, their avid interest in her studies. Never in her life had anyone shown her a portion of the interest in her work that these two girls had.

Smiling slightly, she pulled the small lens from her bodice, easing the long chain over her head and handing it to the younger girl. "Indeed. Do you see that squat thorax?" she asked as the girl peered through the lens to study the specimen. "The faintly pockmarked elytra?"

The girls looked at her blankly. "I don't understand," Miss Eliza said, her brows drawn together.

Bronwyn, feeling a strange thrumming of excitement in her veins at the thought of passing on some of her vast knowledge to these young girls, took up a small stick from the ground and used it to carefully point to each part of the beetle. "This right here is the thorax," she said. "And these plates on the back are the elytra. They cover the insect's wings." Miss Eliza and Miss Nelly took turns then, looking through the small gold lens as Bronwyn, pulling a small notebook and pencil from her reticule, opened it to the sketch she had been working on before her parents' latest mandates. "They are typical of other tansy beetles I have seen illustrations of," she continued as she jotted notations in the margins of the sketch. "Only these are colored a shimmering green with blue undertones and bits of gold. The other *Chrysolina graminis* I have studied have red undertones. After my extensive research," she murmured, more to herself as she settled more comfortably in the grass, hunching farther over her sketch, "I am positive that these specimens are an entirely new species of tansy beetle. Surely, with this discovery, the Royal Society cannot fail to accept my name for membership and publish my paper. Once I manage to send it to them, that is."

She chewed on her lip, the burning determination to succeed flaring back to life in her gut, momentarily overcoming her despair at her parents' latest decrees. Though that exalted society, which was England's premiere scientific institution, had not yet welcomed females into their ranks, they could not fail to see how important her findings were. And then she might finally be recognized as more than a mere hobbyist and secure for herself a place among Britain's top entomologists.

Only how in the world would she ever manage that without her scientific equipment? Even more devastating, she was completely forbidden to pursue her research and was now forced into focusing all of her time into transforming herself into the perfect woman so she could snag a titled husband.

Panic decimated her momentary euphoria. Her parents had already begun to expect more and more from her as far as social obligations went, especially now that the summer season had begun. If they had their way, she would be carted about Synne from house to house, day in and day out, until they were able to squeeze a proposal from some unsuspecting male.

"Shall we look for other tansy beetles in the area for you?" Miss Nelly asked, her voice breaking through Bronwyn's quickly spiraling thoughts.

"Hmm? Oh, yes, that would be lovely. Thank you."

With that the girls scampered off, sending up the faint scent of camphor and rosemary as they brushed past the tansy plants, their happy voices and giggles carrying on the warm summer air.

There was nothing much she could do about her situation, she thought despondently as she bent over her notebook, adding delicate striations along the elytra in her quick sketch. As a young, unmarried female with no fortune of her own, she had no independence, no agency. She was her parents' property, to do with what they wished. And should she somehow manage to extract a proposal from someone, she would then become her husband's property. No matter what path her life took, she had no control over her eventual fate. And that included her entomological work and dreams of success.

But she was growing maudlin, an emotion she did not have time to coddle. Setting her jaw, she went back to work on her sketch, gently lifting the leaf to study the small beetles there, making quick lines and notes in her book. So engrossed was she in her sketch, she did not immediately hear Miss Nelly's voice call to her. Finally, however, the sound of it pierced the bubble Bronwyn was in. Thinking the girls must have located more of the beetles, she held up one finger.

"Just let me make these final notes." She quickly scribbled something more, then held up her hand. "Help me up will you?"

But it was not a slender girl's hand that grasped her own. No, this one was large and strong and decidedly male. Before she could think to snatch her hand back, the unseen person yanked her to standing. And Bronwyn found herself once more staring up into the face of the wickedly handsome, disturbingly intense stranger from the day before.

"Oh," she managed weakly.

"Oh, indeed," he murmured, the deep timbre of his voice sending a jolt of something electric and altogether consuming through her limbs.

She had not forgotten him since that chance encounter outside the Quayside yesterday. No matter if she was following her mother about on her errands, or sitting in on the calls that her mother made to her friends, or listening to her father spout ideologies about duty and family, this man had always been in the back of her mind. And when she had gone to bed...

She flushed hot at the remembrance.

But now he was here in front of her. *Looking just as delicious as before.*

She blinked. *Delicious*? Whatever had put that particular descriptor in her head?

He smiled slightly, his eyes crinkling at the corners. "Miss Pickering, I believe?"

Bronwyn, in the process of hurriedly stuffing her pencil and paper out of sight and self-consciously dusting off her skirts, froze. "How do you know my name?"

"My wards informed me of your identity," he explained, motioning to the two girls standing several feet off to the side.

"Wards?" Bronwyn asked, looking back and forth between the Hargrove girls and the gentleman. She had thought the girls must have a parent about somewhere. Yet she had never thought to ask them. Now she saw the reason for their air of loneliness: if they were the wards of someone, it meant they did not have parents to care for them any longer. They were orphans.

The gentleman inclined his head, watching her with an unnerving interest. "Indeed. I arrived from London just yesterday to join them." He smiled slightly, a small curve of his lips that didn't soften his features one bit. "When I ran into you, in fact. But forgive me; I haven't introduced myself. I am—"

"Mr. Hawkins," Miss Eliza burst in, stepping in front of her guardian. "Mr. Ash Hawkins."

"Yes," Miss Nelly agreed heartily, jumping forward to stand beside her sister. "Mr. Ash Hawkins. Our guardian."

Bronwyn blinked, confused, and looked to Mr. Hawkins. Who looked nearly as taken aback as she felt. He considered his wards closely for a time, some strange, silent interaction seeming to occur between them. Finally he turned back to Bronwyn, smiling stiffly, and held out his hand. "Yes. I am Mr. Ash Hawkins. Owner of Caulnedy Manor."

"I...see." Bronwyn, feeling as if she had missed something, nevertheless shook off the feeling and took the man's hand. Too late, however, she realized she was not wearing gloves. And neither was he.

How could a simple handshake feel so very intimate? Though their palms and the pads of their fingers were the only parts of them that touched, she felt it on every inch of her body. Shaken, more from the fact that the sensation urged her to close the distance between them and do God knew what, she pulled her hand free and stepped back. Yet she stood there, mutely staring. Not quite knowing what to say to this man who made her feel the strangest things in the most private parts of her body.

Bronwyn cleared her throat, shifting from foot to foot, then pulled the watch from the pocket at her waist, giving it a quick glance, more out of nervous habit than anything. She blinked, looking back again.

"Is that truly the time?"

Mr. Hawkins frowned. "I'm sorry?"

"The time. I lost track of it completely." Her parents would be furious; she was supposed to have been home by one to join them for a luncheon at Lady Tesh's house, an invitation they had been angling after for what seemed ages. And it was—she looked once more at her watch, blanching—quarter past?

"I have to leave," she said. "Miss Eliza, Miss Nelly. Mr. Hawkins." She gave him a quick look, a mistake, as the sight of him threatened to send her brain packing once more, before looking back to the girls. "I had a lovely time," she babbled, spinning about to begin the trek back to the manor. "But I really must go."

"Girls," Mr. Hawkins murmured from behind her, "why don't you hurry on up to the house and make certain Miss Pickering's carriage is ready so she might leave all the quicker."

"But we don't wish for Miss Pickering to leave!" Miss Nelly cried plaintively. "It feels as if she has just arrived, and we were just beginning to have fun."

"Yes, I imagine so," the man continued, even as Bronwyn, head down, kept on her course. "But if we do not assist her now, she may not wish to return."

Which was so preposterous that Bronwyn stopped dead in her tracks. Before she could proclaim to the girls that the only way she would not return was if her parents forbade it—something that, unfortunately, was quickly becoming an all too real possibility the more she delayed—the girls darted past her.

"Have no fear, Miss Pickering," Miss Eliza called out over her shoulder, her younger sister's hand tight in her own as they raced full tilt over the landscape. "We shall have your carriage ready for you in a trice."

And they were gone. Leaving Bronwyn quite alone with Mr. Hawkins. Or, as alone as two people could be out in the middle of a meadow where anyone could come upon them.

Suddenly that man was there beside her. In one hand he held his horse's reins—how had she not noticed the horse?—and the other arm he held out to her. "Shall we, Miss Pickering?"

Discombobulated, Bronwyn nevertheless could not allow his comments from a moment ago to pass without mention. "Why would you tell your wards that I would not return?" she demanded. "That was not kind of you."

"I did not mean to be unkind. I merely hoped for a moment alone with you. So we might get to know one another a bit better," he continued when she gave him a suspicious look. "Seeing as the girls seem to have made fast friends with you."

Which made much more sense than she expected. And, as he was still holding out his arm in that solicitous way, there was little else Bronwyn could do. And so, gingerly placing her hand in the crook of his arm, as one they began the walk back to Caulnedy.

But, though Mr. Hawkins had declared that he'd wished for time alone with her to talk, there was nothing but silence between them. It was so charged a silence, in fact, that Bronwyn found herself wishing for that thing she hated so much: small talk. At least then she wouldn't be quite so aware of his arm against her side, or the muscles beneath her sensitive fingers bunching with each movement of his large—ever so large—body. She swallowed hard.

When he spoke, however, she was made achingly aware that she had been a fool to wish for him to speak.

His voice, so deep and gruff, was a sound she felt in every nerve of her overly stimulated body.

"I suppose I can understand now why you reacted as you did yesterday when I nearly swatted those beetles from your skirts. You are a naturalist then?"

Bronwyn flinched, looking sharply up at him, searching for any indication he was mocking her even as she protectively hugged her bag close to her. But no, the eyes that gazed down at her were utterly serious. She blinked, not certain how to proceed. No one except her group of friends had ever acknowledged that what she was working toward was at all valid. And yet here was this magnetic man asking her if she were a naturalist as if it were the most natural thing in the world.

"I am," she finally managed. "An entomologist."

He nodded, as if it made perfect sense. A strange reaction that, as most people tended to sneer or laugh when discussing such things with her.

"My wards seemed incredibly interested in your work," he continued, his voice turning thoughtful. "I have not seen them so engaged in a long while."

Bronwyn felt her cheeks flush. She scoured her mind for something to say, finally settling on, "They are sweet girls."

"Are they?"

Why did it sound as if he was asking her? They were his wards, after all. Wouldn't he know?

Utterly confused, Bronwyn directed her gaze forward and pressed her lips tight, focusing on her footing. That was all she needed, to twist her ankle on a rock. And in front of this incredibly capable, virile male specimen.

Mr. Hawkins remained silent as well. A relief, for she did not think she could speak to him with any coherence. Though it certainly did not help that as they walked he seemed to look down at her with a disturbing regularity. Truly, did she have something in her hair? Perhaps a smudge on her cheek? Surreptitiously she lifted a hand to rub at her face. Just when the house came into view and she was finally beginning to relax, knowing this tension-fraught moment would soon be over, he spoke.

"You are unmarried."

She stumbled. Right away his hand was on her arm, steadying her. She gasped at the contact, her gaze flying to his. To her shock, his eyes had found her mouth. Was it her imagination or did she detect gold sparks of fire in the amber depths?

And then he released her, breaking the spell. She dragged in a deep breath, her head spinning.

"Do you prefer to live on Synne, or would you rather live in London?"

What the ever-loving blazes was he going on about? She shook her head, certain she had heard him wrong. "Pardon?"

"Synne? Do you prefer to live here?"

"Er . . . yes, I do," she answered hesitantly, not quite certain why he was interested in such a thing.

He nodded, as if he had expected as much, seemingly pleased if the small smile that lifted his lips was any indication. Frowning, not at all certain where this strange line of questioning was leading, she opened her mouth to excuse herself and hopefully escape his unnerving presence, when he spoke again.

"My wards have pronounced emphatically that they prefer to reside on Synne as well."

How was she expected to respond to that? Finally she decided on, "That's . . . good?"

"It is."

His enthusiasm took her aback. She glanced over her shoulder. The house was not fifty feet away. If she raised her skirts above her knees and ran, certainly she could reach her waiting carriage in a matter of minutes.

Before she could do so, however, Mr. Hawkins stepped closer. Her gaze snapped to his, all thoughts of fleeing evaporating like mist.

"I wonder if you wouldn't mind living here at Caulnedy," he murmured.

So focused was she on the huskiness of his voice as it vibrated over her skin, she didn't immediately comprehend what he had said. When she finally did, however, she pulled back sharply.

"Stay here at Caulnedy? I don't understand. You mean as a type of companion to your wards?" Which was such an unexpected idea she could not decide how she should react to it.

In the next moment, he suggested an even more unexpected notion. One that quite literally stole the breath from her body.

"Of a type. Though what I had in mind was a bit more permanent." He moved closer still until she was certain she could feel the heat of his body in the small space between them. "I would have you stay here as my wife."

Chapter 5

*E*ver since that one horrific, defining moment when Ash's life had burned down to painful cinders, when he had come home early from term after defending himself from a beating by his schoolmates and found his mother bruised and near death, he had lived his life by taking chances that others normally would not. It had led him to absconding with his mother in the dead of night, making his way to London after her death, joining Beecher in a business venture that outwardly had all the earmarks of failure.

And so when a young, unmarried woman whom his wards seemed to actually like was dropped in his lap like a bespectacled gift from the heavens, and shortly after he had decided it might be wise to marry in order to keep the girls in line, he was not about to ignore it.

Miss Pickering, however, was looking at him as if he'd grown a second head.

"You wish me to be your wife."

"Yes," he responded with that same certainty that had always precluded an important crossroads in his life. This was the right move; he felt it in his bones.

She gaped up at him, her sweet pink lips parted in shock. A shaft of heat shot through him at the sight, but he hastily buried it. This union, should she agree to it, would be a marriage of convenience and nothing more. No matter how delectable the woman in question might be.

"This is madness," she said. "You don't know who my family is. You don't know my financial situation. You know nothing of my interests except that I like to study insects. In truth you don't know anything about me."

It *was* madness. A mere half hour ago he had considered taking a wife. And here he was, proposing to the very first woman he came into contact with. If it had been anyone else doing the same, he would have thought they were meant for Bedlam.

Yet when he recalled how happy the girls had been when he'd come upon them with Miss Pickering—something he had never seen in all the time he had known them—he knew his swift decision to marry this woman was the right one.

"I know you are an unmarried female, and I am looking for a wife," he replied. "And I know you like my wards, and they like you. That, to me, is more than enough."

But she was shaking her head. "I have spoken to you for a total of perhaps twenty minutes," she said in disbelief.

"Many marriages have begun on less."

But she didn't seem to have heard him. Her eyes, which had been glazed with shock, suddenly turned icy, narrowing. "Did someone put you up to this?"

"What? No."

"Are you attempting to teach my parents a lesson through me?"

What the blazes had put such a thought in her head? "I don't even know who your parents are."

"Then why propose so suddenly?" She was growing more agitated by the second. She began to pace, her skirts snapping in the dry grass. "It's absurd. It's a mad scheme of the first order. It's—"

"Serendipity."

She flinched, looking at him with distrust plain in her gaze. "I don't believe in such things."

He pulled back at the bleakness in those clipped words. Had someone hurt her in the past? Was that the reason for her sudden defensiveness? Fury filled him at the very thought. It was an emotion that took him completely off guard. It shouldn't have been a surprise, of course; after the horrors his father had perpetrated, he had developed a deep desire to protect at all costs those who had been wronged.

But with Miss Pickering it was something different, not the cold, controlled anger that typically drove him but a white-hot rage.

Now was not the time, however, to dissect such a response. Apparently, he was going about this all wrong. He would need a different approach, something that would reach a swift conclusion. He had taken enough time and resources from his business dealings as it was in chasing down the girls; he could ill afford much more.

"Ah, yes," he murmured. "You are a naturalist. And I have been remiss in not laying all the facts before you, so you might better understand my reasons for wanting to marry a near stranger."

Something shifted in her at that. She stilled, a calm coming over her, her lovely turquoise eyes, the very color of clear ocean water, steady on him. Yes, this was the approach he should have used from the first.

Clearing his throat, he began. "My wards are very important to me. But they need minding, someone to watch over them and guide them." *Someone to give them the love I can't.* There was a sudden slice of pain at that thought, quickly brought under control. No, he could never provide them the love and affection they so dearly deserved. Not if he was to make certain they remained safe and protected and free of the shame that kept him up at nights.

"I have never in my life seen them respond to anyone as they do to you," he continued. "And, as they have spoken quite loudly on the fact that they would rather remain on Synne, and you would prefer to live here as well, it would be a simple matter of you moving out of your house and into Caulnedy. In short, Miss Pickering," he continued, "I am looking for a marriage in name only. Which would give you all the freedom you could wish for."

Longing filled her eyes at that last bit. But it was quickly gone, replaced by suspicion. "And where will you be?"

"I have a business in London I must see to."

"What kind of business?"

She could be the prudish sort, of course, and balk at the idea of marrying a man who made his fortune in peddling sin. But in for a penny. Bracing himself for her immediate disgust, he stated bluntly, "I own a gambling club."

To his relief, she merely nodded, as if it made perfect sense.

"I will be there most of the time," he continued. "And so, you see, you will have all the independence you desire."

"A marriage of convenience," she murmured, as if testing the words.

"Yes."

"And the marriage bed?" she continued, her cheeks flaming bright pink though she held his gaze steadily.

A vision slammed into his brain at that, an image of Miss Pickering lying in his bed, naked and rumpled and deliciously flushed from their lovemaking. Flames licked him from the inside out.

No, he told himself fiercely, this would not be a physical union. There was no desire involved. Well, he thought ruefully, he did desire her. Obviously. How could he not?

But this would be, as she had stated, a marriage of convenience. There would be no emotions involved. He would make certain of it.

"Physical relations will not be expected," he managed. "This will be a business arrangement."

She blinked, clearly not prepared for such an answer.

Yet he could fairly see the cogs turning in her brain. He already had proof that she was intelligent and incredibly shrewd. As well, she seemed the independent sort; any woman who pursued such an unusual interest, breaking away from societal norms and forging her own path, could be nothing but. Surely she would understand the benefits that she would receive should they marry.

She opened her mouth to speak. He tensed, waiting for her answer. Before she could say yay or nay, however, a cheerful whoop reached their ears. Startled, they both glanced toward the house. Eliza and Nelly were standing on the back of the carriage, waving their arms energetically in their direction. A pinch-faced maid who he assumed had come with Miss Pickering was trying her best to coax the girls down.

It was not the best timing on the girls' parts, but then again, when had they ever done anything they were supposed to?

He feared for a moment the sight of them in such a precarious position, revealing merely the tip of the gargantuan iceberg that was their improper behavior, might frighten Miss Pickering off. He turned her way, his defenses already in place, thinking quickly how he might mend this breach.

But she only looked at him with a healthy consideration.

"Mr. Hawkins," she said.

He very nearly winced at the deception, something he had forgotten in the last minutes of persuasion. He had no idea why the girls had insisted on concealing his true identity. It was something he would have to quiz them on when he had the chance.

For now, though, he was loath to correct Miss Pickering's view of him. It could very well sway her to accept him if she knew he was a duke, of course. Many would be more than happy to be a duchess, even independent spirits such as Miss Pickering. The truth could quite possibly win him the woman's hand all the quicker, thereby ending his search for a bride before it had even begun. Something that desperately needed to happen, he thought as he took in the spectacle his wards were making of themselves with a wince.

But he did not want to secure Miss Pickering that way. He had spent more than a decade forging a successful life without leaning on his father's title, making something of himself without relying on the chance circumstances of his birth. To gain Miss Pickering's hand in such a way was abhorrent to him. If she would marry him, let her marry Ash, not the Duke of Buckley, a title he still saw as his father's, no matter that he had reluctantly worn it since the bastard's death some seven years ago.

"Please, call me Ash," he finally replied.

She pressed her lips tight. "Mr. Hawkins," she repeated, delightfully stubborn. "As you know, I am of a scientific mind, and so you will also understand that I cannot make such a decision in haste. I need to weigh the pros and cons of the situation."

"Of course," he murmured, keeping his expression neutral, though disappointment crashed through him. There was no reason for it, of course. She was not saying no, and so he had hope. And he would lose nothing if she did decide to refuse him. They didn't know each other, after all.

But now that he had decided on the course to take, now that he had planned on making this woman his wife, he found he wanted it, desperately.

"Only, I don't have long on Synne," he continued. "The sooner I receive your answer the better."

She nodded, seemingly all business but for her tightened grip on the strap of her bag. A tell that betrayed her unsettled state of mind. "Of course," she said. "You may visit my family's home tomorrow afternoon, number seven Knighthead Crescent. I shall have your answer for you then."

With that she dipped into a quick curtsy and spun about.

Ash watched her as she fairly sprinted across the ground, climbed into her carriage with a quick goodbye to the girls, and departed with nary a look his way.

"Tomorrow, then, Miss Pickering," he murmured with a strange anticipation as he watched her carriage rumble away.

* * *

The moment Bronwyn departed Caulnedy Manor—fighting the urge to look back at Mr. Hawkins with every bit of willpower she possessed—she had known she would refuse him. It was a ridiculous idea to even think she might accept him; they had met one another a total of twice, both times by chance. And he wanted to *marry her*?

Mr. Hawkins, she surmised, would soon see the folly of such an idea. He had acted without thinking; no doubt having a night to think it over would have him comprehending the utter stupidity of his suggestion. He would not be visiting her house the next day to renew his proposal. She was certain of it.

Why, then, did the idea of him forgetting the entire thing leave a lump in her throat she could not seem to swallow down no matter how hard she tried?

But regardless what the man decided to do on the morrow, it would make no difference to her future, considering she had no intention of accepting him. During the ride home, seated across from her disapproving maid, she told herself she would not think of it any longer.

When she walked in the front door of her parents' fashionable town house, however, the decision to forget was taken right out of her hands. Never in her life, not all those years ago when they had been forced to flee London to avoid the scandal of her betrayal and heartbreak, not even when she had lost the hand of a literal duke the summer before, had she seen her parents so enraged. Between her mother's hysterics and her father's ranting over being forced to miss the luncheon at Lady Tesh's because of Bronwyn's tardiness—how would they react if they knew that part of that tardiness was because a stranger had proposed to her?—Bronwyn did not have time to think, her entire focus on repeatedly apologizing well into the night. By the time she fell into bed, utterly exhausted from the emotional toll of the day, Mr. Hawkins and his ridiculous suggestion had completely fled her thoughts.

Well, perhaps not completely. He remained firmly planted in the back of her mind, a tempting thought. Like the idea of a slice of lemon cake waiting for her, dripping with icing and candied fruit, delicious and decadent and utterly mouthwatering...

Which was probably why she hadn't slept well. And woke much later than usual, craving sweets.

She thought perhaps her tardiness the day before, a mortal sin in the eyes of her social-climbing parents, would nevertheless be quickly forgotten. Mr. and Mrs. Pickering, while ridiculous, were not ones to hold grudges. Therefore, when she descended to the first-floor drawing room the following morning, ready if not quite willing to discover what plans her mother had made for the day, she was shocked to find that her parents were not through with their offense.

"Sit down, Bronwyn," her father said in a voice that brooked no refusal as she entered the room.

Alarmed, for her father was not one to use such firm tones even when deeply upset, Bronwyn approached and sat in the chair facing her parents. What the devil was going on? Was there to be a punishment then for yesterday's thoughtlessness? Whatever it might be, she prayed it was over and done with quickly.

Her parents, however, were not about to make this easy on her.

"We are still very much upset by your actions yesterday, Bronwyn," her mother said, visibly nervous. She shot her husband a quick look. He nodded, as if to encourage her.

Filled with a sudden dread, Bronwyn gripped her

hands together in her lap. Silly and gregarious and outrageous attitudes from her parents she could handle. But
she had never in her life seen them in such a serious,
solemn state.

"It was utterly irresponsible of you," her mother continued. She held a handkerchief in her hands and was
systematically twisting it, as if strangling the life out
of it. "And after all we have discussed in the past days
and weeks, how we expect you to comport yourself in a
proper manner in order to find a husband."

"We had thought you would finally heed our wishes
on the matter," her father chimed in, heavy brows drawn
low over his eyes. "Surely our Bronwyn would not
wound her parents by purposely ruining all chances at
finding a match. But no, you are even more determined
to break our hearts."

"Why, when I think of my mortification, the utter
embarrassment of having to send a letter of apology to
Lady Tesh." Her mother sniffled loudly, bringing her
crushed handkerchief to her eyes to wipe at nonexistent
tears. "She will think we have snubbed her. And so will
everyone else, for it surely must be all over the Isle
by now."

"There, there, dear," her husband murmured, placing
an arm about his wife's shoulders. He shot Bronwyn a
furious look. "Do you see what you have done to your
mother? Her nerves are frayed beyond bearing."

"I'm sorry, Mama," Bronwyn managed, feeling as
low as she ever had. Yes, her parents frustrated her more
than not. She was nothing like them, after all; their
personalities mixed about as well as oil and water. Yet

she loved them dearly and had no wish to give them pain. But she seemed to be doing just that more and more frequently.

"*Sorry* is all well and good," her father said. "But it does nothing to repair the damage you caused yesterday. You are completely unaware of how your every action affects all of our futures. In truth, I don't think you shall ever see the importance of it."

"It's those *Oddments*," her mother bit out, raising her face from her handkerchief, anger stamped across her features. "They've put strange ideas in our girl's head. Oh, Mr. Pickering," she wailed, her mood changing in an instant to one of utter misery. "Those girls have ruined our dear daughter."

Bronwyn gaped at her, stunned at both the pendulum of her mother's emotions and the utter absurdity of her reasoning. "You are blaming this on my friends?"

"Friends who would insist on filling your head with thoughts of independence and bluestocking ways," her father replied, rubbing his wife's shaking back as she sobbed into her handkerchief. "Which is why we are removing you from their influence."

"No!" The word exploded from Bronwyn as she surged to her feet. Though she had fretted that her parents would do just this, the pain that sliced her from the inside out shocked her to her core. "You cannot do this. Mama, tell him he cannot ban me from seeing my friends."

"I can and I will," her father decreed. "No daughter of mine will be a social pariah, an unwed spinster. Why, next you know you'll be telling us your scribblings will be printed in some scientific magazine and you'll be calling yourself a naturalist." He shuddered, even as his wife's sobs renewed with greater volume.

Bronwyn's shock quickly gave way to fury. "I *am* a naturalist," she declared, her voice trembling. "I've worked hard, and I'm smart, and I can make a name for myself, no matter how many of my specimens you might destroy, no matter the equipment you might smash. Besides, there is nothing wrong with remaining unwed. Look at Adelaide, or Seraphina. Both are owners of highly successful businesses and are respected in the community."

"Oh, Mr. Pickering," her mother wailed. "Our daughter wishes to go into *trade*!"

Bronwyn, praying for patience, pinched the bridge of her nose. "Papa made his fortune in trade," she replied, her voice tight with frustration. "There is nothing at all wrong with it."

But her parents, as ever, would not listen to reason. "No daughter of mine is going into trade," her father declared, outrage visible on his face.

"You were right, Mr. Pickering," his wife said, gazing at him with tears in her eyes, her features stamped with her misery. "We have to send her away."

"Of course I'm right," her husband said, patting her back consolingly.

But whatever else her father said was lost in the roaring in Bronwyn's ears. "Sending me away?" she demanded. Surely she had heard them wrong. She had thought they would forbid her from going to her weekly meetings with the Oddments, not that they would remove her from Synne altogether.

Her father glared at her. "You didn't think this latest wrongdoing would go unpunished, did you? We're sending you to live with your brother and his wife in Exeter until you learn that you cannot do whatever you wish."

"No!" Again the word burst from her, this time colored with horror. She could not live with James, so austere and strict. And his wife, who was so needlessly cruel. And in a location so very far from Synne and her friends and her research. Her spirit and her passions and her dreams would be crushed there as surely as an ant beneath a boot.

"No," she repeated, trying and failing to hide the desperation in her words, "I won't go."

"You will, my girl," her father decreed, rising to his feet. "And you shall not return until you are ready to be the obedient daughter we expect you to be." He leveled a look on Bronwyn that left her cold, for there was no softness in it. She would not be able to convince them to allow her to stay. No, her fate was sealed.

The butler stepped into the doorway then. "Mr. Hawkins is here for Miss Pickering," he intoned before stepping aside.

And then there was Mr. Hawkins, looking wickedly handsome in a slate-blue coat and dove trousers, his magnetic intensity clashing with the thick cloud of tension filling the air, sending her off-balance. His amber eyes scanned the room, quickly finding her. His expression was unreadable, but Bronwyn would not have cared if he had reeked of smugness and certainty. She only knew she had never been so happy to see anyone in her life.

"Bronwyn," her father said, eyeing Mr. Hawkins with confusion, "who is this man?"

Before she could think better of it, Bronwyn made her way to Mr. Hawkins's side and tucked her hand in his. Ignoring the man's look of surprise, her parents' gaping, even the now-familiar zing of electricity when their hands touched, she straightened and faced her parents.

"Mama, Papa, this is Mr. Ash Hawkins. My fiancé."

Chapter 6

Well, that was unexpected.

Ash had arrived at Miss Pickering's home in Knighthead Crescent much earlier than was polite for social calls. But he had been at his wit's end after the morning's debacle with his wards. One did not necessarily care about propriety, after all, when one was woken by the pungent smell of burnt food billowing from the kitchens at six in the morning.

Blessedly the damage had been kept to a minimum, confined as it was to the pan of what he supposed was intended to be biscuits. That did not mean, however, that it would not take them the better part of the day to air the kitchens out. Or that he was not doubly desperate to secure Miss Pickering for his wife. The quicker he could get her settled in with his wards, the quicker he could get back to London and Brimstone and away from the constant guilt that he was failing everyone he cared for.

He had expected to still have a fair amount of convincing to do once he arrived at Miss Pickering's house. No one was ready to answer life-altering questions at such an hour, after all. And so he had compiled all manner of reasons why they should marry, each one dedicated to showing Miss Pickering why such a union would be of benefit to her: she would have all the independence she could wish for; she would be provided with all the funds she could desire; she would have his full support on any scientific endeavors she might aspire to.

But he had not thought in a million years she would need no convincing at all.

Her parents—she had called them *Mama* and *Papa*, so he assumed they were her parents, though they looked nothing like her—stared at Miss Pickering as if she had sprouted a pig nose.

"What do you mean, *fiancé*?" her father demanded, looking for all the world like an outraged rooster in his bright yellow coat and red breeches.

"Mr. Hawkins asked me to marry him yesterday," Miss Pickering replied, her voice warbling only slightly. "I have decided to accept."

"But...what...who...?" her father sputtered, his face turning florid, eyebrows as thick as a fox's tail descending low over his blazing eyes.

"Oh, my," his wife said faintly.

"It's a pleasure to make your acquaintance, Mr. Pickering, Mrs. Pickering," Ash said with a bow.

"Oh, my," Mrs. Pickering repeated, her hands flapping

about in the air, the white scrap of lace and linen she held fluttering in front of her like an anxious bird.

"You did say you wanted me married, didn't you, Papa?" Miss Pickering said.

"Yes, but not to—" The man pressed his lips tight against whatever he had been about to say, looking Ash up and down, his face turning a dark red.

"Go ahead and finish," Miss Pickering continued, her voice tight, her body fairly trembling against Ash's arm. "Not to a commoner, isn't that right? You wished me to marry, even planned to send me away to live with my brother as punishment for not finding a husband, yet you will accept nothing less than a nobleman's suit."

"My daughter deserves a title," her father countered, seeming to have forgotten Ash was present.

"I hate to tell you this, Papa," Miss Pickering snapped, "but dukes are not exactly thick on the ground, much less single dukes looking for a wife."

Ash, watching the quarrel between father and daughter with rapt interest, promptly choked. "Er, Miss Pickering?" he tried. Mayhap now was the time to inform her of his true identity.

No, he thought guiltily, the time to inform her had been yesterday, an immediate correction of his wards' deception. The next best time would have been mere minutes later when he had proposed they marry.

But, barring the existence of traveling through time, now would have to do.

The Pickerings, however, seemed not to have heard him.

"There have been a grand total of four eligible dukes

on Synne in the past years who have found brides," her father countered. "Four!"

Mrs. Pickering stepped up beside her husband, her ample bosom pushing into the fray like the bow of a ship plowing through rough waters. "And while there are very good reasons for you losing the majority of them," she joined in, her voice shrill in her outrage, "we cannot forget that you had one in the palm of your hand before he chose another."

Beside Ash, Miss Pickering groaned. "Why must you continue to bring up the Duke of Carlisle?"

"Because you nearly secured him, Bronwyn," her father raged. "You were nearly a duchess. And now you would marry a—I'm sorry," Mr. Pickering said in a ridiculously conciliatory tone, considering the subject, turning to Ash, "what business are you in?"

"Gambling," Ash answered automatically. "But if you would just hear me out—"

"Gambling!" Mrs. Pickering wailed. "Oh, Mr. Pickering. We shall be laughingstocks. What shall we do?"

"We shall not allow Bronwyn to marry this person, that is what we shall do," Mr. Pickering declared.

"You cannot do that," Miss Pickering replied heatedly.

"We can and we shall," her mother stated. "I am so sorry, Mr. Hawkins, but we must ask you to leave."

"You will do nothing of the sort," Miss Pickering countered. She grabbed tighter to Ash's hand, as if she feared her parents would rip him from her side and toss him out on his ear.

"Listen to your mother, young lady," her father said, his chest puffing up in outrage.

Ash might have continued to let the argument run its course; it did not seem they would allow him to speak, though it was his future on the line as well.

But when he looked down at Miss Pickering and caught the telltale glint of a tear quickly blinked back, saw the slight trembling of her lower lip, he decided he was done worrying about propriety and politeness. "I have something to say," he roared, his voice rising above the chaos, feeling ridiculously like he did when trying to stop his wards from squabbling.

They all looked to him, varying degrees of shock stamped across their faces. *Finally.* He opened his mouth to tell these people that he was, in fact, a duke.

Just then, however, the butler was at the door, his voice breaking into the brief moment of blessed silence.

"Lady Tesh, ma'am."

A short, ancient, brightly gowned woman pushed past the man, hobbling into the room. Behind her, a fair young woman followed along nervously, a small, scraggly white pup held in her arms.

"Lady Tesh," Mrs. Pickering gasped, dropping into quite possibly the deepest curtsy Ash had ever seen. "We are honored that you've come to visit. Please allow me to say once again how very sorry we are for missing your luncheon yesterday—"

"Enough." The older woman's clipped tones quieted Mrs. Pickering in an instant. Even in the midst of Ash's confusion and frustration, he couldn't help but admire her for her talent in achieving something of that sort without even needing to raise her voice.

"Yesterday is quite forgotten," she continued, sharp

eyes scanning the Pickerings before coming to rest on Ash. "It is another matter entirely I've come about. Miss Pickering," she said, not looking at that woman though she addressed her, "I hear you have made friends with some new arrivals come to stay at Caulnedy Manor."

"I have, my lady," Miss Pickering said. She exchanged glances with the young woman just behind Lady Tesh, a charged look passing between them. "Two young girls, Miss Eliza and Miss Nelly Hargrove. And this is their guardian, Mr. Ash Hawkins. Mr. Hawkins," she continued, looking up at him with shuttered eyes, "allow me to introduce the dowager Viscountess Tesh and her companion, Miss Katrina Denby. Oh, and her dog Freya, of course."

"*Mr.* Ash Hawkins, is it?" Lady Tesh murmured, her eyes narrowing as she continued to stare at him, as if trying to peer into his very soul.

"Yes," Miss Pickering continued. She gripped his hand tighter. "Mr. Hawkins has asked me to marry him, and I have accepted."

"Bronwyn," her mother moaned.

"There will be no getting her out of it now," her father muttered in a tortured aside to his wife.

But Lady Tesh seemed to have forgotten that the elder Pickerings were present. Her eyes flared wide as her companion gasped. "You are engaged to this man, are you, Miss Pickering?"

"I am," Miss Pickering answered, standing straighter.

"We are so very sorry, Lady Tesh," Mrs. Pickering broke in, her hands clasped beseechingly to her ample bosom. "She accepted Mr. Hawkins without our consent."

"I'm certain my lady can help us to keep this unfortunate predicament under wraps, and perhaps even
assist us in persuading Bronwyn to give up his suit,"
Mr. Pickering said, his voice a pleading whine.

But the dowager viscountess looked at them as if they
were mad as hatters. "Why on earth would you wish to
do something like that?"

"Mr. Hawkins is not a proper husband for our dear
Bronwyn," Mr. Pickering answered, shooting Ash a
furious look, as if to say, *This is all your fault.*

"Not proper, eh? Not keen on having a duke for a
son-in-law?"

The silence at that pronouncement was so thick Ash
could have cut it with a knife. He nearly groaned. Damn
it all to hell, this was *not* the way he had hoped to
tell Miss Pickering of his identity. He looked down at
that woman, expecting to find one of two emotions on
her face: fury at being deceived, or joy that she had
snagged a title. Having seen her stand up to her parents
in the past minutes, he rather thought it would be the
former.

Instead, there was humor in her eyes. "Lady Tesh,"
she said, laughter barely held in check, "I'm afraid you
are mistaken. This is Mr. Ash Hawkins, owner of a
London gaming hell. He's certainly not a *duke*."

"Actually," Ash began ruefully.

Miss Pickering turned to look up at him, the amusement that stamped her lovely features vanishing in an
instant as she took in the seriousness of his expression.
She frowned, dropping his hand and stepping away from
him. "Mr. Hawkins?"

"I meant to tell you," he attempted to explained, the words sounding pathetic even to his own ears.

"You're a *duke*?"

He winced at the disbelief and condemnation in her voice. Ah yes, definitely the former reaction. "Yes," he replied quietly. "I'm the Duke of Buckley."

* * *

Mr. Hawkins looked as uncomfortable as any one person could. No, Bronwyn reminded herself harshly, no longer Mr. Hawkins. The Duke of blasted Buckley.

She should be happy, she supposed. It was her parents' fondest wish that she marry a title. And not just any title, but a bloody *duke*.

Instead, all she felt was a bone-deep hurt. Why did men feel as if they could lie to her? Granted, she had been in love with the man who had last deceived her. But that did not mean this betrayal did not sting as well. Did she seem that naive? Or did they just have so little respect for her that it didn't matter what they told her?

Suddenly tired down to her soul—she didn't know why she had thought this man would be different, but she had—Bronwyn wanted nothing more than to retire to her room and crawl under her covers and pretend she had never woken up that morning. Her parents, however, had quite another idea.

"Oh, my dear Mr. Pickering," her mother shrieked, at such a volume that Bronwyn would have been surprised if the entirety of Knighthead Crescent hadn't heard her.

"Our daughter is marrying a duke. Our daughter shall be a duchess!"

"I always knew you had it in you, Poppet," her father pronounced, his face flushed with pride as he looked at her.

All the while, as her parents fairly exploded with joy, she was painfully aware of Mr. Hawkins—er, His Grace—gazing at her, a kind of apology in his eyes. For what? Making a fool of her? Tricking her? Being found out? Not that he could have hidden it for long. One couldn't marry a woman without certain minor aspects coming to light. Like one being a damned *duke*.

Lady Tesh, it seemed, had finally had enough of the noise. "Dear God," she muttered, waving her cane in the air in a bid for silence and nearly clipping Bronwyn's nose in the process. "You shall make my head ache with all this screeching and going on."

"But, Lady Tesh," Bronwyn's mother gushed, her eyes glowing. "Our daughter is marrying a duke."

"Yes, so I've heard," the older woman muttered dryly. She heaved a beleaguered sigh. "But one would think there was still room for manners. Such as offering your guests a seat and a beverage?"

"Oh!" Mrs. Pickering exclaimed, jumping forward and taking Lady Tesh's arm. "Of course. How forgetful of me. Bronwyn, my darling, wonderful girl, why don't you ring for tea while I get Lady Tesh and His Grace settled." With that pronouncement, she sent the duke an adoring look, batting her lashes.

His Grace blanched and looked to Bronwyn in desperation. She very nearly scoffed. Did the man think she would rescue him? Let him stew in the repercussions of his deceit. Stalking past him, she grabbed Katrina's arm and dragged her to the bell pull.

"Did you know he was a duke?" Bronwyn hissed.

"I knew a duke owned Caulnedy," her friend whispered back, her cornflower-blue eyes wide in her pale face. "Lady Tesh informed me when I discussed it with her last night. But I did not know he was on Synne. Or that you had become *engaged* to him. What in the world could have happened since our meeting with the Oddments two days ago, Bronwyn?"

"I hardly know," she managed, panic beginning to set in. She yanked the bell pull much harder than necessary, sending the tasseled bit of fabric swaying wildly. "It's all run together. Everything has happened so fast. Oh, Katrina, I don't know what to do."

Which was an understatement. It had been one thing to engage herself to Mr. Hawkins, gambling hell owner. It was quite another to find she was set to marry a duke. Not that she had actively attempted to avoid marrying a person with such a title. She had welcomed—though not exactly eagerly—the lukewarm interest of the Duke of Carlisle last year before losing his possible suit. But though her parents had raged when he'd turned his affections elsewhere, Bronwyn had been secretly relieved. After all, to be a duchess, a position where every move would be watched, every word would be dissected, was a terrifying prospect.

Just as it was now, with His Grace's revelation. And what else was he lying about? Did he really intend to let her stay on Synne with his wards? Or would she be expected to give up her interests, to put aside her dreams of making a name in entomological circles and take up the duties of a duchess? If she could not hope to please her parents—though they seemed perfectly pleased with her now, she thought bitterly, casting them a dark glance—how could she possibly live up to the expectations of being a duchess?

Katrina shifted Lady Tesh's dog, who was looking much more interested in their conversation than any canine should be, and placed a comforting hand on Bronwyn's shoulder. "I'm no good at figuring out how to get out of tight spots," she said, her lips twisting in a miserable little smile, no doubt recalling her own scandalous past. "But maybe Seraphina or Honoria or Adelaide can help."

Help with what? Now that Lady Tesh was in possession of the news, and her parents had been apprised that their daughter was marrying a duke, there would be no escaping it.

Before Bronwyn could voice such cold, hard facts, however, her mother's strident voice carried to them. "Bronwyn, darling, do come here and sit beside your fiancé."

Katrina gave her a commiserating look as they made their way to the circle of seats. Quite against her wishes, Bronwyn was quickly ushered to the empty space on the settee beside the duke. Painfully aware of his leg mere inches from hers, she busied herself adjusting her skirts, putting as much distance between them as possible. Dear God, she had never seen a limb so well-formed. A thought came unbidden to her, what it might look like beneath the fine gray trousers he wore, how the muscles might move beneath the skin, how they might feel between her own thighs...

She nearly gasped, putting a swift halt to her gawking of the man's leg. Yes, she was of a scientific mind, had studied creatures, insects and birds and mammals alike, and knew the basics of mating. She had even done her fair share of exploring her own body, wondering what it might feel like joining with another, how they might move together. How it might feel...

Ahem.

But that was no excuse for leering at the man. Especially as he had made it quite clear that theirs was to be a marriage of convenience, with no expectations of physical intimacy.

She should be glad for it. She had known the man but two days, after all; she could not begin to imagine feeling comfortable enough to perform such intimate acts with him.

And yet the naturalist in her was deeply curious to know just what all the fuss was about.

"As our dear Bronwyn will be marrying a duke," her mother declared, giving Bronwyn a glowing look that was full of more pride than the woman had shown her in all of her four and twenty years combined, "I insist on all the pomp such an occasion deserves. A lengthy engagement; balls and luncheons in their honor; visits to all our dear former friends around the country as we shop for her trousseau. And, of course, a lavish wedding at St. George's in London."

"Certainly, certainly," her father said, hands on his

knees, chest puffed up with his importance. "Nothing but the best for our girl. Don't you agree, Your Grace?"

Bronwyn wanted nothing more than to sink into the ground. They weren't considering what was best for Bronwyn at all. These were all things *they* wished, *they* wanted. The better to preen and strut before all those they felt had wronged them; to take, as they often said, their *rightful* place in the world.

She thought back then to that disastrous trip to London. How many times had she hung back, mortified, as her parents forcibly pushed themselves into circles they had not been invited into? How many events had she watched with a kind of fatalistic horror as they made fools of themselves and her by their blind certainty that they would be welcome at all levels of society, that their sizable bank account made them superior to the majority of the population?

And how often had she sat in misery as they voiced their deep disappointment that their daughter did not conform to societal norms?

They had never once considered Bronwyn when making plans for the future. No, everything had centered around their standing and how they would look to outsiders. And this time was no different. No different at all. If anything, it was much, much worse.

"While I am in complete agreement that Miss Pickering deserves only the best," His Grace said, his deep voice dragging her back to the present, "I would very much like as short an engagement as can be managed. By special license if at all possible."

And then he did the thing Bronwyn least expected

him to do: he looked down at her and said, a deep interest in his eyes, as if her opinion was paramount to him, "What do you think, my dear?"

She stared up at him, shocked. And oddly touched. Surely this was just for show. No one cared what her wishes were in this debacle; it was clear as day that there were much more important things at play than what one mere young woman wanted, no matter she was the bride. And soon to be a duchess. She swallowed hard.

Yet the expression on his face, the dark intensity threaded through with a focused curiosity, made it appear as if what she had to say actually mattered to him.

"Come along, Bronwyn," her father said through gritted teeth. "Answer the duke. Forgive my daughter, Your Grace. She's not typically so slow-witted."

"On the contrary," the duke murmured, his unusual eyes never leaving Bronwyn, "I think your daughter is one of the most clever, intelligent people I have ever had the pleasure to meet."

"Oh," Katrina breathed from her place beside Lady Tesh.

But Bronwyn hardly heard her. Something in her had shifted at the duke's words, a softening in her chest she had never allowed before.

Confused, flustered, she cleared her throat. "I am not opposed to a special license," she managed. "Though I would like the wedding held on Synne. With my friends in attendance."

The smile that spread across his face was totally unexpected. It transformed him from wickedly dangerous to affable in an instant. Overwhelmed by her conflicting emotions, she frowned and looked down to her lap.

"Well then," Lady Tesh said, thumping her cane on the ground in a decisive manner, "that settles it."

"But, my lady, Your Grace," Bronwyn's mother tried, distress plain on her face, her hands flapping about, as if ready to take flight before they came to rest on her husband's mustard-yellow sleeve.

"But nothing," Lady Tesh snapped. "Good God, Mrs. Pickering. Both the bride and the groom are in agreement. We should heed their wishes."

"B-but…" Mrs. Pickering tried again.

The look Lady Tesh speared her with leeched all color from her face, leaving only two garish splotches of rouge on her cheeks.

"Are you doubting my authority, Mrs. Pickering?" she demanded. "Or perhaps it is my faculties you call into question?"

Bronwyn's mother flinched. For a second, Bronwyn almost felt sorry for her; there was nothing the woman wanted more than the dowager viscountess's approval after all.

"Of course not, my lady," Mrs. Pickering gasped.

"I *am* Synne," Lady Tesh continued, glaring at Bronwyn's parents in turn. Her pup, too, looked at the couple with disdain, as if daring them to doubt her mistress. "And if I say we can plan a swift wedding that will be fit for a duke and his duchess"—here she gave Bronwyn a nod—"then it shall be done."

Mrs. Pickering, in the process of deflating at the dowager viscountess's pronouncement, perked up at that. "Oh, my lady," she gushed. "Are you saying you shall assist us in planning?"

"Indeed." She turned to His Grace then. "You shall leave first thing tomorrow for London to fetch that special license. When do you think you shall return?"

"As I'll be traveling with my wards so they might pack their things for their move to Caulnedy, I would say a fortnight will suffice," he replied.

Lady Tesh narrowed her eyes. "A move to Caulnedy? Will you be residing on the Isle then?"

As if in slow motion, Bronwyn saw her intended open his mouth to answer the dowager viscountess. Would he admit that he would be leaving Bronwyn and the girls on Synne while he returned to London? That they were to have a marriage in name only?

Mortification flooded her. Ah God, she would not be able to handle the shame of something of that nature being revealed to these people. It was bad enough Bronwyn was aware of what others thought of her, that she was odd and unattractive and could never inspire the more delicate emotions in anyone, much less a magnetic, desirable, utterly male figure such as her soon-to-be husband.

With a suddenness that stunned her, the memory of the most devastating day came back to her, like a nightmare that would not end. She saw Lord Owens's face as he visited their London residence, recalled the surge of happiness in her chest when he asked for her to fetch her parents, for he had something to ask her. And then the confusion, followed by ripping pain when his features turned cruel and he hurled those words at her that would forever be etched in her brain: "Did you honestly believe that someone like me could ever care for a pathetic creature like you? Mayhap now you Pickerings will learn that your place in the world is beneath the boot of respectable society. Do not overreach again."

Now here was another horrible moment, where not only her parents would be witness to proof of her un-desirability, but Lady Tesh and Katrina as well. Would they ignore the fact that the duke intended to leave her as soon as the vows were said, pretending as if it was completely natural for a bride and groom to part so quickly? Or, worse, would they look at her with pity in their eyes? She blanched. No, she couldn't handle it. Before she knew what she was about, she blurted, "Yes, we'll all reside on Synne. For a short time, at least."

There were exclamations of delight all around. All except for His Grace, who was unnaturally still beside her.

"Very good," Lady Tesh said. "A fortnight it shall be then. When you return in two weeks' time, Your Grace, we shall be ready for you."

"Oh, Lady Tesh," Bronwyn's mother gushed, looking at Lady Tesh in a kind of rapturous wonder. "How very generous you are."

The tea arrived then, preventing further discourse for some minutes. A fact that Bronwyn could only be grateful for. Her head was pounding from how quickly everything was changing. In a matter of two weeks she would be wed to a virtual stranger. What had she been thinking? Yes, the idea of being sent off in disgrace to her brother's house had been horrifying. But that at least had been a known outcome, something she could have prepared for. There were so many uncertainties now, from how others would see her to how she would be required to act to what the myriad duties of a duchess were. And they frightened her witless.

A sudden hand on her own made her jump. Her gaze jerked up and met His Grace's frown. Ah, God, for a moment she had forgotten her hasty declaration that they would all reside on Synne for a time. No doubt he was furious at her. She searched his eyes for any signs of anger. But no, there was only a peculiar concern. He studied her, brows drawn together, before turning back to the others.

"As I shall be leaving tomorrow, and shan't see Miss Pickering until our wedding day, I do believe we could do with some time alone to discuss matters."

"Certainly, Your Grace," Bronwyn's mother said with a complacent smile. "You may make use of the back garden."

His Grace stood, holding out a hand for Bronwyn. She looked at it for several seconds, studying his long fingers before, with a trembling breath and a quick glance at Katrina, who was looking at her with wide eyes, she grasped hold of it.

All too soon they were stepping out into the garden. It was not a large space, but it was not small either. Several winding paths snaked in and out of the thick foliage, giving an immediate sense of intimacy. It was the very reason she had taken solace here more times than she could count in the years since they'd moved to Synne. Now, however, it made her even more aware of the man at her side than ever before. The silence stretched on between them as they walked, the sounds of the churning ocean and seabirds and the people of Synne going about their merry lives muted back here in this private place. Bronwyn would have been completely content if they could just keep walking about, circle after circle, not having to face the enormity of what she had agreed to.

All too soon, however, His Grace stopped. Blinking blearily, Bronwyn looked around. They were by the back wall of the garden, ivy-covered bricks and a wrought-iron bench on one side and several well-placed bushes on the other, making it as secluded as anyplace could be.

Gently he turned her to face him. His amber eyes had a strange light to them as he stared at her lips.

Her mouth went dry.

"We have much to discuss, you and I," he murmured, a peculiar tension threading his voice. "But first, I do believe it is customary to seal our engagement with a kiss?"

Before she could think to respond, he lowered his head.

Whatever fears had been simmering in her brain were forgotten at the feel of his lips on hers. How was it possible, she thought in the one corner of her brain still capable of coherency, that something could feel firm and soft all at once?

Then he tilted his head, deepening the kiss as his arms came about her, dragging her against the hard length of his body. The last of her mental faculties disappeared into the ether and her body came alive. Perhaps, just perhaps, being married to this man might not be so bad after all.

Chapter 7

*A*sh hadn't intended on kissing Miss Pickering when he had first suggested they take a walk. He truly had intended to just talk. To give her the space and time she needed to come to terms with what was quickly—much more quickly than he had thought possible—progressing for their futures. After all, the woman had looked as if she was about to keel over on the spot.

But then he had found this private little space in the garden, and had looked down at her lovely, flushed face, and all his previous intentions fled. At least momentarily. He would come back to them, eventually. For now, though, the only thing he could even contemplate doing was tasting her lips.

Which was quite possibly the most brilliant idea he had ever had in his life.

By God, but her lips were soft, just barely pressing

against his own, a tentative exploration. He pulled her body flush to his and felt the soft, slight curves give to him, and very nearly groaned. He gently pressed his tongue to the chaste line of her lips. How was it that one small, fierce woman could affect him so deeply? But then she gasped, and their tongues touched, and there was no more room to wonder. She tasted of sunshine and warmth and coming home. And he needed more.

He splayed his hands against her back, achingly aware of the graceful arch of her spine beneath the layers of fabric, the tips of his fingers just barely brushing the top of her buttocks. She arched into him, a small sound purring from the back of her throat, her hands gripping tight to his shoulders, as if she were afraid of being swept away in a raging current. She was small and slender, her form angular and slight of curve. Yet there was nothing at all childish about her. He breathed her in, luxuriating in the scent of lemon with just the faintest hint of sweetness to soften it. Like the most delectable lemonade on a hot day. Like Bronwyn herself, sharp yet utterly delicious.

What he wouldn't give to explore her to his heart's content, to trace every line of her body, to draw more of those sweet sounds from her lips. But no, he reminded himself severely as he forcibly pulled back, theirs was not a romantic union.

Even so, he could not help but gaze down at her, longing warring with sense in his chest. She remained unmoving, face lifted and eyes closed, and he allowed himself to drink in her features. Her face was long and narrow, her nose pert and pointed, her jaw strong and revealing a stubbornness he felt deep down he had only seen the beginnings of. Her lids fluttered up, revealing those lovely, brilliant turquoise eyes behind the lenses of her spectacles. For a moment he allowed himself to swim in the depths of those eyes. Had she been as affected as he had by that kiss? As simple as it had been, it had shaken him down to his core.

In the next moment her expression cleared and she stepped back. Nervous hands went to her skirts, smoothing the dull green fabric. "I'm afraid, Your Grace," she said in a trembling voice, "that no amount of kissing can prevent us from having a very necessary conversation about your identity, and what it is you expect from this marriage."

No matter that there could be nothing between them, Ash wouldn't mind trying to distract her in such a manner once more. But she was right, this conversation was long overdue.

"Of course. But won't you call me Ash?" At the doubt in her gaze, he continued in a softer tone. "We are to be married after all."

Her cheeks, already flushed from his kiss, burned a bright pink. "Very well...Ash."

My God, how was it possible that his name on her lips, one short syllable, a mere three letters, could sound so utterly decadent? Clearing his throat, he swept out a hand toward the nearby bench.

She sat, quickly tucking herself into the farthest corner, making herself as small as she was able. He sat gingerly beside her, feeling she might bolt if he moved wrong. Goodness knew she looked like a nervous bird, perched as if ready to take flight.

"I'm sorry I didn't tell you who I am from the very moment we met," he began. "It was inexcusable of me."

She appeared shocked at his apology, before her features quickly rearranged to cool censure. "How long did you expect to keep it from me? You asked me to *marry* you, after all. Such things can't usually be kept from a spouse."

"I never intended to mislead you. But then my wards introduced me as Mr. Hawkins, and for reasons I cannot fully recall I went along with it." *And when I proposed I wanted you to accept me for who I am, not my title.* The words hovered on his tongue. But he could not let them loose. They revealed a vulnerability he had not shown to anyone since his mother's death.

She studied him, as if searching for the truth in his words, and he felt inexplicably as if he were one of her insects being peered at beneath a magnifying lens.

"What else have you lied to me about?"

The words were forceful, demanding answers. But there was an undercurrent of pain beneath the question. Once more he wondered if someone had deceived her in the past.

That same fury from before at the idea of her being hurt roared through him again, though stronger this time, and coupled with rage at himself and a deep guilt for his own deception. That guilt grew as he recalled the information he still kept from her. But no, he told himself with fierce certainty, she was not the only one he hid it from, and for good reason. That particular truth would die with him, the better to protect those innocent souls it affected most.

"Nothing," he declared.

She speared him with a sharp glare. "Do you mean to tell me you truly are part owner in a gaming hell in London along with being a duke of the realm?"

She expected him to admit he wasn't. He saw it in the jut of her chin, as if she was preparing for a blow. "I am very much part owner in a gaming hell," he replied. "The name of the place is Brimstone. I have been part owner there for nigh on a decade."

She blinked, her shoulders sagging at his honesty. "Oh."

He reached out slowly and took her hand. She stiffened at the contact but did not pull back, which he would have to count as a win if the guarded look in her eyes was any indication.

"My father and I did not have a good relationship," he explained quietly. It was a massive understatement, but she did not need to hear the entire ugliness of it all, how his father had been renowned for his brutality, how his words had hit as hard as his fists. "I left home quite young and began supporting myself immediately. The rest of what I said is true as well. I am looking for a marriage of convenience, to find someone I can rely on to watch out for my wards. You can live where you wish, can do as you like. I only ask that you care for the girls."

She tilted her head, seeming to mull over his words, testing them for any insincerity. Suddenly her brows drew low over her eyes. "You can easily hire someone to mind them. Why shackle yourself to a stranger for life to see it done?"

"I have hired people. But my wards have not been easy to care for." He gave her a close look, suddenly flooded with tension as he thought of the past years of frustration and trouble, each day bringing with it the deep sense that he was failing the girls. "While you have met Eliza and Nelly, there is also a third, Regina. You may recall seeing her when you and I first met outside the circulating library." At her nod, he continued. "They came to me five years ago, upon the death of their grandmother. It was devastating to them to lose her, and I'm afraid they acted out in the worst ways. I indulged them, letting them run wild, thinking their grief would run its course. A mistake, perhaps, as they have only grown more rebellious."

"I see," Bronwyn responded, her expression thoughtful. For each second that ticked by and she retained that contemplative expression, however, the more his uncertainty grew. Damnation, had he made a fatal error in being so open about the girls' troublesome behavior? Not many would willingly shackle themselves to such an unfortunate family, after all.

But she merely straightened and looked him in the eye. "And who are they to you?"

Again that tension, though this time tenfold. "Their grandmother was my mother's old nurse," he replied carefully, clenching his hands into fists on his knees.

Surely she would have more questions. She had a scientific mind, after all. Blessedly, however, she merely nodded.

"I like your wards," she said. "And I look forward to making the acquaintance of the third." Suddenly her tone gentled. "You've no need to worry about them while they are in my care."

Her softly spoken words moved him in ways he never could have expected. He had assumed she would enter into their agreement in a cool, unfeeling way, focusing on what she could get out of their arrangement and nothing more.

Yet here she was, proclaiming her affection for Nelly and Eliza, showing interest in Regina, and doing what she could to put his mind at ease regarding all three. It had the most unnerving thickness settling in his throat, the strangest warmth and ache in his suddenly damp eyes.

To distract himself from these perplexing—and, if he was being honest, disturbing—reactions to her, he loudly cleared his throat and asked, "Are there any other questions I can answer for you?"

In the space of a moment, Bronwyn's mood changed entirely. Gone was the forthright, assured woman, and in her place was one who was pale and uncertain. She nodded, one stiff jerk of her head before, swallowing hard, she asked, "And...and the marriage bed?"

Ah, of course. He couldn't blame her for her uncertainty and distrust. He had deceived her, after all. And the moment he had managed to get her alone he had pawed at her like an eager green boy.

"Our union remains a business arrangement," he replied gently. "It shall be one in name only. There will be no marital relations between us."

Which, now that he had tasted her lips, sat like bitter gall in his stomach. But he would not go back on his word.

"I see," she said. Why did her voice sound so small? And why did there appear to be regret in her eyes?

But those things didn't remain long. That stubbornness that had been hinted at before took over her features. He didn't know if he should be frightened or impressed at the speed of the change.

"Mr. Hawkins—er, Your Grace—er, *Ash*." She stopped, clearly frustrated, before starting up again. "As you know, I am a naturalist."

Why did he suddenly feel as if he were standing on the edge of a cliff, looking down into an unfathomable abyss?

"And as a naturalist," she continued, "I have more than my share of curiosity in understanding the natural world."

She paused, spearing him with a pointed look. He nodded, not knowing what else she wanted from him.

Blessedly, it seemed to satisfy her.

"While insects are my main field of study, I have always found myself drawn to all manner of creatures, from the very small to the very large and everything in between. That, of course, includes the human body, which, as you know, is part of that natural world. It greatly interests me how it moves, the sensations it might feel." She cleared her throat. "Mating habits."

He blinked. "Mating habits?" His voice sounded hoarse even to his own ears, as muffled with the roar of blood rushing through his veins as they were.

"Indeed." Her face flooded with color, but she held his gaze. Adjusting her spectacles, she shifted, turning more fully toward him on the bench. "I know you said you did not want us to consummate this marriage. Now that we have kissed, however, I have a proposition for you."

"A proposition." The words tumbled from his numb lips. Why did he suddenly feel like a parrot, repeating everything she was saying?

"Yes, a proposition. I would very much like to consummate the relationship. For scientific purposes, of course."

He tried to speak. He truly did. But besides a faint croak, no sound escaped from his throat. Which was probably for the best, as he didn't have a clue how to respond to that request.

She, blessedly, did not seem to notice his shock. Her face became more animated as she warmed to her subject.

"Naturally, I have made a study of the mating habits of other animalia. While my parents have been reticent in allowing me to tackle such subjects, my dear friend, Seraphina, who owns the Quayside Circulating Library here on Synne, has made certain the unmarried females on the Isle have access to information of a more sensitive nature, and supplies us with the means to educate ourselves, the better to arm ourselves for battle in a world dominated by men and their intention to keep women in the dark regarding our very natural sexuality. There is only so much one can glean from books, however." She smiled. "Which is where you come in."

Which was a euphemism, as unintentional as it had been, that he could not fail to be aware of.

"Do I?" he managed.

"Absolutely." She fairly bounced in her seat now

with her excitement. "I, of course, have not had cause to explore such things. While I have come to an understanding of how the human body, in particularly the female human body, reacts to desire, there is only so much I can do myself."

"Oh my God." He groaned under his breath, even as his body burst into flames.

"And so I propose an amendment to our original agreement," she went on, blithely unaware of his discomfort. "We shall consummate our marriage, and we shall live as husband and wife at Caulnedy for two weeks before you return to London. In this scenario, not only shall I gain the research necessary to understand the more intimate workings of the human body, but it shall provide me with a modicum of protection from the gossips of Synne." Here her expression changed, the focused intensity transforming to a wry type of pain. "I am considered an oddity here, as you may not be aware, and would not want anyone to pity me more than they already do. Which they most certainly shall if my new husband abandons me on the very day of our wedding."

His heart twisted at that bit of vulnerability. He had been stunned when she had burst into the conversation earlier, stating that they would live together on Synne for a time. But he had not been particularly concerned; no doubt she was simply trying to save face. They would have a talk before he returned to London for the special license, and he would reiterate his intentions for this to be a marriage in name only, and everything would be planned out nice and neat, wrapped up with a bow.

Now, however, he saw where her hasty declaration had come from, and felt deeply for her reasoning. Even so, the thought of lying with her, her naked skin against his, the feel of her heat wrapped around him . . . Ah, God. He swallowed hard. He wanted that with her, more than he wanted breath.

But he was no good. And she was so damn sweet and innocent.

"I—I'm not sure it would be wise—"

"I know I am not beautiful," she cut in, her voice low and intense, the flush that stained her cheeks spreading down her throat and past the modest neckline of her simple gown. "You must have been with many women, all much more lovely and desirable than me—"

"You *are* desirable," he declared fiercely. He grabbed at her hand, saw her eyes flare wide. "And I desire you," he continued thickly. "Very much."

"Goodness," she whispered. For a moment she gazed at him, longing turning the limpid pools of her eyes to the brilliant blue at the center of a flame. She cleared her throat. "Then you agree?"

What the hell could he do in the face of such vulnerability? She would remain untouched by the ugliness in him; he would make certain of it. Having a consensual, physical relationship with Bronwyn did not mean they would be emotionally involved. And there was no reason to believe she would come to care for him. Hadn't she said herself that this would be purely scientific?

Sending up a quick prayer that he was not making a monumental mistake, he nodded. "Yes, I agree."

The smile she gave him knocked the breath from his

body. "Excellent. Well then," she said, standing. "Shall we return to the others?"

He rose, offering his arm, walking with her back inside. All the while he was achingly aware of the way her body swayed against his and the heat of her hand on his sleeve—as well as the fact that he would soon be bound to this woman, both legally and physically. The next weeks, he mused with equal parts dread and anticipation, would be both the shortest and longest of his life.

Chapter 8

*B*ronwyn would be forever grateful that she had her dearest friends about her on her wedding day. They had been her greatest support in the past fortnight as her mother and Lady Tesh had pulled and prodded and stretched her as thin as any one person could be in planning the *wedding of all weddings*, as her father so eloquently put it.

That did not mean, however, that every moment with the Oddments was all sunshine and roses.

"You don't have to go through with this, Bronwyn," Seraphina hissed in her ear as Mrs. Pickering turned away to converse with Bronwyn's maid over the jeweled crown—a crown! Who was she, the queen?— they were trying to place in her short curls. Lacking a quantity of upswept locks arranged into an intricate mass, they were having difficulty securing the thing to her head.

"Seraphina," Adelaide muttered, "leave her alone. She knows what she's doing. Don't you, Bronwyn?"

There was more than a hint of uncertainty in Adelaide's voice. Yet she stood just behind Bronwyn, hand on her shoulder, a steady support. Bronwyn's heart swelled.

The Oddments had not taken the news of her nuptials well. Bronwyn could not blame them; if it were one of them agreeing to marry a stranger a mere day after meeting him, she would be just as horrified.

But, being the incredible friends they were, they had rallied over the past weeks, assisting wherever they could in the planning and buoying Bronwyn's spirits during the most difficult days.

Like now. A mere hour before she was to step foot in St. Clement's and vow to honor and cherish a man she had spoken to a total of three times.

She drew in a shaky breath, clenching her hands tight in the gold netting of her wedding gown, and raised her gaze to her reflection in the glass. Only to find someone who looked nothing like her staring back at her. There was her same narrow face and plain brown hair and sea-green eyes framed by delicate gold rims. But the familiarity ended there. Her nondescript curls, cut short for ease years ago much to her mother's horror, had been coaxed into soft waves. They framed a face that now held the artificial hint of rouge on her normally pale cheeks, and lips tinted a rosy red. Her clothes, too, looked all wrong on her frame. She was used to wearing simple gowns, ones chosen for comfort rather than fashion, that could withstand treks through knee-high grasses and maneuvering over rocky hills. Now, however, she was garbed in something that could only be described as decadent. The gold and ivory silk underdress was overlaid in gold netting, Brussels lace trimming the low-cut bodice and the small cap sleeves. She fought the violent urge to tug the neckline up to hide her nonexistent bosom.

A hand on her other shoulder startled her back to the present. Glancing up, she caught Honoria's face in the glass. Her friend gave her an encouraging smile.

"Wait until you see the church, Bronwyn," she said quietly. "My sister and cousins and I have turned it into a veritable fairyland. My father—who looks quite dashing in his new vestments, by the way—said he had never seen it look so beautiful." She sent a meaningful glance Adelaide's way.

"Oh! And the cake is quite possibly my best work yet," Adelaide chimed in. "Lady Tesh gave me free rein, and I don't think I have ever had so much fun. It's a garden of sugared flowers and candied fruits. And, of course, I insisted on the cake itself being your favorite, lemon with buttercream."

Honoria and Adelaide looked to Seraphina. That woman pursed her lips, looking for all the world as if she had just sucked on a lemon herself. Then she heaved a world-weary sigh and reached up to scratch Phineas on the neck.

"My sisters have been to Danesford," Seraphina said, referring to the Duke and Duchess of Dane's home, "to help with preparations for the wedding breakfast, and they have come back in raptures over the state of the grounds."

They all fell to talking and laughing, a seemingly

merry bunch. But Bronwyn sensed the undercurrent of tension to it all; their laughter had a hollow ring to it, their smiles just a touch too bright, their eyes tight with strain.

Tears stung her eyes and she blinked them back. She'd hardly had time to think the past two weeks over the monumental change her life was taking. But as she sat at her dressing table, which would soon be her dressing table no more, in a room that already felt no longer hers, in a house she could no longer call home, the beginnings of panic took hold. What if this was a huge mistake? She didn't know this man. And had she truly requested, in a moment of curiosity, still vibrating from the after-effects of his kiss, that they consummate their marriage and live together as man and wife for a fortnight?

No, she reminded herself brutally, she had not requested it. She had all but demanded it, then practically begged him when he refused. Her cheeks flamed hot just thinking of her audacity. The man was gorgeous, and utterly delicious; no doubt he had women throwing themselves at him all the time.

But those women had not been engaged to him. She paused. Or had they? For all she knew, the man had been engaged multiple times over the years. Mayhap he had previously been married. Or he could have a mistress. He could have a battalion of mistresses housed all over London. Didn't men of his station have mistresses? Perhaps he would keep them on after his marriage to Bronwyn. He would continue his affairs in London, his marriage a mere bump in the road.

Bitterness filled her mouth. She forcefully attempted

to swallow it, but it remained, souring her already low mood. Why? She could not possibly be jealous. She and Ash were nothing to each other, after all, merely convenient means to an end. He required someone to raise his wards; she required a husband to escape her parents' quick destruction of her life. It was all neat and perfectly tidy.

Why, then, did the thought of him lying with another woman sit so very wrong with her?

As that question swirled uncomfortably in her brain, Katrina burst into the room, a whirlwind of rose-colored silk and blond curls. She came up short, her blue eyes widening, hands clasped to her chest, when she spied Bronwyn.

"Oh, you look like a fairy princess." She sighed.

"If the fairy princess was marrying the dragon instead of the knight," Seraphina muttered before Honoria quieted her with an elbow to her ribs.

"Bronwyn, we must make haste," her mother said, bustling over. "If Miss Denby is here, then so is Lady Tesh, and it is time for us to depart for the church."

Everything became a blur as everyone bustled about Bronwyn. She felt, quite frighteningly, as if she were in the eye of a hurricane, that if she took one step in either direction she would be swept away in the chaos. Before she quite knew what was happening, she was whisked from the room, accepting greetings and exclamations of delight as she was paraded before Lady Tesh and her father, and bundled into the waiting carriage with her parents.

Years later, when she looked back on this day, she

would remember only disjointed images: the trip to the church seeming at once achingly long and frighteningly short; her parents waving gleefully at each person they passed on the street; the small crowd, gathered before the church, that cheered as she arrived. And then she was inside the small stone building, nearly as ancient as Synne itself, and her eyes met Ash's. Good God, had he always looked quite so handsome? Out of the corner of her eye she saw Adelaide mouth *"Oh my God"* as she gaped at Ash, caught Honoria and Seraphina gawking in disbelief at him as they whispered furiously to one another. As if she needed the reminder that the man was the most sinfully gorgeous person she had ever seen. A fact that did not help her nerves one bit, especially when she considered what tonight would bring.

But she would not think of *that* while she was in a *church*. Mortified, she locked those particular thoughts up tight.

All too soon she was standing beside him, and they were speaking their vows, and he was slipping a plain gold band on her finger. When he turned her toward him, however, and lifted her veil to kiss her, everything else melted away. As his lips pressed against her own for a second longer than was proper she knew she would always remember this very moment, when they became husband and wife. A single moment in time, caught in amber and preserved in her memories where, with a spark of electricity and desire coiling through her, they were bound together.

* * *

There were certain benefits to having perfected a cold stare, Ash thought as, finally having evaded Mr. Pickering's constant attempts to cart him about like some trophy, he looked out over the lavish gardens at Danesford. He had been gracious to his new father-in-law as long as he was able. But everyone had their limits. And Ash had reached his long ago.

A group of young men he could not remember the names of spied him and made a beeline for him. Not caring that he was being an utterly rude arse, Ash deepened his scowl and leveled a stony glare in their direction. He was well aware how dangerous he appeared when adopting such a look and had used it often over the years for keeping at bay those who would seek him out for the sole purpose of befriending a duke. And, of course, he had the added benefit of his father's reputation for violence and cruelty adding even more fuel to that particular fire. As expected, the gentlemen's faces turned ashen, and as one they spun about and scurried off. Thank goodness. If he had to make pleasant talk with anyone, he would scream. He wanted the privacy he preferred and, in this moment, required, as he was still reeling from the ceremony and that not-so-perfunctory kiss with his bride.

What had he been thinking? His lips twisted, for therein lay the problem: the moment he had caught sight of Bronwyn walking down the aisle toward him, he had not been thinking at all. Perhaps it would have been different had they seen each other before the ceremony. He had been gone a fortnight, after all, dragging the girls to London, making certain their things were packed up and sent off to Synne, securing the special license, and coordinating with Beecher on the business of Brimstone for his extended leave. Two weeks apart from his intended was a veritable age when they had gone from meeting to engaged in less than two days.

He had hoped they might find a moment to talk during the drive from the church to Danesford. After all, with her wooden way of moving and the blank look in her eyes, Bronwyn had seemed just as dazed as he himself was. They did manage to greet one another and comment on the loveliness of the weather and the wonder that the church had been. It was a strange thing, as they were now irrevocably married in the eyes of God and man, that their first words to each other could be so mundane. But being seated in an open barouche that was bedecked in ribbons and flowers, followed by a cheerful line of carriages, with groups of people waving and calling out wishes for a long and happy marriage as they drove past, one could not necessarily indulge in deep conversation.

Once they had arrived at Danesford, they had not had a moment alone either. Separated the second they stepped foot on the vast property, whisked from person to person, from toast to toast, there was not a second to breathe. Ash, thank goodness, had managed to finally extricate himself from the loudly guffawing group of men Mr. Pickering had dragged him into with the excuse that he needed to check on his wards—who were blessedly being closely watched by Miss Denby. Bronwyn, on the other hand...

He finally caught sight of her as her ridiculous parents dragged her to yet another group of guests. They treated their daughter like a possession, displaying her to all and sundry, as if she were some golden ticket, a pass to be used to access the highest levels of society. And though his wife—his *wife*, he thought, still stunned that it was over and done with and they were married—attempted to smile and converse with the people around her, he could not fail to see just how utterly miserable she was. Her shoulders would stiffen and her smile wobble before falling away altogether when she thought no one was looking.

Damnation, no matter how much he dreaded diving back into the fray, he could not leave her to their mercies a moment longer. His scowl deepening, he placed his untouched glass of champagne on a nearby stone wall, but then a voice stopped him.

"I was hoping I would get you alone, Your Grace."

He turned, spying a vaguely familiar fiery-haired young woman, one of the many ladies he had met during that long day. A quick glance at the brilliant red and green parrot on her shoulder, however, supplied him with her identity.

"Miss Seraphina Athwart, isn't it? Of the Quayside Circulating Library?"

Her eyes narrowed. "Impressive. But not impressive enough to get you out of this conversation, I'm afraid."

He raised a brow, seeing for the first time the mulish jut of her chin and the hard look in her eyes. Ah yes, this woman was one of Bronwyn's closest friends. And it appeared as if she was ready to go into battle.

Casting a quick glance in Bronwyn's direction, relieved that one of her other friends had managed to extricate her from her parents' grasp, he braced himself for whatever unpleasantness was to come and turned back to Miss Athwart.

"And what conversation would that be?"

If anything, her expression became more furious. "I don't know what you're about in marrying Bronwyn so quickly, but I won't have her hurt."

He pulled back, surprised at the acidic vehemence in her tone. "I assure you, I have no intention of hurting anyone, most especially Bronwyn."

But Miss Athwart seemed not to have heard him. "I know she may appear capable and levelheaded. Which she is; she has a brilliant mind, one far superior to that of most people. But that does not mean she does not have a heart. And it has already been broken once; I won't allow it to happen again."

Once more Miss Athwart managed to surprise him, the third time in as many minutes. This time, however, it woke something dark in him.

"She has been hurt? By whom?" He had, of course, suspected as much on more than one occasion, but to have it verified was something else entirely.

The woman drew herself up. "That is not my story to tell, Your Grace," she replied coldly.

"Ye scabby bawbag," the parrot said in a ridiculously strong Scottish brogue, tilting its head and spearing Ash with a stern glare.

"What I can tell you," continued the young woman, her voice lowering to a threatening growl, "is that the Oddments are watching, and if you wound our friend in any way, you shall rue the day."

Ash very nearly laughed at that bit of absurdity. *The Oddments are watching*? What secret society code was this? But his amusement was short-lived. The woman did not stand down; if anything, her glare became more pronounced, her lips pressing into a thin line. She was as serious as sin.

"I do not take my vows lightly," he replied gravely lest she think he was toying with her. "Bronwyn is under my protection, and I will guard her with my last breath if I have to."

The words were said with a surety and gruffness that she could not fail to hear. Finally there was a crack in the ferocious mask she wore, and a vulnerability shone through. He saw the wild worry for her friend that she had no doubt been trying valiantly to hide. She opened and closed her mouth several times, as if unsure of how to respond. Just when it seemed she had gathered herself together to form words, however, Mrs. Pickering burst upon the scene.

"Your Grace," Bronwyn's mother exclaimed, grabbing his arm. "My darling son-in-law. We cannot have you hiding from your guests. There are ever so many people we have yet to introduce you to." She turned to Miss Athwart with a cool smile. "Do forgive us for stealing Bronwyn's husband away, my dear. Duty calls and all that."

Miss Athwart's eyes turned glacial. "Of course, madam," she replied stonily.

"I'll gie ye a skelpit lug!" the parrot screeched, flapping its wings, sending tendrils of Miss Athwart's hair flying.

"Oh, that horrid beast," Mrs. Pickering muttered as she dragged Ash away. In the next moment she turned a sickeningly sweet smile toward him. "I do hope Miss Athwart was not disturbing your peace, Your Grace. She is much more opinionated than an unwed woman should be. I have tried for years to nip Bronwyn's friendship with her in the proverbial bud but have failed horribly in that regard. Perhaps you might succeed where I have not."

Good God, how had Bronwyn dealt with such idiocy for so long? "I assure you, Mrs. Pickering," he said with deliberate firmness, "I have no intention of forbidding my wife to socialize with any of her friends. Ever."

Mrs. Pickering stumbled to a stop, gaping at him. But her look of surprise quickly melted away to one of condescension.

"Dear, sweet boy." Which was something he had never been called in his entire life. "You are, of course, newly married, and do not yet know the mischief such women can do to a happy home life. If you require advice, I am certain Mr. Pickering would be more than happy to assist you."

Before he could think to respond to that outrageous suggestion, the woman spotted someone and waved energetically, her hand flying wildly about in the air.

"My dear Lady Grinton, you are here," she exclaimed. "Would that I could have given you more notice. But you know these young people. Love at first sight and all that, and they could not wait a moment longer to marry. Why, the duke even hied off to London for a special license. How grand is that? Ah, to be young and in love again. But let me introduce you to my son-in-law."

Here she turned to Ash with a cat-that-licked-the-cream smile. Thus began a blatant preening as she introduced Ash to her friend, dropping his title with frightening frequency. By the time the two women linked arms and waddled off, graying heads bent together, Ash's own head was spinning as fast as a top. Truly, he didn't know whether to be offended or impressed.

A soft, strained voice sounded at his elbow. "I'm sorry about that."

He looked down to find Bronwyn at his side. And he promptly forgot the last minutes. Now that he was the recipient of her steady, solemn gaze he felt suddenly grounded as he had not all day. Well, except for that one shining moment at the altar when he had lifted her veil and kissed her, binding them together.

But she was still talking. "I know she is a little... much." She winced, her hands tangling in the gold netting of her gown. "I know both of my parents are, really. But you needn't worry that they believe a word of what they say about us." Her expression darkened. "And no one else will believe them, either."

He frowned. "Believe them about what?"

Her face flushed red. "That ours is a love match. It is a known fact that I am not the kind of person to inspire such feelings."

They had, of course, never intimated that they were blissfully enamored of one another. But the stark, certain way she spoke the words dredged up a deep anger in him. He had seen her interact with her parents before, of course. But their relationship had to be so much worse than what he had witnessed to have her thinking such a thing of herself.

Moving closer, he took up her hand in his. "It is a ridiculous notion to think you cannot inspire love," he murmured.

She gazed up at him, seemingly stunned by his fervent words. For a moment there was a softening of her turquoise eyes, churning waters stilling, and he felt himself sinking into their depths. In the next moment, however, they went flat, her expression smoothing, devoid of all emotion.

"That is kind of you to say," she murmured. Then, gently extracting her hand from his, she turned and walked away.

If he could have kicked himself, he would have. While he had meant his words to be kind, he saw now how needlessly cruel they had been, as well as how much he had stolen from her by marrying her. It was obvious, though she had friends who cared about her, that Bronwyn had been starved for love from her own parents. They had somehow made her believe that no man would love her, so much so that she had accepted Ash's offer of a cold, heartless marriage of convenience less than forty-eight hours after meeting him. She would never know romantic love, would never have proof that she was not the unlovable person her parents had made her believe she was.

And what a selfish bastard he was, he thought with no little guilt as he gazed at her retreating form. For he was drawn to his bride in ways he never expected, and would not change having married her for the world.

Chapter 9

Within the hour, Bronwyn and Ash were off for Caulnedy.

Blessedly, the drive was a quiet one, each of them mired in their own thoughts. Bronwyn was glad for it. After that horrid moment in Danesford's garden, being confronted with Ash's pitying kindness, she did not think she could handle conversation with him.

Mayhap she should attempt to smooth things between them. She had seen the flash of horror in his eyes after his well-intentioned comment, which had only managed to highlight the truth of her situation: she was so unlovable she had been forced to marry a stranger.

But it was not Ash's fault. He was providing her with the life she had wanted, after all, one free to pursue her passions. He didn't deserve such distance from her. A short conversation would do wonders for chipping away at this slab of ice that seemed to have settled between them. Bronwyn, however, had always been rubbish at small talk, with a social ineptitude that bordered on pathetic. It was doubly so now as the gravity of what she had just done in marrying him hit her with all the force of a brick to the head. She was married. She was a wife. No, not just a wife; a *duchess*. She didn't know the first thing about being a duchess—well, she didn't know the first thing about being a wife, either, but she especially did not know anything about being a duchess. And a duchess who was now responsible for three young girls. Yes, she liked them. And they seemed to like her, or at least the two younger ones did. She had only seen them in passing all that long day, the first she had seen them since her acceptance of Ash's proposal. But what little time they'd spent together had been filled with talk of how thrilled they were that Bronwyn was marrying their guardian, the fun and adventures they would have on the Isle, how much they looked forward to assisting her in her research.

Even so, how was she supposed to help guide a duke's three wards in all the things they would need to take their places in the world? To help them find husbands and begin lives of their own?

Especially when she had been such rubbish at it herself. Current position notwithstanding.

The carriage emerged from the thicket of trees, and the setting sun streamed into the window and across her lap, highlighting just how tightly she was grasping her hands together. She peered outside, suddenly unaccountably nervous as she spied Caulnedy. Golden light bathed its brick facade, a sight that she supposed should be welcoming but instead only filled her with a deep uncertainty. This was her home now for the foreseeable future. This grand place had an old-world elegance, which her parents had tried so desperately to copy in their bright, new, fashionable town house. Lady Tesh had insisted that Regina, Eliza, and Nelly remain with her for several nights, to give Bronwyn and Ash time together as newlyweds. Seacliff had been much too quiet and lonely, she had declared, since her dear granddaughter had married the Duke of Carlisle, and she looked forward to having young people about the house again. Judging by how frazzled Katrina appeared during the wedding festivities while watching over the girls, however, Bronwyn rather thought it would not be the sweet experience the dowager viscountess assumed it would be.

But as the carriage stopped and her new husband hopped down to the gravel drive to hand her down, Bronwyn sent up a quick prayer of thanks that she had been unable to talk Lady Tesh out of her plan to have the girls stay with her. This whole situation was strange and difficult enough.

A thought that was compounded as, stepping down from the carriage on shaky legs, she looked up to find a long line of servants, hired on with impressive speed to ready the house for habitation, waiting for them.

"Your Graces," the butler intoned, bowing deeply. "The staff and I would like to wish you our felicitations on your marriage. We pray everything at Caulnedy is to your liking—"

He had not finished before a slight, ancient woman

pushed past him. "Master Ash," she declared with a wide smile. "So you are married are you? Good, good. Let me see the lady then." With that she turned to Bronwyn, looking for all the world like an insect, her eyes magnified in an almost ridiculous fashion by her spectacles.

Bronwyn stood frozen, stunned, as the woman looked her up and down. Ash leaned down and said in her ear, "This is Mrs. Wheeler. She has been housekeeper here since I can remember."

"And I'm nearly as old as the foundation Caulnedy was built upon," the woman quipped before she took Bronwyn's hand and patted it. "I've heard of you, of course. I may not leave Caulnedy, but that does not mean I don't know a fair bit about the Isle and all the comings and goings. Your parents are said to be somewhat ridiculous, but you, I hear, have a good head on your shoulders. And you're a lovely little thing as well. I'm certain Master Ash's mother, dear Miss Mary, would have liked you immensely." Her happy expression fell, a quiet sorrow entering her eyes. "God rest her soul, the poor dear."

Bronwyn, not knowing what to say to that, glanced up at Ash. And was stricken by the deep grief that had etched itself into his features.

It quickly cleared, however, an impenetrable mask seeming to fall into place. "Mrs. Wheeler, Mr. Hugo," he said, speaking to the housekeeper and butler, "if you would be so kind to introduce your staff to the duchess?"

"Of course, Your Grace," the butler said, jumping forward and beginning the long process.

Sometime later—how long, Bronwyn hadn't a clue, for her mind was still spinning with the incredible number of faces and names she had to learn—they entered the house. And she realized she had never seen the interior. Strange, that, as it was to be her home now.

Ash, too, seemed to realize as much as well. He paused in the front hall and looked down at her. "Would you like a tour of the house?" he asked quietly. "Or would you like to retire right away?"

It would be the proper thing to do, she supposed, to allow him or one of the many servants to introduce her to the house. She was now its mistress, as inconceivable as that might be. And as he had married her for the express purpose of having her take up residence here to care for his wards, she had best hit the ground running.

But as she gazed up at her new husband, the awkwardness of the past hour disappeared, replaced with an awareness of what they would be doing when they were alone together. In the space of a single heartbeat, she realized that she didn't care about propriety. His kiss in her parents' garden when she had accepted his proposal was still seared into her brain, and the memory of it had disturbed her sleep more than once over the past fortnight. All her questions and curiosities would be assuaged tonight with this man. And she found that she wasn't prepared to wait a moment longer than necessary.

"I would very much like to retire," she whispered.

He sucked in his breath, his eyes snagging on her lips, his cool expression transforming to one of deep hunger. For her?

And then her hand was in his, and he was guiding her up the stairs, and the only sound she could seem to hear was the mad pounding of her heart.

* * *

How long was one supposed to wait before heading to one's wife's room to consummate a marriage?

Ash, in the process of pacing before the hearth in his dressing robe and bare feet, stumbled. *Wife*. She truly was his wife. Good God, he was married, a fact that still had the ability to stun him nearly immobile.

But he was being ridiculous, he told himself brutally as he resumed his pacing, his footsteps quicker than before. People married every day. This particular occasion was nothing uncommon. If anything, it was incredibly ordinary.

And yet this did not feel ordinary. In fact, it felt quite unbelievably extraordinary.

Enough. This was getting him nowhere. He had promised Bronwyn they would consummate this union, and that they would live together as husband and wife for a fortnight. He could not remain hiding away in his bedchamber all that time.

Dragging in a deep breath, he looked to the connecting door that led into her chamber. Was she ready for him? He paused, listening, attempting to make out even a whisper of sound on the other side of the door. But no, there was nothing. Had she finished preparing for bed then? Was she waiting even now for him, sitting up in the huge four-poster bed, perhaps garbed in a soft nightgown that he would take great pleasure in removing from her body?

He groaned as his cock throbbed to life beneath his dressing gown. If he didn't gain control of himself, he would finish before he even got started. Like some green boy bedding a woman for the first time.

Taking a deep breath, he strode to the connecting door and knocked.

Her voice, trembling and hesitant, reached him. "Come in."

Before he could think better of it, he grasped the latch and opened the door.

The sight that greeted him was much more erotic than he could have imagined. And, ironically, he did not think she was even aware of just how utterly desirable she appeared. She was on the bed, yes, but she was not tucked under blankets. No, she was kneeling in the center of the mattress, in a nightgown that was much more revealing than he ever expected her to wear. No doubt the doings of her mother and Lady Tesh; judging by the deep red that stained Bronwyn's cheeks and the way her hands fluttered over her breasts, she did not seem to be used to wearing such garments.

For the first time ever, Ash found himself fervently thankful to the two older women.

She looked about the room and to the pillows behind her. "I wasn't certain where I should wait," she began, her voice faint, barely reaching to where he stood. "This is all quite new to me."

"I assure you," he replied as he moved closer, "this is all new to me, as well."

Her eyes flew to his, shock stamped across her features. "You are a virgin?"

"What? Oh! No, I have been with women." His lips quirked. "Just not a wife."

"Well, that's good," she said, her visible relief making her shoulders sag. "I had hoped at least one of us would know what they were about. It will make this whole thing much easier, don't you think? Not that I don't know the basics. As I mentioned, I have done a fair amount of study into the process through extensive research in books. But reading about it and seeing drawings are much different than experiencing it oneself."

By God, she was a delight. And the pictures she was painting in his mind were achingly erotic. "Did you truly make a study of the sex act?" he asked, his voice turning husky as he sat on the edge of the bed.

"I would be a sad excuse for a naturalist if I did not," she proclaimed, seemingly oblivious to his quickly growing desire. "Many of the pictures I viewed seemed simple enough. But others seemed impossible to pull off. I just cannot comprehend how limbs can twist in such ways."

He moved across the bed, closer to her, until he could fairly smell the sweet citrus scent that seemed to follow her wherever she went. "I assure you," he murmured, "the human body is capable of all sorts of things when in the throes of passion."

Finally, she seemed to grow aware of his proximity, as well as the meaning behind his words. She blinked, swallowing hard, her eyes dropping to his lips. Her voice, when she spoke, was a mere breath of sound. "Is that so?"

"It is. May I?" he asked as he reached out, slowly lest he startle her, gesturing at her spectacles. At her jerky nod he gently removed them, placing them on the bedside table before cupping her cheek, dragging his thumb across it in a slow caress. "Though, of course, before we begin to experiment with positions—all in the name of your research, of course—it's wise to make certain a woman's body is ready for the man."

"Ready?" she replied faintly, her eyelids drifting lower as his fingers trailed down the side of her neck. "Do you mean like when I touch myself and I grow wet?"

"God, Bronwyn," he groaned, desire flooding him. Unable to help himself, he drew her against him and covered her mouth with his.

There was no surprise on her part this time; she was an eager participant from the first touch of lips. Her arms came about his neck, her breasts pressing flush to his chest as she lurched toward him. There was no maidenly modesty, no shyness as he had expected. Instead, she threw herself into the kiss with an enthusiasm that stunned and delighted him. He had guessed there might be deep passions hidden beneath her scholarly exterior; however, he had not expected them to be so explosively glorious.

Growling low in pleasure, he pushed her back against the pillows, covering her body with his own. Though there were no stays and layers of clothes between them, though they were separated by only his dressing gown and her lacy concoction of a nightgown, he wanted—no, needed—more. He needed to feel her skin against his, to sink into her delectable body, to touch and taste her until he didn't know where one of them ended and the other began.

And judging by the way she squirmed against him, she felt the exact same. Her hands roamed over his back and shoulders, her tongue tangling with his, her legs rubbing against his own. He tore his mouth free, moving his lips across her cheek to trail kisses down her neck. She arched her head back, gasping.

"You have no idea what you do to me, Bronwyn," he rasped against her skin. He dragged a sleeve off her shoulder, down, down, until he freed her breast. It was small and pert, a perfect plum with the most delectable strawberry tip. And he wanted to taste it so badly he felt he might weep.

But Bronwyn stilled. And then she tried drawing her nightgown back over her breast. The light was dim, yet when he glanced up he could see uncertainty in her eyes.

Mumbled words poured from her lips, falling over each other, mingling into an incomprehensible jumble. All but for two words that stood out from the rest.

"...too small..."

Ah, God, was that what this was about? Did she think her body displeased him? Could she not see how she affected him?

Tenderness sweeping through him, he placed a gentle hand over hers but made no move to uncover her again.

"Bronwyn, listen to me, and listen well," he rasped.

"Your breasts are not too small. To me you are perfect, in every way."

Her kiss-swollen lips parted, a ragged sigh escaping from them even as her eyes widened, her uncertainty replaced with a passion-laced shock.

"Will you let me prove it to you, sweetheart?"

The next seconds were torture for him as she paused, considering. Funny, that, as he had been the one who had not wanted anything physical between them. But suddenly it was all he wanted, all he needed.

Finally she nodded. "Yes."

That one word, spoken in that sweet huskiness, was like salvation. Gently easing her hand from her chest, he replaced it with his own, cupping the soft mound in his palm. He lowered his head and drew her nipple into his mouth, barely hearing her incoherent cry as the gloriousness of it sent jolts of pure lust through him. His free hand trailed over her body, tracing each slight dip and curve, reveling in the strength under his fingers. This was a woman who hiked over hills and valleys and rough terrain day in and day out. She was no squeamish society miss, his Bronwyn.

His Bronwyn. The words reverberated through him, and the satisfaction that realization brought him only stoked the fire of his need for her. He had hoped to find a woman who could provide a good life for his wards. He had not thought to find someone who drew him like a moth to a flame.

But mayhap these thoughts were dangerous. Wasn't it possible, after all, that these emotions, along with their new physicality, could lead to feelings much stronger?

He very nearly reined himself in; no matter that he did not believe they could become enamored of one another, it was much too risky a chance to take. But she gasped then, pushing his dressing gown from his shoulders, her small hands roaming greedily over his back, and he forgot everything but the feel of her beneath him.

Quickly shrugging off the garment, he tossed it aside before, grasping the hem of her nightgown, he tugged it up her body and over her head. Now there was nothing between them. And there was nothing to stop him from exploring every sweet inch of her body. He trailed kisses lower, over her rib cage, across the soft expanse of her stomach, down across her hip. Each cry and moan and sigh that escaped her lips as she moved eagerly beneath him drove him on with increasing frenzy. He had to have her, and soon. But first...

Shifting, he pushed her thighs wide, settling his shoulders between them. He allowed himself a moment to look up her body and drink her in. She looked glorious, her head pressed back against the pillow, her short curls a halo about her head. Her breath came hard and fast, pushing her small breasts forward as she clutched at the sheets beneath her.

And the thatch of curls between her legs...

He let out a harsh breath at the beauty of her. It stirred those most private curls, and she gasped, her head jerking up and her passion-hazed eyes meeting his. But there was no fear, no shock, her uncertainty long gone. Only an eagerness remained that made his aching cock even harder.

He held her gaze, trailing his fingers over her sex,

as light as a butterfly wing, wanting to see what his
touch would do to her. Her eyelids fluttered, her mouth
opening in a small oval, a low sound of need escaping
her lips.

And he had not thought he could desire her more.

"I want to taste you, Bronwyn," he said, his voice low
and urgent. "Will you let me taste you?"

"Yes," she gasped.

He did not waste a second more. Lowering his head,
he closed his mouth around her, and the taste of her hit
his tongue, fairly drugging him with her very essence.
If this was heaven, he did not want to ever return
to earth.

* * *

Bronwyn had seen illustrations of just such an act
being performed, of course. But never in a million
years could she have guessed what sensations it might
awaken in her.

Ash's mouth moved over her, drawing her in, his lips
and tongue doing the most gloriously wicked things to
her. She could not imagine anything on earth that felt
better than this.

Until he pushed a finger into her.

She could not think, could not reason. Immediately
abandoning any attempts to keep her approach to this
at all scientific—not that she had been particularly good
at that from the moment he'd touched her—she gave
herself up to sensation. He moved his finger in and out
of her, his mouth growing more insistent, and she felt as

if she were shooting up, up, into the atmosphere. Surely she would come crashing back to earth soon. But no, the sensations bombarding her body, so much more potent and overwhelming than the pleasure she had given herself with her own fingers in the close darkness of her bedroom, continued to build. When he added a second finger, however, and he caressed her swollen womanhood with his tongue, she fell apart. Light burst behind her eyes, as brilliant as fireworks, the explosion that began at the center of her vibrating through her entire body, rippling over her skin.

Before those sensations were done pulsing through her, he was over her. His chest dragged across her sensitive nipples, and the desire she thought had been sated proved that it was not quite through with her yet. By the time the blunt tip of him pressed into her, she was eager for more.

"Bronwyn," he groaned. He cradled her face in his hands and gazed down at her, his eyes burning with need, though he paused. "Sweetheart, are you ready for me?"

But Bronwyn was unable to speak. Instead, she planted her feet on the mattress and pressed up into him beseechingly.

He did not need further urging. Taking himself in hand, he guided himself into her with aching slowness, each inch stretching, burning. Yet nothing had ever felt so good. Finally he stopped, buried to the hilt. His arms trembled on either side of her, sweat dotting his brow, the muscles in his back flexing with the effort.

"Are you well?" he rasped.

Something unexpected unlocked in Bronwyn's chest, an emotion she did not understand, one that brought tears to her eyes. Cradling his cheek, she gave him a small smile. "Oh yes."

Groaning, his mouth came crashing down on hers even as his body began to move inside her. Each thrust of his hips came quicker than the last, the feel of him sliding in and out of her bringing her to the same heights as before, carrying her even higher.

"Ah, God, I can't wait any longer," he gasped. "Come for me, sweetheart."

And then his hand was between their bodies, and he was stroking her. And she shattered, his shout joining her cry of completion.

Chapter 10

*B*right light assaulting Bronwyn's eyelids the next morning was what finally woke her. That, and the cheerful humming of...someone. Frowning, she fumbled for her spectacles on the bedside table, fighting back a growl of frustration when her hand came up empty. Peeling one eye open to locate them and learn just who was the origin of such an annoyingly happy sound so early in the morning, she promptly froze in horror. Who was that person bustling about? What room was this? And why was she *naked*? She gasped, pulling the sheets up to her chin.

Suddenly the woman spied her. In a blurry haze Bronwyn watched as she smiled widely, rosy apple cheeks lifting and nearly swallowing her eyes as she came closer. "Good morning, Your Grace. I pray you slept well?"

Your Grace. It all came flooding back to her. She was

married, and a duchess, and this was her bedroom at
Caulnedy Manor. The woman before her was Veronica,
the lady's maid who had been assigned to her—she had
refused to bring her previous lady's maid with her, considering that woman's firm allegiance to Mrs. Pickering.
And last night Bronwyn had done the most intimate,
private things with Ash. Who was now her husband.

Cheeks flaming hot, she looked wildly about for her
spectacles before finding them and somehow managing
to get the delicate things on one-handed. She cleared
her throat. "Er, yes," she replied in as proper a voice as
she could muster, considering her position in bed and
the fact that her mouth was currently being muffled
by the sheets. "Thank you, I did." She peered out
the window, her muddled mind unable to comprehend
where the sun was in the sky. "What time is it?"

"Nearly ten, Your Grace."

"Ten!" She lurched upright, just barely catching the
sheets before they revealed her breasts. It could not
possibly be ten; she never slept so late. Of course,
she was certain the woman would not lie to her about
such a thing, yet she nevertheless grabbed the small
clock beside the bed and peered at it. Blast, the maid
was right.

Veronica, blessedly, seemed unaware of her distress.
She brought a silk dressing gown over, so much finer
than what Bronwyn preferred to wear, laying it on the
bed at Bronwyn's feet. "I'll have breakfast prepared and
brought up to you right away, shall I?"

She had never in her life had breakfast in her room.
Typically she was up with the dawn, hurrying down to

the breakfast room for a quick piece of toast before rushing out to begin her work for the day.

Her mother, on the other hand, had always indulged in a leisurely morning, reading the latest gossip columns, eating breakfast in bed, not leaving her sanctuary until close to noon. Bronwyn supposed it was expected of married women.

But the thought of doing something of that nature made Bronwyn's skin itch. "Er, no, thank you," she mumbled, reaching for the dressing gown, attempting to wiggle into it and keep herself covered at the same time. "I'll take my meal in the breakfast room." Wherever the devil that was. But she was resourceful; she would find it, somehow.

Finally covered, she threw the sheets back. "Is His Grace up?" she asked with no little nervousness. The last thing she recalled of the night before was Ash collapsing beside her in bed, pulling her into his arms, their ragged breaths mingling in the quiet of the room. And then... nothing. Good God, had she fallen asleep? And when had he left her bed? Had it been immediately? Or had he slept beside her all the night long, leaving only this morning?

Before she could rise, however, Veronica answered her. "His Grace woke some time ago and headed out riding. He said not to expect him back until this evening."

Bronwyn blinked at that bit of news, falling back against the pillows. It should not be unexpected, of course. They had agreed that this was to be a marriage of convenience. There was no affection between them;

though they would be living as man and wife—while in bed, at least—at the end of these two weeks he would be off for London, and Bronwyn would remain on Synne, and they would go on with their lives with only a name between them.

Why, then, this surge of disappointment?

But she would not think of him now. "If that is the case," she said with more certainty than she felt, swinging her legs over the side of the bed and rising, "I will have that breakfast sent up, thank you. And after I dress I would like Mrs. Wheeler to show me about Caulnedy." There, that sounded properly duchess-y.

It must have been the right thing to say, for the maid smiled and curtsied and hurried from the room. Bronwyn was left blessedly alone to make her way on strangely sore legs to the washbasin.

As she bathed her face and ran a brush through her chaotic curls, however, casting a glance out the nearby window and over the unfamiliar grounds below, she found that, no matter how she tried, she could not be easy. The tension, already present in her muscles, grew until she thought she might claw herself out of her own skin. It did not take her long to realize why: she was frightened. Her life, she knew with stark certainty, would never be the same again. Dragging in a shaky breath, she found herself sending up an impotent wish that she had the Oddments with her. Or, barring that, Ash's wards. For she had never felt so alone in her entire life.

* * *

Mrs. Wheeler, while as ancient as anyone Bronwyn had ever seen, was nevertheless incredibly spry, if a bit rambling in her speech and prone to branch off on the most unexpected tangents. Over the next hours, as the afternoon wore on, the woman carted Bronwyn about Caulnedy with impressive energy. Each nook and cranny of the place was gone over, every bit of history repeated with genuine pleasure. It was obvious even to Bronwyn, who was as horrid at reading people as any one person could be, that the woman loved the place and the family she worked for.

At the end of some hours they reached the portrait gallery. The woman took her down the long line of paintings, each one an ancestor of Ash's on his mother's side. Bronwyn's head, already spinning with the amount of information that had been crammed into it, could only silently nod as the housekeeper chattered on.

"Now this here," she said as they moved to a small painting of a young girl of about fourteen or fifteen with pitch-black hair and dark eyes, "is Master Ash's mother, Miss Mary."

That finally snagged Bronwyn's attention. She gazed at the portrait, looking for any similarities between this pretty young girl and her husband. There was a hint of it in the dark, wavy hair and the Romanesque nose. But there the similarities ended. The girl before her appeared delicate and trusting and happy, the glow in her eyes and the small smile on her lips making it seem as if she had just heard something that pleased her greatly.

"She was such a sweet thing," Mrs. Wheeler

continued. "I never knew such a creature, so loving, so ready to help anyone in need."

Her expression fell, making her look even older as that same look of muted grief washed over her features that she had worn the previous night when she'd spoken of the late duchess.

"She seemed so very happy when she left to marry the duke. And we were all so thrilled for her, certain that she was about to live a veritable fairy tale. But then Master Ash appeared in the dead of night years later, still a boy, so secretive as he bundled his mother inside. Miss Mary was heartbreakingly different from what we remembered, pale and sickly and sad. It was as if every bit of joy and life had gone out of her. And then she died not long after." She sniffed, pulling a handkerchief out of her bodice and reaching under her spectacles to blot at her eyes. "At least her suffering was over."

Bronwyn felt as if a veil had been teased back, giving her a hint of understanding into the muted grief that had been on Ash's and Mrs. Wheeler's faces the evening before, when the previous duchess had been mentioned. The housekeeper's disturbing description, however, only brought about more questions than answers. "What happened to her?"

But the woman did not hear her; already she was shuffling off to the next portrait, the moment of grief past as she began spouting some new information about another ancestor of Ash's who Bronwyn would never remember.

As Bronwyn followed after her, her mind whirling, she couldn't help but think once more of the look on

Ash's face the night before, the mask quickly dropped into place to disguise it. What had happened to his mother? And what had happened to Ash after his mother died? Mrs. Wheeler had mentioned that Ash had been a boy when he had brought his mother here for her final days. No, she thought, frowning, she had specifically said he had come in the dead of the night, that he had been secretive. And Ash had mentioned before that he and his father had not had a good relationship. Had Ash smuggled his mother to this house to escape his father?

Too many questions, each one making her feel more in the dark regarding the man she had married.

Blessedly the tour of the house and grounds ended shortly thereafter. Bronwyn, exhausted and confused and feeling the pressure of her new position more than ever, made her way back to her rooms. Each servant she passed bowed or curtseyed with a "Your Grace," making her feel as if she would jump out of her skin. As she gripped the banister to ascend the stairs, she stopped, unable to lift a foot to the first tread, a sense of being closed in overwhelming her. She had to get out of here. She had no idea what she would do, where she would go. But in that moment she unerringly knew she needed to escape these walls, which seemed to press in on her more every moment.

Without a second thought she spun about and, taking up the brilliant blue skirts of her new gown—her mother and Lady Tesh must have had every seamstress from here to Whitby working on her new wardrobe to have it done in time for the wedding—she sprinted out the front door.

The band constricting her chest eased some the moment she was able to breathe in the fresh air blowing off the sea and felt the setting sun on her face. But it was not enough; she needed to put greater distance between herself and her new home, to a place where she did not feel a stranger to herself.

Pivoting in the gravel drive, she strode off then, unerringly making her way through the side gardens, to that place that felt home to her more than anywhere else in the world.

Chapter 11

*T*hough he hadn't been in residence at Caulnedy for long, Ash had already made it a habit to spend as much time out of the house as he was able. There were too many memories at every turn; wherever he looked, he saw his mother in those final days, when her body, broken and weak, could no longer house her battered soul. The guilt that he hauled around like a lodestone doubled in weight at the image, making it almost unbearable to carry.

Except when he had been with Bronwyn. In those moments, when he'd held her in his arms and joined bodies with her, there had been nothing but the two of them.

Which had been the thing that had prompted not only his leaving her bed as soon as she'd fallen into an exhausted slumber the night before, but also his early morning flight from the house. The strength of their connection when they had come together had shocked him to his core; he had never known the like before, with anyone. Granted, he had always made certain that any affair he entered into had strict rules put into place before it was even begun; it must be a short-lived relationship that was based on physical needs alone, with no expectations for more.

With Bronwyn, however, while it had been determined beforehand that it would merely be for scientific purposes—on her part, at least—and had a set end date, there had been an intimacy, a closeness that had taken him by surprise.

It should, perhaps, not have surprised him. They were bound together for life now, after all. Despite their mutual agreement that this portion of their relationship was to be temporary, there was nevertheless an awareness of that lifelong bond. No doubt something of that sort would make a person feel differently about the intimate aspects of a relationship. And she, who was so innocent, who had never been with another, could very well confuse physical intimacy for emotional connection. No, he could not allow that.

But that was not his only reason for leaving the house to gallop over Synne's landscape. No, it was only the more palatable. The other reason he had fled, the more potent of the two, was that he had ached to remain in her arms.

He had not realized until just then how starved he was for a connection to another person. And it troubled him. Over the years he had become an expert at keeping people at arm's length. Even with Beecher, whom he was closer to than anyone else, there was a wall he kept up between them. The silent shame he suffered under guaranteed that, a shame and guilt that no one truly knew the extent of. While the world was aware who his father was, a man who had been needlessly cruel, who had seemed to take pleasure in hurting others, they did not know the full scope of that horror. How he had beat his servants, had forced himself on the helpless women in his employ. How even his own wife, the delicate, sweet, kind creature that had been Ash's mother, had not been safe from such brutality and had ultimately lost her life when she had attempted to step in and save another woman from such an attack.

And Ash, who had sensed something was wrong but, in his innocence, had not understood what, had been so damn selfish that he had only thought of himself and the beatings he was avoiding by going away to school. Not once had he considered that the women left at home, his mother included, had been forced to bear the full weight of the old duke's wrath. And when Ash had finally returned, and become aware of what had been happening beneath his very nose, he had been too late to save his mother. He'd been too late to save any of them.

He shuddered, running a hand over his face, as if he could erase the memories that haunted him even now. His horse, no doubt sensing his disquiet, threw its head in agitation, dancing to the side. He welcomed the distraction of pulling the animal to a stop on the grassy hill that overlooked a wide valley, of calming it with a soft voice and pats to its quivering neck; the focus needed for such a thing helped to dispel those horrifying memories.

No matter how much time he took in tending to the horse, however, he could not stop thinking of Bronwyn. What was she doing just then? Was she settling into Caulnedy? Did the house please her? Was she thinking of him and their night together as well? He had been trying to quiet those questions all day, with little to no success. But the day was lengthening, the sun beginning its descent toward the horizon, and he knew he could not stay away from Caulnedy any longer. Dragging in a deep breath, he turned his horse back toward the manor house. Surely now that he knew what to expect from the more physical aspect of their relationship, he reasoned, he would be better prepared to handle it. And he would not look too closely at just how much he anticipated returning to her.

As he cantered through the tree line into the front drive, there she was, as if he had created her from pure longing. His heart sped up at the sight of her and he drank her in: how lithely she moved and how the sun hit her light brown curls and transformed them into a fiery crown about her head. So focused was he on how lovely she looked, however, he did not immediately realize how quickly she was walking. With her hands fisted at her sides and her footsteps swift, it appeared as if she were anxious to get somewhere. Or she was running from something.

She hurried through the side garden and made her way toward the meadow where he had found her and his wards that first day. Frowning, it took him only a moment to decide what to do, and in short order he was cantering his horse to the front step, dismounting, and handing the creature over to a footman before he started off after Bronwyn.

It didn't take him long to find her. Even so, he might have missed her if he hadn't known where to look in the first place. She was seated in the dirt near a tansy plant, her slight frame, though brightly garbed, nevertheless camouflaged by the low bushes and dry grasses surrounding her.

She flinched as he approached, eyes wide and startled as a fawn's rising to meet his. In the next moment she twisted, as if to hide whatever was in her hand from his sight. As if she feared he might take it away from her.

His heart wrenched. For some instinct told him her reaction to his presence had less to do with her being surprised and much more to do with some fear that had been cultivated in her in the past.

"I'm sorry," he hurried to say, palms up to show he meant no harm. "I didn't mean to disturb you. What have you got there?"

Her gaze lost its fear, turning wary before dropping from his altogether. Nevertheless, she seemed to relax, her fingers uncurling from whatever it was she hid in her palm. He looked down to see a small green beetle there, the same type of insect she'd had with her when he'd come upon her outside the circulating library.

She watched it intently, as if studying the way it moved and how the dappled sunlight hit its brilliant exterior. She was so quiet for so long, he thought maybe she had forgotten he was there. Then, her eyes still on the creature as it merrily walked from finger to finger, she spoke.

"Did you know that tansy beetles overwinter by burrowing underground for months at a time? Of course, this specimen is slightly different from the *Chrysolina graminis* I have read about previously. I have researched this particular Coleoptera extensively and am certain it is a new subspecies never before discovered. I am in the process of writing a scientific paper on it, and hope to one day have it published with the Royal Society of London. They are the premier scientific society in Britain, you know, and really my best option, since the Entomological Society has disbanded."

Her voice was quiet, conversational, as if they had been speaking of such a thing for some time. Just beneath the surface, however, was the slightest warble, though from defiance or fear or deep emotion he could not tell. Her hands, too, trembled faintly.

With great care he lowered himself to the ground beside her. He was achingly aware of her proximity, his body holding a physical knowledge of her now that had been lacking before. But though he wanted more than anything to touch her, he held himself apart. She looked as if she would shatter if he moved wrong. He cursed himself ten times a fool. As much as he had thought it imperative that he leave her this morning, he saw the strain in her now and realized he had made a serious error in judgment. She was newly married, and no matter how they had come into this union, it had to have stung to be abandoned by your husband of less than twenty-four hours.

He watched her as she allowed the beetle to walk from hand to hand. The creature's bright blue-green body shimmered in the waning sunlight, like a brilliant jewel. He could see the draw of it; it was a fascinating creature. Yet not at all a subject that interested most people, let alone females.

"What drew you to study insects?"

The question popped out of his mouth quite without him meaning for it to. But he was glad it had, for he was deeply curious what had led her to delve into such a subject.

She shrugged, her gaze still glued to the creature. "I was lonely as a child, and often preferred solitariness to the chaos of my home life." Her lips quirked in a hollow kind of amusement. "You have met my parents. They have not changed much from when I was a child. If anything, they have only grown worse. And I, unfortunately, have always been...me."

"I don't think that's an unfortunate thing at all," he murmured softly. "You're an incredible woman."

The only indication she heard the softly spoken compliment was a slight start and a blush staining her cheeks. "My elder brother is the opposite of my parents," she continued, "though still quite different from me. Where they are flamboyant and outgoing and dream incredible dreams, my brother is austere and unfailingly strict, with a very rigid idea of a female's place in the world. And I could please none of them. No matter where I turned, I was confronted with disappointment and censure. I took to spending most of my time outdoors, immersing myself in the natural world. I was already a curious child, and so it did not take me long to begin wondering about the animals around me, the fish in the creeks I waded in, the birds flying over my head. But most especially I was drawn to the creatures that crawled in the dirt at my feet: What was their purpose, what were their habits, why did they look as they did? And the more I learned, the more I realized how utterly fascinating they were, these insects that seemed everywhere. And," she said, her voice dropping to a near whisper, "I could be myself around them. They didn't expect things of me, and I didn't disappoint them."

Ash's heart constricted. He pictured her as a small child, without a single friend, turning to insects in her need for companionship. How lonely she must have been. And yet how resilient, to find light in the darkness and passion from barrenness.

"I'm glad you found something that could bring you happiness," he replied. "And you are writing a scientific paper on these beetles?"

She nodded, cheeks turning crimson, then shrugged. "I was. Before my parents destroyed the equipment and specimens I had managed to collect."

He stilled in shock, studying her stiff profile. "They did what?"

Again that shrug, this time more jerky than the last, as if she were shrugging off a bad memory with it. "I suppose it was my own fault. I was so consumed with my research I was not paying attention to other important aspects of my life." Her lips twisted wryly and she sent him a sideways look. "Such as finding a husband."

He found himself smiling in return. "That's something you definitely don't have to worry about any longer," he murmured. "And so you may continue your research to your heart's content. What is the next step in completing your paper and sending it off to that society you were talking about?"

To his surprise, she frowned. "You cannot have any interest in that," she muttered, her tone telling him she thought he was merely humoring her.

Once more his heart wrenched, this time at what she must have gone through with her parents in regard to her scientific pursuits. Life was not easy for women, especially ones with such aspirations. He had seen enough of her enthusiasm for her insects to know that losing all those things she had spent so much passion and effort into compiling must have been devastating. For a moment he felt a burning anger simmer beneath the surface for what her parents must have put her through in their need for her to marry well. But instead of instinctively smothering that anger, he felt the strange desire to cultivate it, to use it to...what? To turn back time and change how her parents had treated her? An impossibility. And yet...

But she was looking at him, hurt in her eyes. "I assure you," he replied, slowly lest she misinterpret him, "I am very much interested."

Still she peered at him, a small frown creating a divot in between her brows. But there was something soft in her gaze now. Then, before he knew what she was about, she held out her hand.

"Would you like to hold it?"

It was nervously said, as if she expected him to recoil in disgust. In answer he held out his hand, palm side up, beside her own.

Her eyes, those beautiful turquoise eyes, softened even more. She gently nudged the beetle, and soon it was walking from her hand to his.

It was so small, so light, he barely felt its delicate legs as it scurried across his palm. Yet he sensed the true weight of it, for there was something incredibly important about this moment, as if Bronwyn was entrusting something precious to him.

Shaken by such a revelation, he passed the insect back to her. She accepted it, her hand brushing his, sending ripples of awareness through him before, with infinite care, she moved her hand close to the plant beside her, letting the insect make its way back to it. She was quiet for a time, watching its progression across the leaf. Ash remained quiet as well, aware of a deep contentment coming over him by just sitting here beside her. There was a stillness in his soul he had not felt in too long.

Suddenly, shifting slightly, she turned to look up at him. "Why did you leave Caulnedy this morning?"

He could lie, of course, and claim he'd had business elsewhere. She need never know that he left to keep distance between them.

But he could not. He recalled the pain in her eyes when she learned he had concealed his true identity from her. She deserved nothing but honesty from him. At least in the things he could be honest about.

"I thought it would be best."

Her brows puckered. "Best?"

"Yes." He sighed, plucking a blade of dried grass from the ground, studying it closely so he might not have to look her in the eye. "I'm leaving in a fortnight. And though we have become...physical with one another, we have agreed this is to be a marriage of convenience and nothing more. I thought it best to make certain there was no emotional attachment between us."

He didn't know what he expected her reaction to be at his confession. Whatever it might have been, it was not the quick bark of laughter that burst from her lips.

"Did you worry I would fall in love with you?" she asked, disbelief and humor coloring the words.

No matter that it had only constituted a portion of why he had left, no question had ever made him feel quite so thick-headed before. He had thought he was well beyond blushing at this time of his life. Nevertheless, his cheeks warmed uncomfortably. "Well, it sounds ridiculous when you say it like that," he grumbled.

"That is because it *is* ridiculous," she returned, with a flippancy that should have relieved his mind on the subject and yet did not. "I assure you, I have learned my lesson in regard to losing one's heart, and shan't be doing that again. No, I have no intention of falling in love with you."

While he was relieved she thought the idea of falling in love with him was comical and completely without merit, he also felt an absolute idiot for even suggesting that he was so irresistible that she would fall in love with him after one night together.

But both of those emotions were forgotten in the face of her revelation that she had been in love before. Yes, her friend Miss Athwart had said as much yesterday when she had confronted him at Danesford after the wedding. But this was proof positive that someone had hurt Bronwyn, and badly. It woke something almost feral in him, a troubling emotion, indeed.

But Bronwyn continued, dragging his attention back from the edge of the cliff where he had been teetering. "Are you planning on falling in love with me?" she asked softly, her face turning a becoming shade of pink.

"No." That one word burst from him, quick and certain.

She smiled brightly. "Well then, there is no danger. We may spend time together without fear, isn't that right?"

There was a surge of warmth in his chest that might have worried him if they hadn't just basically vowed that they would not fall in love with one another.

"Yes," he answered with a small smile.

"Good," she replied. She looked down to her skirts, smoothing them busily with suddenly nervous hands. "And...and we might continue to do the things we did last night without worry as well?"

How was it that one breathless question from her could affect him in such a physical way? He reached out and took her trembling hand in his, needing to touch her more than he needed anything just then. "Oh yes," he rasped.

She looked at him, her eyes seeking out and snagging on his mouth. "Excellent." She licked her lips, her breath coming faster. "Though do we really need to wait until tonight?"

"God, no," he groaned, pulling her toward him, crushing her to him even as his lips found hers.

* * *

The following morning Bronwyn woke much the same as she had the day before: she was alone and quite naked in bed, the sun already beginning its ascent into the sky, Veronica bustling about the room and whistling merrily. Panic set in, an instinctual reaction as she once more clutched the sheets to her bosom. She had thought yesterday would change the way things would be going forward between them. But what if it had changed nothing at all?

"Good morning, Your Grace," the maid said with a bright smile, once more delivering the silky dressing gown to her.

"Good morning," Bronwyn managed. "Is...er, is His Grace up?"

"Oh, yes," the maid said cheerfully, laying out a sea-green gown over a nearby chair and smoothing the delicate folds. "He's an early riser, he is."

So once more he had already left for the day. Bronwyn fought back the wave of disappointment. Of course their conversation and the increased intimacy of yesterday had not altered how things would be. And truly, she should be happy. He was here for only a short time, after all. There was no sense in getting used to his company when she would be without it soon enough.

Veronica's next words, however, managed to decimate that small bit of reason.

"He asked to be informed when you woke so he might join you here for breakfast if you're amenable."

She really should be concerned that such news so quickly replaced her disappointment with joy. But she was too excited in that moment to care.

That did not mean, of course, that she had to advertise her excitement. Attempting to school her features to an expression of unconcern, she grabbed at the dressing gown and once more squirmed into it beneath the cover of the sheets. "Yes, I am amenable to such a plan," she said with what she thought was impressive gravity. "Please inform His Grace I would like that very much."

With a smile and curtsy the maid was off. The moment Veronica closed the door behind her, Bronwyn bolted from the bed. She raced into the adjoining washroom, taking a brush to her chaotic curls, scrubbing her face and teeth, and taking care of those more sensitive needs. She was no longer surprised at the slight soreness of her inner thighs; rather, she wondered how the rest of her was not equally sore as well.

With an enthusiasm that had delighted and excited her, Ash had taken to her suggestion to try out the different sexual positions she had read about. Even just remembering what they had done in the chair in her room the night before had her body aching in the most interesting manner. The washcloth she was briskly sponging herself off with slowed then, drifting lower, tracing the same path his mouth had taken. How was it, she wondered as her hand dipped between her legs, that the human body could contain such sensation? And how was it, she thought as she moved the washcloth against her suddenly aching flesh, that something touching one spot on her could be felt in every inch of her?

So focused was she on the faint abrasion of the cloth that she did not immediately hear the door open behind her. Suddenly strong arms came about her, and she was dragged back against a broad chest. She gasped and dropped the washcloth, embarrassed that she had been caught in such an act, and tried to close her dressing gown over herself even as she attempted to squirm from Ash's embrace.

His hot mouth on the side of her neck and his large palm cupping her breast, however, banished all thoughts of escape. She felt his manhood pressing against her lower back, and the heat that had begun to build between her legs blossomed into something potent.

"Were you touching yourself, sweetheart?" he rasped, his breath caressing her skin, making her shiver. He took hold of her hand and guided it back between her thighs. She gasped, her head falling back against his shoulder as sensation washed over her.

"Show me how you like to touch yourself," he said. There was no demand in the words. Rather, he seemed to be begging her, desperation making the words come fast and breathless. He rocked against her, and she arched her back, pressing her buttocks against him. And then, because she could not have refused him even if she wanted to, she began to work her fingers over herself. Her folds were slick, the natural wetness from her body easing the path of her hand. He groaned, his mouth finding the sensitive place where her neck met her shoulder, sucking on the skin there, sending her spiraling even higher. And then he did the thing that sent her over the edge: pressing one hand as a support against her lower belly, he reached behind her with the other, searching for and finding the opening to her sex. Suddenly one finger was slipping inside her, then another, moving in and out of her even as she touched herself. And she broke apart in his arms.

But that was not the end of it. Not by any means. As her legs gave out from the force of her release, his arms slipped beneath her, lifting her against his chest. He strode back into the bedroom and to the still unmade bed, dropping her to the mussed sheets. One quick flick of his fingers at the fall of his breeches, and he was between her thighs with a hiss of pleasure, his manhood sinking into her.

The pleasure that had still been reverberating through her body came back with a force that stunned her. She gasped, twining her arms about his neck, wrapping her legs about his waist to bring him even deeper inside her.

"My God, you're incredible," he growled. He pumped in and out of her, his breath hot against her neck, the feel of him fully clothed while she wore nothing but a scrap of silk seemed erotic in a way she had never thought possible.

They moved together, the pleasure climbing, her blood rushing in her ears. Suddenly there was a rapping against her bedroom door.

"Your Graces, your breakfast," Veronica called from the other side of the panel.

"Leave the bloody food by the door," Ash growled.

Then, before Bronwyn could think to understand what had just occurred, he slipped a hand between their bodies, his fingers finding her, mimicking the movements she had performed on herself just minutes ago. Her body exploded in sensation just as his mouth claimed her own, swallowing her cry of completion.

Chapter 12

*I*n all his life, Ash could not recall a time he had been more content.

Holding out a hand for Bronwyn to grasp, he helped her across several flat stones that spanned a slow-moving river. They had spent the day out of doors, leisurely riding over Synne's softly rolling hills, walking through shady groves. The majority of their time had been spent in silence. He'd expected something of the sort to be highly uncomfortable. He'd never spent time with any-one who was content with a lack of conversation.

Yet with Bronwyn, it felt as natural as breathing.

So much so that, when it had come time to return to the house for luncheon, he'd been loath to put an end to their time together. And so he'd suggested a picnic in a place of her choosing, an idea she'd seemed equally eager for.

She pointed up the slight incline as they reached the

far side of the river. "It's just up that rise," she said, her voice quiet.

Shifting the picnic basket they'd fetched from Caulnedy more securely in his grasp, he held out his free arm to her as they took the path up. "What did you say this place was again?"

"The Elven Pools. There is quite a bit of local lore regarding the pools, having to do with the Viking invasion and a romance between a Norseman and the namesake of the Isle, an Anglo-Saxon maiden named Synne." She smiled up at him, a wicked gleam in her eye. "Apparently the brute spied on her while she was bathing naked."

He raised a brow, fighting an amused smile of his own. "That is quite a scandalous tale."

"Oh, very scandalous." Her eyes glittered with mischief behind her spectacles. "Especially as she stabbed him, nearly killing him in the process."

He let out a bark of laughter at that, startling a nearby bird from the bushes. "Not a romance, then."

"Oh, no. It is a romance. By all accounts they did fall in love. Eventually. But that, of course, is not what draws me to the place."

"Oh no?" he murmured, taking in the growing excitement in her gaze. "What is it that you like about these famed Elven Pools?"

She didn't answer, merely dragged him more swiftly up the path. And then they crested the hill, and his question was answered for him.

"Oh," was all he could think to say.

She gave a small chuckle. "Oh, indeed," she murmured.

But in that moment he couldn't care less that she was laughing at his reaction. He had never in his life seen a place like this one.

The thick woods they had meandered through had opened up, the land turning craggy and seemingly unforgiving. Yet there was movement and life. Water had carved pools out of the rock, wearing bowls into the stone with dozens of trickling waterfalls that filled the air with their music. Each basin grew in size the farther down the hill they were, one after the other, each one clear and colorful as stained glass, like the holiest of nature's churches. How was it that such colors could exist? Azure and emerald and an indigo bordering on amethyst, all mingling together, like brilliant watercolors splashed across a water-soaked page. And the color that stood out to him the most, a soothing turquoise, the same color as Bronwyn's eyes.

"It's...it's..."

"Yes." He heard the smile in her voice. "But to witness the true beauty of the place, you have to look closer."

She started off down the incline, a path paved in flat shale steps, her stride almost eager. Bemused, he followed, coming up beside her as she stopped at the edge of the largest pool.

"Most visit and see a beautiful landscape," she said, her voice quiet as she looked out over the water. "It's a place they come to on occasion, to swim or lounge about, and then they are gone. All without seeing the lives lived within the scope of the pools." Here she pointed.

He frowned, not having a single clue what she was referring to. Nevertheless, he followed her finger. Then he saw it, a small, brilliantly blue creature, darting across the top of the water.

"*Coenagrion puella,*" she said, awe plain in her voice. "The azure damselfly. They're quite common, of course." She smiled, a kind of peace falling across her features. "But that does not make them any less incredible."

He could not take his eyes from her. The transformation that came over her as she observed the creature stunned him. Gone was the faintly cautious look that always seemed present. Instead, her face was relaxed, happy even. It was an expression that turned her from quietly beautiful to stunning. He felt, quite thoroughly, as if he had been hit by a bolt of lightning.

"And there is more life around these craggy rocks," she continued, oblivious to the baffling emotions coursing through him. She dropped to her haunches, peering at the ground. He followed suit, unable to do anything but.

"You see there?" She pointed to a line of tiny reddish ants. "And there?" She motioned toward a small brown cricket, then toward a delicate spiderweb strung between two rocks. She gave a happy sigh. "There's life everywhere."

She was quiet for a time, looking about, her lips curved in an easy smile that he felt clear to his toes. He could have stayed there for the rest of the day, gazing at her while she took in the natural world around her. Was it always like this for her, these moments of peace and clarity? Allowing herself to do nothing but sit and observe and appreciate even the smallest lives? His heart ached, and he rubbed at his chest, confused. What was this emotion that was quickly taking over him? Regret? No, that particular feeling he knew only too well. Longing? But for what? To experience life as she did, to slow down and live moment by moment?

It was not something he indulged in. Not since his mother's death, when his innocence had been dashed to pieces. Since then he had kept moving forward, throwing himself into his work, the better to forget his origins, and the shame and guilt his memories never failed to expose. Brimstone had been the foundation of all that busyness, a beast that had constantly needed tending, and he had welcomed the labor it had required from him. Never once had he been tempted to take stock of what was going on around him and sit still and just *be*.

Until now, here with Bronwyn.

She looked up at him, eyes bright behind the lenses of her spectacles. "Shall we eat?"

She chose a flat, shady spot near the largest pool, beneath the only tree that had dared to grow in the rocky ground that surrounded it. He might have wondered that she did not choose a more sheltered spot—despite the peculiar starkness of the ground surrounding the water, the area that cradled it was lush with vegetation, with a thick wood on one side and a vast meadow on the other—but as he laid out the blanket and sat beside her, he was glad she had decided on this place. The water splashed merrily into the basin beside them, the sound of it washing over him, relaxing his muscles in a way he could not remember ever feeling before. As Bronwyn busied herself with setting out the food, Ash found himself utterly transfixed by the ripples in the water. Such chaos under the falls, churning into a white mass, then spreading out to gentle waves that lapped ever so softly at the pool's edge. It made the myriad-colored stones beneath the water appear as if they were dancing. As if the elves the pools had been named after had cast a spell on them.

"I think the girls would like it here, don't you?"

Bronwyn's question snapped him back to the present. Of course, the girls. They were the entire reason he was on Synne, after all, and married to Bronwyn. His time on the Isle was short-lived, mere duty, and soon he would return to his old life with an easier mind, now that he had someone who would take care of them.

Yet the thought of going back to London alone was like a knife to his gut.

He looked down to his plate, frowning, hardly seeing the chicken leg and pile of berries and hunk of cheese Bronwyn had filled it with. It should be a relief, knowing he no longer had to worry quite so much about his wards. Yet it only made him feel hollow.

But Bronwyn was waiting for an answer.

"Yes, I think they will enjoy it here."

"Nelly told me it has been years since they have visited the countryside, that they have never seen a place like Synne."

Ash glanced back to the pool of water. "I don't think there's a place quite like this anywhere in the world."

She paused. And then, "Won't you tell me more about them?"

He looked to her sharply, feeling the walls he had erected about his heart surge back up around him. "What do you mean?"

But she didn't back down from his gruff tone. Instead she nodded, as if he had confirmed something. "You are very protective of them."

He shrugged, suddenly feeling horribly exposed. "They are my responsibility," he replied, taking a piece of hard cheese and biting into it. But it was too dry in his mouth. Taking up the glass of lemonade she had poured for him, he took a deep draught, then immediately regretted it. The sour and the sweetness of it, so at odds with one another and yet amazingly compatible, was too much like Bronwyn.

All the while she watched him, silent. As if he were some specimen that she was studying.

Finally, she spoke again. "Most men would not take responsibility for children they were not related to, much less marry a woman to see they were cared for."

He flinched, an instinctual reaction. Had she guessed? But no, her gaze was steady, curious.

Clearing his throat, he placed his plate aside, all the while wondering how much he could tell her without revealing the truth. Yes, he owed this woman the utmost honesty. But no one, not even the girls, knew the full truth of their parentage; it was a secret he would take to his grave.

There was one thing he could tell her, however.

He sighed and raked a hand through his hair. "The girls grew up without parents. It was difficult for them; though Mrs. Hargrove, my mother's old nurse, did what she could to fill the void, she was elderly, and not at all well, and the girls had to care for her as much as she cared for them. Most of the responsibility fell to Regina, as she is the oldest. Yet she was only eleven when she came to me, and so you can imagine the burden she had on her shoulders. In truth, none of them have had much of a childhood at all."

He fell silent, unable to continue, remembering the lost look in their eyes when they had arrived on his doorstep. That shadow had never disappeared and broke his heart whenever he happened to catch sight of it. It sharpened the blade that scored his guilt, torturing him down to his very soul.

And he would do anything to make certain the grief they had experienced was not compounded by the shame they would no doubt feel, that same shame that sat so heavily on his shoulders, if they were to ever learn the truth.

Suddenly Bronwyn's small hand was on his sleeve, grounding him. "You've no need to worry about them, Ash," she said, her voice quiet and gentle and yet fierce with a protectiveness that reverberated through him. "Though I have not been blessed with close female relations, I have always wanted some. I shall treat your wards as if they were my own sisters."

He looked into her eyes. How was it that his chest could feel so very full? She would never know how deeply her words touched him. He cupped her cheek with his palm, rubbing a thumb over her high cheekbone. Everything about her was sharp and narrow, from the pointed tip of her upturned nose, to the stubborn line of her jaw, to the slash of her brows. When he'd first met her, he'd wondered how many people she'd put in their place. Now he knew that what lay behind her ferocious expression was a strong will and heart. And he knew he had never seen anything or anyone more beautiful in his life.

He lowered his head to hers, claiming her lips in a kiss so much gentler than the previous kisses they'd shared. Those had been hungry, born from desire.

This, however, was something different. He took his time, savoring the taste of her, breathing in the small sounds she made as if they alone could give him life. She reached for him, but this was not the hot need from just that morning; rather, her hands trailed over his shoulders, his arms, his chest, as if she would memorize him.

Their tongues twined, their breaths mingling. And then her hands were unbuttoning the flap of his fall front breeches.

"Ash, I need you," she whispered into his mouth.

He gasped, his body bursting into flames as a sudden urgency flared between them. He rolled onto his back, the better to protect her from the hard ground, and pulled her atop him. After only a moment's hesitation she came eagerly, straddling him, hiking her skirts up to her waist. And then she freed him, grasping his member, positioning him at her entrance, and slid down.

She was heaven. He arched his head back as the feel of her over and around him overwhelmed his senses.

"My God, Bronwyn," he rasped, his hands finding her thighs, the feel of her garters driving him nearly wild. She remained still, her hands planted on his chest, her thighs trembling on either side of his waist. In a haze he realized she might be uncertain what to do and would need instruction.

But one look at her face and he knew that was not it at all. Her eyes were closed, her cheeks flushed, mouth open in a small oval, a mirror of the same overwhelming ecstasy that was quickly taking over him. And then she began to move, hesitantly at first, then more certain, the rhythm of her hips driving him half out of his mind. Everything in him urged a quick release, to grasp her about the waist and pump into her until he was spent.

But no, he did not want to miss a bit of this exquisite moment. He closed his eyes, savoring each rise and fall of her body over his, the achingly beautiful slide of flesh on flesh. But, more than that, he savored the connection between them. It was as if she was burying herself inside him, straight to his soul.

Suddenly her movements quickened, her breath coming faster and more ragged. Gasping, he opened his eyes, desperate to see her in her release. The beauty of her features, transformed as she reached the pinnacle, sent him over the edge. As her muscles squeezed about him, he gripped her hips and thrust up into her, his own climax taking him over, their cries of completion ringing across the ancient waters of the Elven Pools.

* * *

Ash didn't realize he had fallen asleep until he opened his eyes to find that the sun had passed its zenith and was now beginning its leisurely descent toward the horizon. The air around the Elven Pools was still pleasantly warm, the chirp of birds and the lazy call of insects humming in the air, mingling with the melodic sound of splashing water to create a kind of lullaby. He yawned, his body deliciously sated, more relaxed than he could ever recall being. It was no wonder he had drifted off.

He lurched upright, a kind of panic taking over him. Bronwyn. Where the devil was she? Yet was there any reason to panic? It wasn't as if she couldn't do as she pleased. And he could certainly find his own way back to Caulnedy. She had not abandoned him, for goodness' sake.

Yet when he scanned the landscape and spied her not far away, sitting cross-legged beside the pool, bent industriously over a notebook, the relief that rushed through him was strong enough to make him light-headed.

She must have heard him stir, for she suddenly looked up. "Oh, hello. I hope I didn't wake you."

Shaken by his peculiar reaction, he pointedly ignored it and shifted so he could peer over her shoulder at her notebook. "What is that you're doing?"

She smiled shyly, holding the book up for his inspection. "I thought of a way to revise my scientific paper on that new subspecies of tansy beetle and wanted to get it down before I forgot."

He peered at the open notebook, his eyes scanning over the jumble of words, most of which he could not decipher or understand until they came to rest on a small, incredibly detailed sketch in the corner.

"Bronwyn," he murmured, more than a bit awed, "that is beautiful."

Her cheeks burned red and she snapped the book closed. "Nonsense," she mumbled, reaching over to tuck the book into the bag she had brought with her.

He stopped her with a hand on her arm, then gently took the book from her and began to flip through the pages. Illustration after illustration leapt up at him, each one more detailed and lifelike than the last, and each accompanied by carefully listed instructions on color, movement, habitat. He had known she was passionate about entomology. But he had not fully understood it until now.

"You are brilliant," he said in awe.

"Nonsense," she replied again, though this time the word was barely a whisper.

He recalled then what she had said the day before, when he had come upon her with the tansy beetles in the meadow. Her parents had destroyed her work? They'd had the gall to look upon such talent and strip her of every means she had to put her work out in the world? What monsters were they to do such a thing?

Well, he would not allow her to squander her talents. He glanced at her. "When will you send in your paper to the Royal Society?"

She shrugged, quickly busying herself in packing up their things. "Eventually," she replied evasively. "It is not yet up to the caliber of work they publish. If I can refine my paper, it might be worthy of consideration." Her lips twisted. "And I shall need to create new finished illustrations, of course; the ones I had managed to complete are gone now, along with the rest of my things."

Again that fury at what she had been forced to endure at the hands of her parents. But now was not the time. He looked back to Bronwyn's illustrations, impressive even in this rough state, and the carefully penned notations, and he knew without a doubt that her decision to delay sending in her work was only partly due to the loss of her equipment and supplies. No, the main reason for her hesitation had to do with her own feelings of self-worth. Or, rather, lack of them.

"I am not a naturalist, of course," he murmured. "But I think they would be foolish to refuse you. You have an incredible talent."

To his shock, the look she sent his way was tight with hurt. "You needn't patronize me."

He blinked at the venom in her voice. "I assure you, I am not patronizing you."

But she shook her head furiously. "You flipped through a single notebook. You cannot possibly know if my work is worthy of publication." And then, in a voice so quiet he nearly didn't hear it, "I don't like to be lied to, Ash. I am not a fool."

He very nearly retreated. It was obvious he had upset her.

Instead he moved closer to her, gently taking her hand in his when she refused to look his way. She tensed but didn't pull away.

"If there is anything I am certain of," he said, low and intense, "it is that you are not a fool." When she remained silent, he asked, gently, "Who was the man who hurt you, Bronwyn?"

Her eyes were wide and pained when she looked up at him, pulling her hand from his grasp this time. "It doesn't matter."

"It matters to me." The words slipped out without him meaning for them to, stunning him. Why did it matter so damn much to him who had hurt her before? They were not to become emotionally entangled, remember?

But no matter that stark fact, he found it did matter, very much.

"Who was he, Bronwyn?" he repeated quietly.

She shrugged. "It doesn't matter who he was," she whispered. "It's in the past."

"The past can still hurt," he found himself saying, achingly aware of just how large an understatement that was.

Her lips twisted wryly. "Yes, I suppose it can." She looked back up at him before heaving a defeated sigh. "I was seventeen, in London for the first time and preparing for my debut. My parents had the idea that they could ingratiate themselves into society early and garner more invitations during the season, thus ensuring my popularity." She winced. "But they were not exactly welcome in those *exalted* circles, and they wound up offending more people than not."

She swallowed hard, her gaze dropping to the basket in front of her, her fingers nervously picking at the wood panels. "With all of that embarrassment and strife, I was shocked when one particular man began showering me with attention. He seemed so kind, so interested in what I had to say. And I began to fall in love with him. No," she corrected herself harshly, "I *did* fall in love with him, head over heels. Or, at least I fell in love with who I thought he was, who he presented himself to be. And how could I not? It was like a fairy tale. I had been ignored all my life. And here was this handsome, elegant man paying attention to *me*. When he arrived at our town house, we all believed he was about to ask for my hand. In actuality, his intentions were quite cruel. He had wished to teach my parents a lesson, you see. To show them they did not belong in the higher circles of society, and that they would never belong."

She straightened. "I fear my reaction was not... gracious. I dumped a pot of tea over his head. He threatened to spread it about that I had been loose with my favors, that I was an uncultured hoyden, and that they would make certain we were never welcome in society. My parents agreed to quit London for good, banished, rather than be the subject of a scandal."

While he knew she had been hurt, he'd had no idea the person responsible had been so cruel. He ached to demand she tell him who the blackguard was; if he was a noble in London, there was a good chance the man had crossed paths with him at Brimstone.

But no, she had every right to keep the bastard's identity a secret. He had to respect her privacy.

In his battle with himself, however, Bronwyn must have taken his silence as disapproval. She sent a brittle smile his way. "But enough of that. Now then," she continued, standing and shaking out her skirts, "the light is beginning to wane. If we are to make it back to Caulnedy before nightfall, we had best leave. I've no wish to stumble through the woods in the dark."

He stood as well. But when she would have reached for the blanket to fold it up and pack it away, he stalled her with a hand on her arm.

"I am very glad you dumped that tea over his head."

The cautious look that had made her features appear

frozen melted and she gave him a small, shy smile before turning back to the task at hand.

Within minutes they had finished packing up and were headed back toward Caulnedy, something Ash found he was loath to do. He wished he could stay here with her forever, cut off from the ugliness of the world, in a bubble of contentment. The more he got to know Bronwyn, the more he admired her, and wanted her to find success and happiness. It was something that should have had alarm bells peeling away in his head. He did not get close to people, after all, and certainly never welcomed affection. Yet holding her hand as they ascended the shale-stepped path, all he could think of was how he never wanted this time with her to end.

Chapter 13

*T*he last thing Bronwyn wanted—or expected—upon their return to Caulnedy after the exquisite trip to the Elven Pools was to see a familiar carriage in the front drive. Her boots skidded to a stop on the gravel drive and she dropped Ash's hand. Dear God, she had been married a mere two days; did her parents have no sense of decency?

That question, as rhetorical as it had been, was answered moments later when the front door opened and the elder Pickerings appeared. They were talking animatedly with Mr. Hugo, their voices carrying in the late afternoon air.

Ash, who had stopped beside her and was looking at her quizzically, gave a start. "Your parents are here?" he asked, disbelief coloring his voice.

"I'm so very sorry," she moaned.

Before he could answer—God knew what he would say—her mother's voice carried to them.

"Oh, but please do let the duke and duchess know we have been to call." She gave the butler a condescending smile. "I'm certain our dear daughter will be beside herself to know she missed us."

"Indeed," her father chimed in, his narrow chest puffing up with his importance. "She is ever so attached to us, you know. I daresay you shall be seeing much of us about Caulnedy in the years to come."

Dear God.

Bronwyn swallowed hard. "Perhaps if we move fast enough we might duck into the side garden before they see us," she whispered.

Ash, who held the picnic basket in front of him like some sort of shield, nodded quickly. "I agree."

Before they could take a single step, however, the elder Pickerings spotted them. Bronwyn froze as her mother leveled a delighted smile on them. "Oh, but here is our daughter now," she exclaimed. She hurried down the front step toward them, the wide ribbons of her bonnet flying behind her, arms outstretched. Bronwyn barely had time to brace for impact before she was enveloped in plump arms that carried with them more than their fair share of perfume. Bronwyn, for her part, stood frozen. Their family had never been one for affection. Yet here was her mother, hugging her as if she had not seen her in a decade and this was some joyous reunion.

"My darling Bronwyn," she said. "And dearest Buckley. We could not wait another day to see you. It feels as if it has been forever."

"It has been two days," Bronwyn muttered, extricating herself from her mother's embrace. She straightened her bonnet, all the while fighting the urge to hide her bag behind her back so her parents might not see that she had been indulging in research. She did not have to worry about their decrees any longer, did not have to fear they would send her away from Synne. Yet the fear was still there in spades.

She cleared her throat. "What are you doing here?"

"Now, Poppet," her father replied with mock sternness, "is that any way to greet your loving parents. You must know how dearly we've missed you." He turned to Ash then. "Buckley, good to see you, my boy. Treating our Bronwyn well, are you? You must, for she's looking decidedly flushed right now." He laughed, loud and long.

Bronwyn wanted to close her eyes in mortification and slink away, especially when Ash drew in a sharp breath at her father's crassness. Instead she said, head held as high as she was able, "If I am flushed it is because the day is warmer than I took into consideration and our walk was a long one. But please excuse us; we have just returned and need to ready ourselves for dinner."

"Oh, certainly, certainly," her father said expansively.

"Oh, yes, completely understandable," her mother joined in. "Just have your butler show us to the drawing room and we shall make ourselves at home while we wait for you." She smiled brightly all around while Bronwyn gaped at her. "I say, this shall be lovely, our first dinner with our daughter the duchess." She tittered.

Bronwyn felt the blood leave her face. Ah, God, now

what? Ash must rue the day he married himself to such a family. She cast him a horrified look, mind whirling at how she might get them out of this mess.

But he was not looking at her. No, he was looking at her parents, and with a disturbingly blank expression.

"Perhaps you misunderstand my wife," he said softly. "We are still newlyweds, after all, and are not yet ready for guests."

Her parents, however, either did not hear the tension under his calm tone or did not care. "Oh, but we aren't guests, my boy," her father said with a wide smile. "We're family now."

Bronwyn winced. Ah, God, he was only making things worse. "Papa," she tried again, "what the duke is trying to say is that we would prefer some privacy, for a little while longer at least."

"Privacy, eh?" He leered at Ash before sending a knowing look to his wife. "That we can understand. Gad, but I didn't let you leave our bed for a fortnight after our wedding, my dear."

How Bronwyn didn't cast up her accounts then and there, especially when her mother blushed and simpered like a bride, she would never know.

Ash stepped forward. "I'm glad that you understand." Then, with a talent that Bronwyn would be in awe of for the next decade at least, he herded them all toward the waiting conveyance.

In short order they said their goodbyes to her parents and, before that couple had even stepped up into their carriage, she and Ash were safe behind Caulnedy's doors.

After they had handed over their things to the butler, Bronwyn wasted no time in apologizing. "I'm so sorry," she said in a low voice.

But he held up a hand, halting her apology in its tracks. "There's no reason to apologize. You are not your parents, Bronwyn, and have no control over what they say or do. I more than anyone should understand that."

Why, she wondered, more than a little stunned, did his gentle tone turn so bitter at that last bit?

But she had no time to think on it. In the next moment he bent his head, taking her lips in a swift kiss. "Go now, and ready yourself for dinner. I'll see you momentarily."

With that he hurried away toward his office. Bronwyn, frowning, made her way to her room.

* * *

Ash had not cared for the elder Pickerings from the moment he had met them. Over the past two days, upon learning what they had done to Bronwyn in an attempt to suffocate her talents, he had begun to actively dislike them. Now, however...

He hurried through his office to the French doors that opened into the side garden and to the front of the house, hoping the Pickerings had not left Caulnedy just yet, for he had something to say to them and he did not want to put it off a moment longer. Blessedly their carriage was still on the gravel drive, Mr. Pickering having taken it upon himself to reprimand his groom on something or other from the carriage window. When he saw Ash, he waved the man off and stuck his head farther out, smiling expansively.

"Your Grace, have you changed your mind about that dinner then?"

"Not in the least," Ash answered curtly, stepping up beside the carriage. "No, it is something altogether different I wish to speak to you about."

"Oh dear." Mrs. Pickering bit her lip, poking her head out her window. "Has Bronwyn displeased you in some way, Your Grace? I know she is not classically pretty, and her form is not pleasing."

What the devil? He gaped at the woman in disbelief. "There is nothing at all wrong with Bronwyn's appearance," he exclaimed.

"Yes, well." The woman gave him a look that said she did not believe him one bit. Before Ash could think how to react—whatever it was, it would not have been at all pretty—she spoke once more.

"It must be her odd notions of a woman's place in the world, then." She nodded mournfully, as if greatly grieved, before giving him a brilliant smile. "But, truly, I'm certain if you're patient you can turn that right around."

"That's right, Buckley," Mr. Pickering pronounced. "You're a man of the world, and can surely nip such behavior in the proverbial bud."

Ash saw red. "I assure you," he gritted, "there is nothing at all wrong with Bronwyn. Not in the least."

"Newlyweds," Mr. Pickering said in a knowing aside to his wife.

"We are so relieved to hear it, Your Grace," Mrs. Pickering said, giving Ash a knowing smile that said she did not believe him one bit.

"You may not be relieved when you learn the true purpose of why I wished to speak with you," he growled.

At once the couple appeared alarmed, their smug complacency of a moment ago gone.

"I…I don't understand, Your Grace," Mr. Pickering stuttered.

"You shall in short order," Ash replied, his voice as tight as the hold he had on his quickly growing anger. "Bronwyn, as you know, has a deep interest in entomological studies."

The attitude of the pair before him shifted once more, this time to acute discomfort. But he was soon to learn it was not because of any guilt they might feel at attempting to stifle their daughter's talents, as any parent worth their salt would have felt. No, it was quite a different reason.

"We know we have failed in purging her of any of those more unladylike interests, Your Grace," Mrs. Pickering said in an almost whine, her hands gripping the windowsill tight. "We indulged her for too many years, allowing her oddness to run unchecked. But I am certain, if you continue where we left off in gently redirecting her interests to those that are much more proper for a woman of her years and station, she will soon see reason and abandon those unfortunate pursuits."

Ash, however, had heard enough. Drawing himself to his full height, he glared at the duo. They blanched and reared back within the carriage interior, their faces going as white as the belly of a fish as they blessedly fell silent.

"You know nothing about your daughter at all," he bit out. "She is your own flesh and blood, and yet to you she is merely a piece of clay to be molded to align with your own likes and preferences and designs. But she is a person, and a brilliant one at that. One who has incredible talent, who has hopes and dreams and aspirations of her own."

"I say," Mr. Pickering managed weakly, looking to his wife in confusion, "I don't know where this is coming from—"

But Ash wasn't about to let them turn this conversation around. "Did you or did you not discard Bronwyn's scientific equipment and specimens?"

The Pickerings paled even further. "It was necessary—" Mrs. Pickering tried.

"Necessary to what purpose?" Ash demanded. When they continued to look at him in stunned muteness— a blessing, really, for he could not take much more of their selfishness and inanities—he glowered at them. "Why would you destroy those things that were so very important to your daughter?"

"But we didn't destroy them," Mrs. Pickering burst out, turning a sickly green when Ash turned his glower her way.

"We told Bronwyn we destroyed them, of course," Mr. Pickering added. "How else could we keep her from searching out her things and using them again? We would have been back to square one with the girl. No,

we stored them in the attic." Then, in an aside, and oblit-
erating whatever crumb of goodwill Ash might have felt
for the man, Mr. Pickering said, "They were much too
expensive to destroy. Better to recoup the money from
reselling them, after all."

How was it, Ash wondered as he stared at these two
people who should have loved their daughter uncondi-
tionally yet had always made her feel less than, that
Bronwyn could have come from such a union? Lowering his brows, he glowered at the couple.

"Hear me, and hear me well. You will return home
immediately and fetch Bronwyn's things from the attic,
and you shall have them delivered here tomorrow afternoon. Is that understood?"

They both gaped at him, and for a moment he thought
he might have to repeat his order. Finally, however,
they both nodded. Knowing that if he continued this
conversation with them, he was bound to say something
he would regret, he nodded curtly and, stepping back,
indicated to the driver that he could now go. Within
moments the Pickering carriage was trundling down
Caulnedy's drive and out the gate to the darkening road
beyond.

Ash stood in the drive, taking deep, cleansing breaths
of the fresh island air, letting the briny scent of the
ocean and the greenness of the trees and the richness of
the earth fill him up. How had Bronwyn grown up surrounded by such people and still retained her incredible
individuality? The more he learned about her, the more
impressive he found this woman he had married.

A warmth blossomed in his chest then as he turned and

gazed up at Caulnedy. Before he could think twice about it, he strode back to the house. Perhaps he could steal a few moments alone with Bronwyn before dinner...

* * *

It was late afternoon the following day when Bronwyn and Ash returned to Caulnedy. But they had not spent their time together visiting the sights or riding over Synne's rolling hills, as Bronwyn had expected when they rode out for the day. No, much to her surprise, Ash had insisted they visit the meadow.

She had gaped at him. "Surely you don't wish to sit and watch me study insects."

But he had smiled. "I would like nothing more."

Bronwyn had not needed further urgings. There had been a time, after all, when she had feared she would never be able to return to that place, when first her parents' decrees and later their intention to send her away from Synne had threatened to forever put an end to her research. And so she and Ash had traveled the short distance to the meadow. While Bronwyn sketched and observed to her heart's content, Ash had propped himself against the trunk of an obliging tree, alternately reading and watching her sketch and asking questions about her work.

There was still that voice in her head that told her he didn't truly care, of course, that he was merely placating her. But as the afternoon marched on that voice grew quieter and quieter until, by the time they returned to the house, it was merely a whisper. And then, at Ash's suggestion, they visited the library, and that whisper was completely silenced.

She froze in the doorway as she took in the changes surrounding her. The room had been a stuffy space, with its large carved desk dominating one wall, the seeming acres of bookcases interspersed with all manner of heavy tomes, the uninspired landscapes that covered any bare bit of wall space, the large floor-to-ceiling windows that should have looked out into the back garden but were so suffocated with heavy velvet drapes that they made one feel even more closed in.

Now, however, it was quite different. Most obvious, of course, were the windows. The dull velvet drapes had been removed, only gauzy white swaths of fabric remaining, pulled back with silk tassels so it seemed the outdoors was part of the interior. The landscapes were gone, the pale green wallpaper unencumbered, giving the room a fresh, clean look. The desk, previously sparse of material, was topped now with quills and pencils and piles of creamy paper. The bookcases were different, too. The majority of the books had been condensed down to one wall, and the rest of the shelves were now empty, except for one filled with what appeared to be brand-new leather-bound journals.

And in the center of the room stood several chests, opened wide, their contents fairly spilling from them. It was not until she took a hesitant step closer to see what was within those chests, however, that she could discern that what they held was achingly familiar to her.

"Oh," she breathed, her gaze wandering greedily over the framed specimens and magnifying lenses and books upon books upon books. Precious things she thought to never see again. But surely she must be dreaming. Her parents had told her they had destroyed her things, after all. She took off her spectacles, used her skirts to rub at the lenses, placed them back on her face. But no, everything was there. This was no dream at all, but the most beautiful reality.

She gingerly reached in and picked up a framed butterfly, her gaze roving over the carefully pinned wings, lovingly preserved by her own hand. She shook her head in disbelief. "I...I don't understand."

Ash's footsteps came closer until he was at her elbow. "I stopped your parents before they left yesterday and asked them about your things," he said quietly. "It seems they did not have them destroyed after all. They'd had them all stored away in the attic. I asked that they return them to you."

She gaped up at him. He had spoken alone to her parents, had gotten them to return her things to her? But even with the proof right in front of her, she could not fathom it. Why would he do something like this? For *her*?

He smiled. "You mentioned the loss of your equipment. And you cannot very well become an acclaimed naturalist if you don't have the necessary supplies. That, and a space to do your work in. I thought perhaps you could utilize the library for that. We can change the wallpaper if you don't like the green, can have new drapes made up, buy new furniture..." His voice trailed off as she remained still, staring up at him in a mute shock. Again he smiled, though now there was a hint of nervousness to it. "I admit, I did not think until this very moment that I might have overstepped."

Tears stung her eyes. Had anyone ever done anything of this magnitude for her before? Yes, she had the support of her dear friends, and they never failed to bolster her spirits and cheer her on.

But this... this was something different altogether.

Bronwyn carefully placed the specimen back within the chest before she took Ash's hand in hers.

"It's the most wonderful gift I could ever imagine," she whispered, the words watery with unshed tears. "Thank you."

He looked as if she had handed him the moon. Which was ironic, she thought as, with a soft kiss, he left her to peruse the contents of the room at her leisure. For she felt the exact same.

Chapter 14

*T*he following day saw Bronwyn not in the library as she ached to be—she had hardly left that room since Ash had revealed it to her the day before, only to eat and to retire in the evening for another night in Ash's arms. No, instead she was in her room, anxiously pacing the rug, waiting for the expected arrival of the girls.

It was not that she dreaded seeing them. In fact, she was looking forward to it. As much as she enjoyed spending time alone with Ash—something she had not thought possible three days ago—she was nevertheless eager to begin the process of settling in with the girls before Ash returned to London.

She frowned as she adjusted her spectacles and smoothed her skirts in preparation for the day ahead. In the past few days of domestic bliss, she had brutally ignored the fact that he would be leaving Synne at the end of the fortnight. It was an inevitability, something that had been discussed and agreed upon before they wed. These two weeks with him were merely an interlude until life as they would know it began.

Now, however, after their time at the Elven Pools and the meadow, and more importantly what he had done to reclaim her scientific supplies, showing her in not only words but deed as well that he supported her research, the thought of him leaving, something she had looked on with disinterest at best, loomed on the horizon like a gray storm cloud.

Which was ridiculous. Yes, they enjoyed their intimate times together, the latest having been just that morning before they had separated to prepare for the girls' arrival. And yes, he had surprised her with just how thoughtful and caring he could be. For a moment her chest warmed, thinking of all he had done to make certain she could continue her work, giving her back all she thought she had lost.

But this was temporary, she told herself firmly. They had always meant for it to be a short-lived interlude. She would not allow his leaving to devastate her. In just over a week and a half, things would go on as they had planned, and they would separate. She would be as independent as a woman could be, remaining here on her beloved Synne with Ash's wards and her dear Oddments, continuing her research and making a name for herself in the entomological world. It was the life she had always dreamed of having.

But was it the life she wanted now?

The question whispered through her mind, throwing her off-balance. Where the devil had that idea come from? Of course it was the life she wanted. Her wishes for her future had not changed. And anyway, even if they did—which they would *not*, but hypothetically if they did—it would make no difference. Ash's departure was not up for debate; he had to return to his business in London, and she had to remain on Synne.

Which did not seem nearly as satisfying a plan as it used to be.

Before she could begin to understand what was happening to her, Veronica was suddenly at the door.

"The Misses Hargroves are just arriving."

Splendid, she thought with no little pleasure as she hurried from the room, more than happy to bury the strange thoughts she'd begun to have. This was exactly what she needed, the girls to ground her in reality. She and Ash had been in a virtual bubble these last days, separated from the outside world, and it was time to remember who she was, and who she would always be.

She reached the front door just as the carriage pulled up. Before it could rock to a halt, the door was thrown open, a figure vaulting to the ground. But it was not one of the girls. No, this was large with black and white coloring and decidedly canine.

"Mouse," Katrina cried from the carriage.

Bronwyn hardly heard her, however, for the booming woof that bellowed from the dog as he galloped toward her was almost deafening. She could only watch, frozen, as the animal careened across the drive and up the steps. She braced for impact.

But the only thing she felt was the wind rushing by

her as he passed, fleeing into the house as if he were running from the devil himself.

Bronwyn blinked, looking back as the beast tore through the front hall, nails scrabbling on the tiles, nearly toppling a footman in the process before racing out of view.

Stunned, she looked back at Katrina, who was still poised in the carriage door, her face a mask of horror.

"Oh, dear," Katrina said faintly.

"What the blazes is wrong with Mouse?"

Before her friend could answer, a great commotion went up from the interior of the carriage behind her. A footman, poised to help Katrina down, barely had time to catch her as she was jostled from behind. And then Nelly and Eliza tumbled out to the gravel drive.

"Mouse!" Nelly cried, running after the dog, her tangled hair streaming behind her. "Hello, Bronwyn," she chirped with a grin, not breaking stride as she tore into the house in hot pursuit of the animal.

"Nelly, it is my turn to ride Mouse," Eliza called out, hurrying after her sister, not bothering with greeting Bronwyn at all.

Bronwyn, feeling as if she had just narrowly escaped a whirling tornado, looked back to Katrina. Her friend gave her a sickly smile.

"Lady Tesh thought it would be best if Mouse accompanied the girls back to Caulnedy. She...er, she apparently wanted, as she put it, *some peace and quiet in her house.*"

"Oh," Bronwyn managed weakly.

Just then Regina appeared. She descended from the

carriage without a word, approaching Bronwyn and sinking into a curtsy.

"Your Grace."

Bronwyn was stunned by the coldness to her tone. She had not had much interaction with the girl; Regina tended to blend into the background, a result of her sisters' boisterous energy, and Bronwyn hadn't had time alone with her.

Recalling what Ash had told her of what the girl had been through and how much she had suffered, Bronwyn gave her a gentle smile. "Please call me Bronwyn."

"It would not be proper, Your Grace," Regina replied before, raising her chin, she marched into the house.

At a loss, and strangely hurt, Bronwyn could only stare after her.

"Don't mind her," Katrina murmured as she came up beside her, linking arms with her. "I'm sure she doesn't mean any harm."

Which, to Bronwyn, seemed highly unlikely. Regina had stared at her with what appeared to be deep loathing, as if her aim had been to hurt Bronwyn.

But Katrina was forever looking for the good in others, and Bronwyn doubted she could persuade her friend to see life differently if she tried. Which she most certainly did not. There were too many cynics in the world already, herself included.

She heaved a sigh and guided Katrina inside, trying to ignore the sounds of shouting and banging that echoed back at them from deep in the house. "Was it truly that bad?"

Katrina patted her arm. "Don't worry yourself on

that score," she said with false brightness that didn't fool Bronwyn one bit. "We've more important things to discuss. Such as your new status as a married woman. What is it like?"

Bronwyn couldn't help how violently her face heated, no doubt a raging blush staining her cheeks. "It's been...very enlightening."

Katrina's cornflower-blue eyes lit up like lanterns as she leaned closer to Bronwyn. "Is it everything the books say it is?" she whispered.

Bronwyn, mortified down to her toes, nevertheless could not lie. Though she was tempted to, especially when thinking of that incredible incident at the Elven Pools two days before. She cleared her throat, looking about for prying ears, before whispering back, "Even more so."

Katrina gasped. "You must tell me. But no!" she exclaimed before Bronwyn could answer her—which she most certainly was *not* going to do. "You must wait until our next meeting. You can tell all of us at once. I know the others will be equally curious. Especially as your new husband seems to be a most virile specimen."

Before Bronwyn could choke out a refusal to such a horrifying proposition, the virile specimen in question appeared, descending the stairs.

Katrina squeaked at the sight of him before dipping into a deep curtsy. "Your Grace."

"Miss Denby," he said warmly as he approached them. "Please call me Ash. But how lovely to see you again. I pray my wards were no trouble."

In answer, a great cacophony arose from somewhere

in the house, growing louder by the second. Suddenly Mouse burst into the front hall, tongue lolling, drool flying. He skidded to a stop when he saw Ash, his ears perking up with interest. And then, with a look Bronwyn knew only too well, he started off at a gallop for him.

"What in the blazes—" was all Ash managed before Mouse's giant snout found its target: Ash's nether regions.

He yelped, stepping back, trying to escape the beast. But Mouse was not to be denied his greeting.

"I am so very sorry, Your Grace," Katrina babbled, lunging for her dog's collar. "He does like people, ever so much."

"What the devil is it?" Ash managed while trying and failing to push the animal's nose from his person.

"He's my dog, Your Grace—er, Ash," Katrina panted, finally managing to get ahold of the heavy leather collar and tugging with all her might—which, unfortunately, had about as much effect on the creature as a fly on a bull elephant.

"His name is Mouse," Bronwyn added, joining Katrina in her attempts at pulling the dog back and at a safe distance from Ash.

"Mouse?" Ash asked incredulously as, finally, Bronwyn and Katrina succeeded in gaining control over the exuberant beast.

Katrina flushed bright pink and gave him a nervous smile. "He was the runt of the litter."

"If he is the runt, I would hate to see what his siblings look like," Ash muttered, tugging at his waistcoat.

Nelly and Eliza tore into the front hall just then,

squabbling like peahens. Upon catching sight of their guardian, however, they skidded to a halt, their mouths snapping shut with audible clicks.

Bronwyn might not have thought anything of it—no doubt they were embarrassed at being caught going for each other's throats—if Ash had not reacted to them in the same manner.

"Eliza, Nelly," he said, his voice solemn. "Welcome home. I trust you behaved yourselves for Lady Tesh?"

"Yes, Ash," Nelly responded, her typically cheerful voice devoid of inflection.

"Miss Denby," Eliza said, ignoring her guardian entirely, "may we play with Mouse?"

"Oh! Er, actually, I must get back to Lady Tesh."

But such reasoning had no effect on the girl. "I'm certain she wouldn't mind you staying for a short time," she wheedled.

"Eliza," Ash growled. "Miss Denby has told you she cannot stay."

The only indication that she had heard him was a slight roll of her eyes. "Or you could leave Mouse here," she continued with an encouraging smile.

"Oh, yes," Nelly chimed in, looking up from rubbing Mouse's ears. "That would be great fun. We'd take such good care of him, we promise."

"I don't...that is, I'm not sure..." Katrina, looking as panicked as Bronwyn had ever seen her, cast a desperate glance her way.

"Actually, I have need of you girls this afternoon," Bronwyn said to them. "Ash has managed to get ahold of my specimens and books and equipment, and I'll require help unpacking and sorting them. Do you think you could assist me?"

"Specimens!" Nelly stepped back from the dog, seemingly forgetting the creature was even there as she bounced on her toes in excitement. "What kinds of specimens?"

"Insects, you ninny," her sister scolded before turning to Bronwyn with an expression that was even more excited than Nelly's. "We would love to help. We'll go prepare ourselves right away."

Giving Katrina and Mouse quick farewells, the two girls hurried up the stairs, their footsteps clattering like a herd of cattle as they each tried to outrace the other.

Bronwyn let out a breath of relief, then turned back to Ash and Katrina with a smile. But it froze on her face when she caught sight of her husband's expression. He looked, quite literally, as if he were in physical pain.

"Ash, are you well?"

His features rearranged in a moment, leaving no trace of the former anguish. "Of course I'm well. I've just come to tell you I'll be heading out and won't return until this evening. I'll see you at dinner. Miss Denby," he murmured, bowing slightly. And then he was on his way, striding out the front door. And Bronwyn had never felt more confused.

But there was no reason for confusion, or hurt feelings, she reminded herself as she saw Katrina and Mouse on their way. The time they had spent together thus far had been a short tangent from the path their lives were to take, no matter how wonderful it had been. This was not a marriage based on affection.

Even so, she could not help but reflect on his reunion with Eliza and Nelly. They had all appeared painfully uncomfortable with one another, as if they were nothing more than strangers. Yet she knew, from her conversation with Ash at the Elven Pools two days ago, that he cared for the girls, perhaps much more than he comprehended. She also knew, from his actions yesterday, that he was capable of great kindness. Why, then, the cold greeting and the sudden change in mood?

But she was overthinking things. It had been an interaction of a mere moment. She could not base any conclusions she might have on so minor a conversation, if you could call it a conversation at all. She had more important things to tackle, such as the care of three girls, one of whom appeared resentful that she was there at all.

She looked up at Caulnedy's brick facade and took a deep breath, feeling somehow as if she were about to cross some invisible line that she could not come back from. But she was no missish miss. Ignoring the shout that echoed through the house and the pale, angry face that peered at her from a second-story window—Regina's room, she knew—she straightened her shoulders and strode inside.

* * *

Bronwyn had not thought, in a million years, that two girls could have quite so much energy and enthusiasm.

Looking out over the destruction of the library, she blew out an exhausted breath. Though Bronwyn had managed to get through a good number of the chests, filling the empty shelves with books and equipment, even hanging some of the framed specimens and illustrations upon the walls, the majority of her things were still packed away, awaiting their turn.

Well, she reflected wryly, they *had* been packed away. The moment Eliza and Nelly had descended upon the library—Regina could not be coerced into leaving her room—they had dived into the chests, removing items and piling them up in chaotic mounds. It was all Bronwyn could do to keep up with them and prevent anything from being damaged. All the while they talked faster than she could comprehend, about Mouse and Seacliff and Lady Tesh until Bronwyn's head was spinning.

"And did you know Mouse is in love with Lady Tesh's dog, Freya?" Nelly asked, giving Bronwyn a dreamy sigh. "It's so romantic."

"There's nothing romantic about it," Eliza snapped. "Firstly, they are dogs. Secondly, how would they be able to have puppies? Freya is much too small. She would explode." She grabbed at a wooden case with a glass front containing a pinned butterfly before tossing it aside as if it were nothing of import. Bronwyn grabbed for it but she was a second too late; she winced as it clattered along the ground, the delicate creature within jarred by the impact. Upon closer inspection, however, she saw the Rhopalocera was intact. She gave a small sigh of relief.

But this was getting out of hand. Rather, she thought with a wry twist of her lips, it had gotten out of hand the moment the girls had arrived in the library to *assist* her. It had been one thing to be with them outdoors, as she had on every other occasion she'd spent with them. There they had been able to expend their energy in the fresh air and sunshine. This, however, was another situation entirely. And made her understand much better why they had run off so many governesses and nurses— and why Ash had been so very desperate to find some-one to care for them that he would marry a stranger to see it done.

Not that he felt like a stranger now.

Her face burned as she focused back on the girls. She would not think of *that* now. She had to gain control of this situation. "Eliza, such talk is improper," she said as she wrestled a freestanding brass magnifying glass from Nelly's sticky fingers—what sweet had the girl managed to pilfer that she had sticky fingers? If she did not remove the girls from her research equipment immediately, she would lose everything she had worked so hard for. Again.

"Now," she continued firmly, "why don't we put these chests aside and take a walk?"

Their reaction was swift. "Oh yes, let's," Nelly exclaimed, tossing the notebook she'd been flipping through on the pile beside her and jumping to her feet. "Lady Tesh was ever so strict about where we could go when we were at Seacliff. Apparently she feared we would get too close to the edge of the cliff and tumble right over."

"That is because you nearly did, you ninny," her sister said. "You should have seen it, Bronwyn. Miss Denby barely had time to grasp Nelly's hand. A second later and she would have fallen right into the sea."

Bronwyn felt faintly ill at the image that particular description painted but managed to hold on to her composure. Good God, what had she gotten herself into? The two occasions she had spent with the girls before Ash's arrival and proposal had done nothing to prepare her for the reality of what life would be like with them. As the girls sprinted out of the room and toward the entrance hall, she realized that she knew nothing at all about children. Granted, Eliza and Nelly were not toddlers; she had been informed they were twelve and ten, respectively, and so there was no changing nappies or spoon-feeding them. If duchesses even changed nappies. Which she doubted very much they did.

Yet they seemed to require much more minding than she had ever imagined they would. She thought of her own childhood, of the endless lessons and expectations and need for escape. Was that what these girls needed, to be reined in and molded like her mother had tried to mold her, turning her into something she wasn't?

She frowned as she followed Eliza and Nelly. A lot of good that had done. Such a life had only made Bronwyn miserable, and had taught her nothing so much as the fact that she could not be loved for who she was, but rather for who she should be.

Yet it was all too obvious these girls needed guidance and boundaries. Ash had told her that none of them had been able to experience a childhood. He truly cared for them, no matter how he might deny it, and had no doubt indulged them, giving them much more freedom than they should have had.

And now it was up to her to set things right. Despite the fact that she had no idea what she was doing. But when had she ever backed down from a challenge?

* * *

Some challenges, Bronwyn realized dejectedly several hours later, were much harder than others. In fact, attempting to build up the nerve to send her paper to the Royal Society seemed like it was a walk in the park compared to dealing with three headstrong girls.

"Regina," she called once more, knocking on the girl's door, "we are about to eat luncheon; won't you join us?"

"Is that an order, Your Grace?" the girl said. Though the words were muffled by the thick wood panel, there was no ignoring the sarcasm and disdain that dripped from them.

"No, Regina," Bronwyn replied. "It is not an order. But I would like you to join us. We have not had a chance to get to know one another, after all." Not that she was particularly talented in doing something of that nature, especially if the other person was highly reluctant. But she would do her damnedest.

"That won't be necessary," the girl said. "I am not expecting you to stick around long enough for that to matter."

Bronwyn pulled back, stunned by the venom in the girl's voice. Frowning, she tried again. "I assure you, I am not going anywhere. We shall be living together for some time. Won't you join us?"

But there was no answer except for the slamming of the girl's washroom door, a clear indication she was done with the conversation, such as it was. Heaving a sigh, Bronwyn turned about and made her way to the drawing room.

The day had not gone as she'd hoped. While there had been much less for the two younger girls to damage in the great outdoors, that did not mean they had kept completely out of mischief. From their near constant bickering, to the deep apologies Bronwyn had been forced to give to an elderly farmer when the girls had spooked his horse, to the game of hide-and-seek in which Bronwyn had thought for nearly an hour she had lost Nelly, she had been hard-pressed to keep her composure.

Now they were back at Caulnedy—the girls had been quite vocal over the past hour about the fact that they were "starving" and needed to eat—and Bronwyn was exhausted. How could she possibly set the boundaries they needed to prepare for their futures, especially as one of the girls seemed bound and determined to pretend Bronwyn did not exist?

"You must see the scrumptious fare we've been given," Nelly exclaimed as Bronwyn entered the drawing room, bouncing in her seat and nearly knocking over the very tray of food she was in raptures over.

"Nelly," Eliza said, plucking a bit of cheese off the tray and taking aim at her sister, "open your mouth. Let me see if you can catch it."

Immediate visions of that bit of cheese lodging in Nelly's throat flashed through Bronwyn's head. She hurried to them, gently lowering Eliza's hand, even as Nelly opened her mouth like a bird. "Perhaps that is not a good idea. I would not want to see your sister choke."

Eliza rolled her eyes and attempted to take aim once more. "She shan't choke."

"You cannot guarantee that," Bronwyn insisted through gritted teeth, physically taking the cheese and popping it into her own mouth, quickly chewing and swallowing. "Now," she said as Eliza grumbled, "I do believe we should look into hiring you a proper governess soon. I would not want you to fall behind on your studies."

"We do not want a governess," Nelly declared, sidling up beside Bronwyn and securing an arm through hers, giving her an adoring look. "Our time on Synne shall be one long holiday."

"Besides," Eliza added, "what use will we have for learning? I'm certain we know all we need to."

Bronwyn gaped at them. "No use for learning? Why, feeding your mind with knowledge is the greatest gift you can give yourself."

"It has not done you any good," Eliza muttered as she dissected a watercress sandwich, making a face at the innards. "It is not as if you have made a career for yourself with your learning. You married and are a man's property just like every other woman."

If the girl had slapped Bronwyn she would not have been more shocked. Or hurt. As she sat reeling from that blunt little speech, Nelly spoke.

"The same shall happen to us. Ash has said on more than one occasion that his goal is to see us married off. Which means he cannot wait to be rid of us."

The young girl's morose tone was enough to pull Bronwyn from her hurt. "That is not true," she said.

"It is," Eliza confirmed with her own brand of direct bluntness. "We are a burden he never wanted. It only makes sense that he would wish to pawn us off elsewhere." She stilled, then looked to Bronwyn, a curious tilt to her head. "Though I suppose he has already done that in a way, in marrying you."

Before Bronwyn could think how to respond, the girl continued. "But he shall be gone soon enough anyway. Not that we shall see him much while he's here on the Isle. He does prefer to remain far from Caulnedy whenever possible."

"Mayhap it is because of his mama," Nelly said, her voice soft and contemplative.

"His mother?" Once again Bronwyn was struck that Ash's mother should be brought up in such sad terms. "Because the house reminds him of her?"

"Of course it reminds him of her," Eliza replied around a hefty bite of biscuit. Crumbs dropped to her skirts but Bronwyn was too interested in what she was about to say to reprimand her over the mess she was making. "The whole reason we came to Caulnedy was because we located his mother's diary and read about her childhood here. It sounded so very magical, we just had to come." Suddenly her expression turned and she sent a dark glare at the door. "But then Regina found the journal and realized where we had gone and told Ash. It would have been ages before he found us if she hadn't."

Bronwyn was stunned. "Do you mean to tell me you ran away? You left London on your own and traveled all the way to Synne? Just the two of you?"

She expected at least a modicum of remorse. Instead, Eliza smirked. "Oh, we weren't alone. A maid in the house next door to ours was heading to Whitby, supposedly to visit her parents. Only she wasn't visiting her parents, but a young man she was sweet on. I simply asked that she bring us along with her—in exchange for our silence. And Whitby is so close to the Isle, it was easy enough to make our way here from there."

Nelly grinned, her narrow chest puffing out with what could only be described as pride as she looked at her sister. "It was a brilliant plan. Eliza captained it; she's quite clever."

Bronwyn gaped at Eliza and Nelly in turn. "But why would you do such a dangerous thing?" Not to mention committing bribery. But that was another matter entirely.

Eliza shrugged. "The stories were like fairy tales, and we wanted to see what all the fuss was about. We could have asked Ash to bring us, I suppose. But I'm certain he would have refused. All he does is work, and he does not like to spend more time than absolutely necessary with us. That, and he doesn't like to speak of his mother. He had all her things locked away in a chest in his rooms back in the London town house, so he never had to see them."

Which, of course, brought up the question on why Eliza had thought it acceptable to break into his trunk and riffle through his private things. But that was for another day. For now, there were more pertinent matters at hand. Namely, their thoughts on Ash's feelings toward them. Or, if they were to be believed, his lack of feelings, which Bronwyn had seen firsthand was not at all true.

"I assure, you," she said firmly, "Ash cares for you all very much."

The noise that came from Eliza could only be described as rude. "We must not know the same Ash. But come along, Nelly," she said, standing and brushing the crumbs from her clothes. "I've heard there is a new litter of kittens in the stable."

"Oh, yes!" Nelly squealed, jumping up and sprinting after her sister, knocking over the picked-over food tray in the process.

Bronwyn, sighing in exhaustion, put her head in her hands. This was all getting so much more complicated than she had ever thought. Was that why they acted out as they did, because they thought their own guardian didn't want them and wished to be rid of them at the earliest convenience? But Bronwyn knew differently; she had seen herself that Ash cared for the girls and worried terribly about them.

Surely there must be a way to rectify that, she thought as she began the job of cleaning up the mess Nelly had made. No matter how stubborn or reluctant each person involved would be.

Chapter 15

$\mathcal{H}$e was a coward, a bloody pathetic coward.

Ash climbed the stairs to his bedchamber to dress for dinner later that evening. He had been gone for most of the day, blindly riding, walking, anything that could take him far from Caulnedy and the girls and the guilt they all dredged up in him. Leaving Bronwyn to take on the burden of caring for it all.

But wasn't that the reason he had married her? And she had agreed to that arrangement. In fact, she had seemed just as eager for it as he had. She was brilliant, and determined, and it would give her exactly what she wanted out of life, the independence to forge a name for herself.

And she was so damn passionate she made him ache for her.

But no, he could not think of her in that way. He could not remember how she had straddled him by the

Elven Pools, how her sweet face had been flushed with passion and her beautiful turquoise eyes had become heavy-lidded as she'd gazed down at him.

And he certainly would not remember how deeply she'd touched his heart when she'd talked of caring for the girls as if they were her own sisters...

He flung open his bedchamber door with more force than necessary, slamming it behind him as he tried to eradicate the sudden heavy ache in his chest, so much more potent than the desire that coursed through him. And so he did not immediately see the slender figure perched on his bed.

Bronwyn. He stumbled to a halt, though he wanted nothing more than to lay her back on that bed and sink into her, forgetting for a time the troubles he carried.

"Bronwyn, what are you doing here?"

Her face was impassive. "Waiting for my husband so we may discuss our situation."

Ah God. His heart raced so fast he feared it would burst out of his chest. She wanted to dissolve the marriage already, did she?

Ready as he was for her to put an end to things, he was wholly stunned when she finally spoke again.

"The girls, as you know, have run wild for some time now," she began, standing and beginning to pace like a disapproving governess. "And while I am more than willing to watch over them and prepare them for adulthood as you wish me to, I feel I cannot begin this particular journey alone. Especially," she continued, her lips twisting in a kind of pain, "as I cannot seem to even entice Regina to leave her rooms."

She turned to face him fully, spearing him with a stern look. "This, of course, is where you come in."

He blinked. "Me?"

She nodded. "You are their guardian. Right now you are the authority figure in their life; I am merely a friend they made by chance who somehow married their guardian. And to Regina, I am nothing more than a nuisance. So I shall need a kind of passing of the torch, if you will."

He set his jaw, nodding. "Of course. I shall speak to them immediately."

As he turned away to do just that—best to get it over with—she stopped him.

"It will take more than a quick talking-to, I'm afraid," she said. "What I need from you requires a bit more involvement on your part."

He cautiously turned back to her. Why did that sound so horribly ominous? "I don't understand," he managed through numb lips.

"I will need to get them on a schedule of some kind, with expectations set in stone. Especially for Regina. She, of course, may have the privacy she requires; being so much older than her sisters she will not want to learn lessons and go on hikes and such." Suddenly she stilled, her brows drawing together. "Or perhaps she would. I'm not certain what her interests are at all." She chewed on her lip for a moment before shrugging. "Regardless, I would have her know that she may pursue her interests but shall be required to join the family at specific times, such as luncheon and dinner and after in the drawing room. And, on occasion, on family outings about the

Isle. To give that schedule the gravitas it needs to get through to her, and indeed Eliza and Nelly as well, I will need you to join us at those times as well for the remainder of your stay on the Isle."

Why did he feel both anticipation and a dread so potent it made him nauseated?

When he did not reply, she came closer to him, taking his hand in hers. Her voice, gentle now, washed over him. "Please say you'll help me, Ash."

Ah, God, how could he refuse that? He gazed down into her eyes, feeling as if he were drowning in them. "Very well," he managed. "I agree. I'll help you."

The smile she gave him made her face glow with happiness. And as she gave his lips a lingering kiss and slipped through the adjoining door between their rooms, he thought he would do anything to see that expression on her face again.

* * *

While Bronwyn felt a sense of accomplishment—and rightly so—in persuading Ash to agree to her terms, and she could pat herself on the back for getting him and the girls, even Regina, in the same room together for more than a few moments at a time, there was no denying that it would be an uphill battle to see the quartet find any kind of reconciliation.

Though it really wasn't a reconciliation, was it? That implied they'd had a relationship of sorts before now. And it had quickly become obvious, even to someone as socially inept as Bronwyn, that Ash had never had a

relationship at all with the girls. For the remainder of
the evening, first at dinner and then in the drawing room
after, they had not seemed to know what to do around
each other. Between their stilted conversations—when
they attempted to converse at all—the great quantity of
eye rolls from the older girls, and Ash's harumphing and
throat clearing, Bronwyn realized she had never seen
them truly interact. Good God, and she thought *she* was
awkward.

The evening had been got through by some miracle.
And the night. Her cheeks flushed hot as she recalled
how Ash had come to her long after she thought he
would, when she had just about given up hope and was
drifting off into a fitful sleep. He had climbed beneath
the sheets, taking her in his arms, and kissed and
caressed her until she was writhing with unimaginable
need. And not a word had passed between them the
whole while.

Bronwyn might have thought it a dream if she hadn't
woken naked, just as she had the past several mornings.
But today was a new day, and she would not lose
momentum on this plan she had created for Ash and
his wards. And so here they were, on their first family
outing, a trip to Admiralty Row to window-shop and
breathe in the fresh sea air. The girls had not truly seen
the town center. And maybe, just maybe, she might gain
an inkling about where Regina's interests lay.

But no matter the myriad shops they passed, the girl
did nothing more than sniff and turn away, to glare out
over the busy street. Such as now, as they stood before
the bakery.

"Oh, please, Ash, may we buy something?" Nelly wheedled, jumping from foot to foot on the pavement even as she eyed the abundance of baked goods within. "I'm ever so hungry."

"You ate just before we left Caulnedy," Regina snapped.

"And I am hungry again," her youngest sister said, her small face scrunching with anger.

"I am hungry, as well," Eliza declared mutinously, linking arms with Nelly even as she glared at her elder sister.

Regina glared right back. "You are making a spectacle of yourself," she hissed.

"No more than you, with your sour face," Eliza shot back, her voice rising, gaining the interest of more than one passerby.

"Damnation," Ash grumbled. He reached into his pocket, retrieving some coin. "Here, buy whatever you like."

"Hoorah!" Nelly cried in triumph as she snatched up the coins without a thank-you and dragged Eliza within the shop.

Regina, giving her guardian a look of disgust, marched to the next shop and stared blindly into the window.

Ash gave a sigh and ran a hand over his face. "This was a mistake, Bronwyn. I should not be here."

Bronwyn, for her part, didn't know if he was referring to the outing, or the Isle of Synne completely. But she could not back down now.

Though how was she to move forward? She could insist they spend time together, but she could not force them to interact. If only she wasn't so rubbish at things of this nature.

Which was why she had sent a letter to Honoria just that morning. She only hoped her friend arrived soon with reinforcements.

As if she had heard her name echoing through Bronwyn's head, Honoria appeared, her younger sister and cousins in tow.

"Bronwyn, imagine seeing you here," she exclaimed, giving Bronwyn a surreptitious wink before she turned to Ash.

"Your Grace, how lovely to see you again. You, of course, remember my sister, Miss Emmeline Gadfeld, as well as my dear cousins Miss Felicity Gadfeld and Miss Coralie Gadfeld?"

"Of course," Ash said with a smile and a bow. Though Bronwyn could not fail to see how strained that smile was. He looked, quite literally, as if he wished to be anywhere but here.

Bronwyn bit her lip anxiously and looked to Honoria. Her friend motioned with her eyes to Regina. Of course.

"Regina," she called out to the girl, "have you met the Gadfelds?"

Having been backed into a corner, Regina could do nothing less than acknowledge the newcomers. Heaving a sigh, she approached.

"Yes, we met at the wedding," she said mechanically. "How do you do?"

The Gadfelds all smiled and bowed. Coralie, ever bright-eyed and curious, sidled up beside Regina. "What is it you were looking at there?" she asked, pointing to the shop window.

Regina blinked, flushing, even as she peered back in confusion at the window in question. "I...I'm not certain."

Coralie nodded, as if that made perfect sense. "Mrs. Jensen's hats are odd concoctions, aren't they? But the tourists do seem to like them. Are you interested in millinery?"

"Not particularly," Regina answered stiffly. Suddenly, giving Ash a rebellious look, she turned back to Coralie and said, "I prefer to wear men's hats, actually. And trousers."

She no doubt expected scandalized shock. Instead, Coralie nodded once more. "That sounds wonderfully freeing. I think I should like to try it myself sometime. But where were you all off to? If you have no other plans, perhaps you might accompany us to the Quayside Circulating Library?"

Regina, looking suddenly lost, as if she could not quite comprehend Coralie's kindness, cast an uncertain glance in Ash's direction.

Bronwyn's hand was tucked in his arm, as it had been since their arrival in the town center, and she could not fail to feel his small start. Her heart twisted, not only for his reaction to Regina looking to him for support, but also that the girl had actually done so. Why could these two not see that they needed each other dreadfully?

Squeezing his arm, she prodded him to answer the girl's silent question.

"Ah, er, yes." He cleared his throat. "That sounds like

a lovely idea. Why don't you go ahead while Bronwyn and I wait for your sisters?"

Regina's face relaxed as she turned back to Coralie. "I have never been to a circulating library," she replied in as soft a voice as Bronwyn had ever heard her use.

"You will love it," Coralie replied with a wide smile. "And they have just received the latest *Gaia Review and Repository*. I'm aching to get my hands on it. S. L. Keys has been writing the most delicious gothic romance as a serial for it, and we are all waiting on tenterhooks to see what comes next."

"*Gaia Review and Repository*?" Regina asked, not pulling back when Coralie moved closer and linked arms with her.

"A wonderful periodical," she explained, eyes bright with excitement in her dark face. "Gaia, as you may know, was said by the ancient Greeks to be the mother of all life…" They moved off, heads bent together. Honoria and the other girls moved off after them as well. Leaving Bronwyn and Ash alone on the pavement.

He remained silent beside her, his body stiff against her arm. For an anxiety-ridden moment, she feared she had overstepped by getting the Gadfelds involved.

When she cast a glance up at his face, however, it was to see it flooded with emotion.

"Ash?"

He swallowed hard, his gaze on Regina's retreating form. "She has never had a friend, you know," he said, his voice hoarse. "Can you imagine, sixteen years old and never had a friend?"

Tears burned Bronwyn's eyes. "I can imagine, very well," she replied softly.

He looked down at her, understanding lighting his face. "You can, can't you?"

They stood that way for a time, gazing at each other. And Bronwyn, for the first time in her life, felt truly seen. It knocked the breath from her.

Eliza and Nelly chose that moment to tumble from the bakery, arms full of brown paper packages, mouths full of sweet buns. Bronwyn fully expected the moment between her and Ash to have been shattered with their appearance, that his mood would revert to the same tension-filled one as before.

Instead, he instructed them where they were headed, and gave Bronwyn a small smile as they all started for the Quayside. And Bronwyn felt she wasn't walking so much as she was floating beside him.

* * *

A strange kind of truce had cropped up at Caulnedy since the trip to the town center three days ago. And while the time Ash spent with Bronwyn and the girls was not without tension, there was a new, cautious politeness among them.

And it was all due to Bronwyn.

He glanced across the library to the large desk in the corner, where she sat surrounded by piles of papers and books and stacks of shallow wooden display cases. Eliza and Nelly were hovering about her, seemingly captivated by what she was working on. As he watched, she answered one of the myriad questions the girls were peppering her with, handing Eliza a small magnifying glass and pointing to a specimen in one of the cases.

"Here you can see the life cycle of the tansy beetle," she explained as the girl hunched over the case in question. "I managed to collect specimens from all aspects of the cycle, and I've pinned them here in this case. This stage," she continued, indicating something out of Ash's view, "is called the larva stage. It's much like the beetle's adolescence."

Nelly pushed forward, trying to squirm her way between her sister and Bronwyn. "Let me *see*, Eliza," she demanded.

Ash frowned, preparing to reprimand her. Bronwyn, however, quickly defused the situation.

"While you wait for your turn," she said, firmly yet gently as she maneuvered the girl to the seat beside her, "shall I tell you how the beetle transforms from such an unassuming creature to the brilliant jewel that it eventually becomes?"

"Oh, yes please."

Bronwyn riffled through the piles before her, finding a portfolio and opening it to a series of watercolors. "Here you can see how the larva burrows underground. Over the winter its body makes the most fascinating transformation..."

She rambled on, her passion for her subject obvious. Nelly, to his surprise, remained rapt, hanging on her every word. Eliza, too, soon lifted her head and focused her full attention on Bronwyn.

His chest swelled with emotion. The expression on

both the girls' faces was, for the first time he could recall, full of absolute wonder. They always seemed defiant, as if they were preparing for anger or disappointment. Now, however, there was none of that.

This was how it should have been for them. They should not have experienced so much upheaval and uncertainty in their lives. Perhaps, just perhaps, he had finally done right by them in marrying Bronwyn.

But they, of course, had not been the ones to suffer the most. He looked to Regina, who sat curled up in an overstuffed chair not far from him. When last he'd looked her way, her nose had been pointedly buried in a book, one of the large tomes on fossils she had borrowed from the Quayside. He fully expected her to still be in that defensive position, neither joining the others nor inviting conversation. Which would be a sight better than her typical open defiance.

Yet instead of reading, her book lay forgotten on her lap as she craned her neck, trying to see what it was that had the rest of them so transfixed.

His heart ached for her, looking from the outside in. It had not always been thus; Eliza and Nelly had used to look up to her and rely on her when he had first taken them in. Three ferocious, defensive kittens clinging to one another.

As the years passed, however, the two younger girls had branched out on their own, becoming increasingly rebellious to Regina's attempts to care for them. And Regina had responded by lashing out, drawing into herself, pretending she did not care. Though hadn't Ash seen hints that she did care, very much? Her determined sleuthing to learn where her sisters had run off to, insisting on purchasing sweets for them before their arrival at Caulnedy, and now the longing in her eyes as she gazed at them; these all were proof that she loved her sisters and mourned the loss of the closeness they'd once had.

Pressing his lips tight in uncertainty, he nevertheless put his own untouched book aside—truly, he'd forgotten it was even in his hands—and leaned forward in his seat. "I'm certain they wouldn't mind your company," he said softly.

Regina started guiltily, as if being caught doing something embarrassing, before she shrugged her shoulders and, schooling her features into cool unconcern, turned back to her book. "I don't know what you mean," she muttered. "I don't have any interest in insects."

After the past several days of carefully tiptoeing about one another, her reaction cut deeper than it should have. Sitting back in his chair, he cursed himself for his misstep. He should have let well enough alone.

As he picked up his book once more, however, he sensed Regina shift. And then, her tentative voice, "Bronwyn is very smart, isn't she?"

He glanced up sharply, not certain if he had heard her right. To his surprise, Regina was once more gazing at the trio across the room, the longing in her eyes more pronounced than before.

"She is," he answered softly. "In fact, I daresay she is brilliant."

She nodded, swallowing hard. Suddenly her face scrunched. "But she cannot do anything with such a mind. She is a female, after all."

He blinked at the vehemence in her voice. "She can do anything she wishes," he answered.

She looked at him then, her eyes narrowed in suspicion. "You are her husband. Surely you don't support her pursuing such interests."

"Actually, I do." When she continued to look at him with a determined distrust, he was tempted to turn away and let her continue on with her pique. Or to argue with her, as he would have done in the past.

Instead, he remembered Bronwyn's gentle way of handling confrontation with Nelly and Eliza. His raising his voice and arguing with them had never had the success that she'd had with her patient forthrightness. And so, taking a deep breath, he looked Regina full in the face.

"Do you know what Bronwyn's dearest dream is?" When she said nothing, he continued. "To have a paper published in the Royal Society of London, to have that scientific body acknowledge her findings."

She frowned, looking Bronwyn's way. "She is a woman. That will never happen."

"I daresay," he replied, "that Bronwyn can do anything she puts her mind to. As can you."

She sucked in a sharp breath and looked back to him, her eyes wide, vulnerability and longing swirling in their dark depths.

When she turned back to gaze thoughtfully at the book in her hands, a faint hope making her face fairly glow, Ash looked to his wife. To his surprise Bronwyn was gazing at him, her eyes moist, a proud smile on her face. And for the first time in his life, he felt a pride in himself as well.

Chapter 16

*I*n all his years of running one of London's premier gambling hells, living his life in shadows and sin in keeping with the darkness of his soul, Ash had never imagined himself on a family outing to the beach. Yet here he was, hiking over sand, climbing over rocks, the laughter and chatter of Bronwyn and his wards in symphony with the calling of the gulls in the bright blue sky above them. And, to his everlasting shock, he was enjoying himself.

The trip had been decided upon just that morning. Bronwyn, it seemed, had noticed Regina's particular interest in fossils, and had written to her friend Miss Athwart of the Quayside for any particularly fertile fossil hunting grounds on Synne. Miss Athwart had pointed them to this remote beach, located near the mouth to one of the rivers that cut through the Isle. The cliffs rose in a sharp slope on one side of the river, a shale wall that by all accounts held all manner of treasures. And it was there, beneath that wall, that their efforts were focused.

"Bronwyn," Nelly cried, looking up from where she crouched near a collection of broken bits of shale and stone. "I have found some. I have found more fairy coins!"

Bronwyn made her way over the rocky ground toward her. Nelly, for her part, gingerly plucked several small items from the ground, placing them with infinite care in the palm of her hand and holding them up for Bronwyn to see.

"There must be a dozen at least," she said with pride, beaming at her.

They were all busy searching for the small star-shaped fossils Bronwyn had told the girls about. Crinoids, she had called them, a marine animal that had lived long ago and could be found imbedded in the rocks at the river's mouth. The long, slender arms of the creatures often broke apart, she had told them, and looked very much like small star stones. Nelly had naturally latched on to the more magical mythology of the fossils, that fairies used them as currency. Eliza was making a game of how many she could fit into the small leather pouch she had brought for just this purpose. And Regina, garbed in her beloved trousers to make it easier to move about, had taken to scouring the rock face for more intact specimens.

Ash, on the other hand, had been content to watch from a distance. While the truce existed among them all, that did not mean he had been willingly invited into their conversations. He was still very much an outsider, though a grudgingly accepted one.

Until, that was, Nelly looked in his direction and waved an arm to gain his attention.

"You must come and have a look. This one is so very tiny, I think you could balance it on a pinhead."

Ash looked about, certain she must have meant some-one else. But no, there was no one else near him at all. But she was still staring at him expectantly, so he started off across the sand toward her.

By the time he reached her she was on her feet, fairly bouncing in her impatience. The moment he reached her she grabbed his hand, depositing her collection in his palm.

"They are even smaller in your hand," she said in awe as she gazed down at the tiny dark gray star-shaped stones. Her eyes were glowing with excitement when she looked back up at him. "Aren't they beautiful?"

"They are," he agreed.

She beamed at him, then closed his fingers about her prize. "You shall keep them safe for me, won't you? Eliza is finding ever so many, and I am determined to beat her. But I have forgotten to bring a pouch."

"I shall guard them with my life," he replied with utmost gravity, depositing them into his waistcoat pocket.

Again, that brilliant smile that took his breath away. It was an expression he had never seen on her face before, one he had never thought to see. It made him think that maybe she did not despise him, that she might care for him.

She crouched back to peer into the sand and stones, looking for more treasure. But no, he did not want her to care for him. He had fought hard over the past five years to make certain she, and indeed all of them, did not become attached to him. The only way he had believed he could protect them, after all, was by separating them from everything that had to do with the Dukes of Buckley—himself included.

He tried to rebuild that old barrier he had erected between them. But it was a weak thing. And when Eliza bounced over, proudly showing him her own collection of fairy coins, he couldn't hold on to it a moment longer. Especially when the two girls, now openly competing, began to good-naturedly fight over him, each begging him to assist them in their endeavors. He found himself on his hands and knees in the sand, scouring the ground alongside them. And he wished for the day to never end.

* * *

Bronwyn had never thought the sight of a grown man talking and laughing with two girls as they all crawled around on the sandy ground searching for bits of fossilized sea creatures would bring her to tears. Yet that's just what it did.

Sniffling, she ran a surreptitious hand across her eyes before, breathing deeply of the briny sea air to clear her head, she made her way to the basket they had brought and extracted her notebook. The past days had inspired her more than anything else ever had to complete her paper and finally send it off to the Royal Society. With Ash's interest and appreciation for her work, as well as Nelly's and Eliza's near constant enthusiasm, there was nothing she wanted more than to make them proud of her.

In all her life she had never wanted to make anyone proud. Or, rather, she had never dared to try, knowing beyond a doubt she would fail.

Yet now, with Ash and the girls, she felt as if she finally might succeed. She had begun to steal away at every spare moment she could in order to polish her work, readying it for that terrifying date when she would finally send it off.

This particular spare moment, however, did not last long at all. Though for the most surprising reason.

"May we talk?"

She looked up, shielding her eyes from the glaring sun. But it was not Eliza or Nelly who required her; those two were still happily engrossed in searching out every last crinoid they could find with Ash. No, it was Regina who stood before her.

As of yet, she had not managed to reach the girl. Though she had agreed to the new expectations put on her with minimal grumbling, Regina had yet to speak to Bronwyn without being spoken to first. Nor had she referred to Bronwyn as anything but *Your Grace*, something that Bronwyn had tried and failed to ignore. The girl would come around when she was ready, she had firmly told herself... all the while trying not to contemplate the fact that she might never come around.

Now, however, here Regina was, her typical cool indifference replaced with a vulnerable uncertainty.

But the girl wanted to talk. And Bronwyn was doing nothing but staring at her as if she had grown two heads. "Of course," she replied haltingly, her face heating. She made room on the rock. "Won't you have a seat?"

Was that relief in Regina's eyes? But, no, she must have been seeing things, for it was quickly gone as the girl, after a moment's hesitation, sank to the rock beside Bronwyn.

And then...nothing. The girl sat silent beside her, rubbing her hands up and down her trouser-encased legs. Bronwyn had the feeling that, if Regina had been wearing a skirt, she would have twisted it into a wrinkled mess.

But what was Bronwyn supposed to do now? Did she quiz Regina on why she had need of her? Did she wait until the girl was ready to talk? The latter might mean they would both sit in awkward silence for who knew how long. The former, however, might be the height of rudeness.

She caught sight of Ash. He glanced at her, smiling slightly, and her heart stalled in her chest. The moment was quickly gone, as his attention was snagged again by the younger girls. But that small look decided things for her. If he could overcome years of distance to make a connection of sorts with his wards, she could certainly make an effort with this young girl who was apparently as lost as she was.

Dragging in a deep breath, she closed her notebook and placed it aside. "Did you need to speak with me about something?" she asked in a voice that trembled only slightly.

Regina's dark eyes flew to hers. "No. That is, yes. That is—"

She looked lost, and Bronwyn thought she might bolt. She remained completely still, holding her breath, having the utterly ridiculous fear that if she moved wrong the girl would jump up and run off and this chance with her would be gone forever.

Instead Regina shook her head and looked Bronwyn straight in the eyes. "I wanted to thank you. For this outing."

"Oh." She blinked. That was completely unexpected. And it touched her heart deeply, much more deeply than she thought possible. "You're welcome. I had seen your interest in fossils and thought it might please you."

The girl nodded, her lips pressed tight together, and she looked toward her sisters and Ash. The trio were intent on their goal, the sounds of their laughter ringing out over the sand. Then she swallowed hard and blinked rapidly, as if staving off tears.

"But it is more than the fossils," she murmured thickly. "In all the time I have known him, he has never spent so much time with us. We thought—" She cleared her throat, tried again. "We thought he despised us."

"But why would he despise you?" Bronwyn asked.

The girl shrugged, still not looking at Bronwyn. "We are a burden on him. And an embarrassment, I assume. He is a duke, after all, and forced to raise three girls in his household from a completely different station that have no blood connection to him."

She finally turned to look at Bronwyn, and her dark eyes were filled with so much pain Bronwyn wondered how she could bear it.

"And our own mothers did not want us; why would he?"

Shocked by this revelation—not only by the fact that the girls had separate mothers, but also that their mothers had abandoned them—Bronwyn did not know what to say. My God, what had this girl been through in her short life?

Regardless of her own state of mind, however, Bronwyn did the only thing she could think to do: she remained quiet, keeping her gaze firm on Regina, letting her know through her actions that she was still listening.

"I thought he would be only too happy to discard us here on the Isle, where he did not have to deal with us anymore. But then he married you."

She gave Bronwyn a smile. It was the merest ghost of one, the slightest curve of lips. Yet it was a smile all the same.

"I am glad he married you," she said softly.

Without another word Regina stood and walked off. Bronwyn, mutely watching her go, fought back tears, feeling as if, with the olive branch the girl had offered, she had been handed the most priceless treasure.

* * *

When Ash had first entered into this agreement with Bronwyn, conceding to her request that they live together as man and wife for two weeks, he had been certain that it would be an easy thing to confine their intimate moments to mere physicality. Even after they had begun to enjoy their time together outside of bed, and had seen their bed sport blend into some of their more private daytime activities, he had made certain that one specific line was never crossed: that they would never sleep in the same bed once their lovemaking was done. They would never remain with one another in the intensely vulnerable act of slumber, would never wake in one another's arms.

Tonight, however, after the joy of their outing, feeling his armor crumble beneath her gentle hand...

He pulled her snug against his side, their ragged breaths mingling in the night air. He had thought his desire for her would surely have abated by now. Yet each time they came together was more powerful than the last. And each time he was about to leave her bed, it was harder to do so. Which should be alarming. He was to depart for London in less than a week, after all. But he comforted himself with the fact that he still had five more days with her—and five pleasure-filled nights to satisfy his hunger. Surely by the time he departed, he would be more than ready to do so.

But the thought of leaving, as comforting as it had been in the beginning, was not comforting any longer. In fact, it seemed each time he so much as thought about ending his time on Synne a vague panic began to build in him. Which was ridiculous. He and Bronwyn still held fast to their original agreement, and she talked of the end of their time together with unexpected frequency.

Which was lowering, really, but he would not look into that too much.

She stirred against him, and he was dragged back to the present. Or, rather, he came willingly. There was nothing he wanted more just then than to be in her arms, but it was time to go back to his own bed.

Yet he was loath to leave her. Unconsciously he hugged her tighter to his side, reveling in her slight, lithe form, so warm and soft, and yet amazingly strong, reposing against him.

"Ash?"

Her voice, husky from sleep, curled around him like a caress in the darkness. "I'm sorry, did I wake you?"

"I'm glad you did."

The soft admission tugged at his heart. He should leave, he knew. They did not talk after their lovemaking. She fell asleep, and he left her alone in her bed, and he was happy with that arrangement. Talking brought on too much closeness for his liking.

Or, at least, that was what he used to think. He wasn't so certain now. Especially when her arm tightened about his middle and her slender leg brushed against his own.

As a way to distract himself from the sensual feel of her thigh as it dipped between his, he cleared his throat and said, his voice only slightly hoarse, "That was kind of the Gadfelds to visit today after our return from the beach. Eliza and Nelly, I think, enjoyed the extra attention. And Regina and Miss Coralie have become fast friends."

"Coralie is a sweet girl," she replied. "She will be

good for Regina, I think. She, too, had her life upended when she was a child, forced to come to Synne and live with her uncle and his family when her parents died. But she has adjusted well, and I think Regina will, too."

His throat felt suddenly thick. Clearing his throat again, he said, "And Eliza and Nelly? Do you think they shall adjust?"

"I do," she said with soft certainty. There was a moment of stillness as her fingers traced lazy circles on his chest. He thought she might fall asleep again.

But she spoke up, her voice hesitant. "Several days ago Eliza and Nelly told me that they ran away from London, and that is why you came to Synne, in order to find them."

It seemed a lifetime ago, those days of panic and fear. "Yes."

"They said they chose Synne because of stories your mother had written in her journal."

Instinctively his body tensed at mention of his mother. Bronwyn's fingers continued to trace gentle circles on his chest, as if she knew he needed soothing. Eventually he relaxed enough to find his voice. "Yes."

"Your mother's descriptions of Synne must have been beautiful indeed to entice two young girls to leave everything they knew behind and travel such a distance."

"They were very beautiful," he managed. "*She* was beautiful."

There was a moment of silence. And then she asked, with utmost care and gentleness, "Won't you tell me of her?"

Ash sucked in his breath at the request, memories bombarding him. But where a deep grief usually accompanied any thought of his mother, now there was only a sad longing. He should change the subject, then excuse himself and leave her to sleep.

Ash, however, found he didn't want to ignore her request, nor did he want to leave. Then, without meaning to, he spoke.

"She was amazing," he began, the words a whisper. "Always kind, always gentle, always giving. She thought of others before herself, even to her detriment—"

The words caught in his throat, as if stopping him from revealing just how detrimental her giving spirit had been to her.

Bronwyn seemed to sense his distress. She kissed his chest, then said, "I saw her childhood portrait when Mrs. Wheeler gave me a tour of the house. She grew up here?"

At once the panic in him eased. His chest expanded, a kind of relief washing over him that their talk had turned to safer waters. "Yes. Her name was Mary Caulnedy then, an only child. She used to tell me the most fantastic stories when I was young, of the folklore of Synne, and the adventures she had, and how happy she had been here. It was why—"

Once more his throat closed as grief took control again. But he was suddenly tired of keeping her hidden, like some dirty secret, when in fact she had been such an incredible blessing.

"It was why I brought her here when she was about to die," he finished, his voice hoarse with effort. "I wanted her last memories to be in the place that had made her so happy."

His voice hitched on the last word. Bronwyn immediately rose up, leaning over him. She gazed down into his face, her brilliant eyes glittering with surprising moisture in the faint firelight. Was she crying? But he did not realize he had been crying as well until she ran a finger along his cheek, wiping away a tear.

"I wish I had known her," she said.

He cupped her cheek, overwhelmed by emotion. "I wish you had as well," he replied. He dragged her head down and took her lips in a kiss, his soul lighter than it had ever been.

How was it that his life could so totally turn on its head in such a short time? Lying here with Bronwyn, thinking over the past days of happiness, he could not now remember why he had been so determined to keep her at arm's length, or any of them, for that matter. When he recalled the smiles on the girls' faces, at how he had shared laughter with them—something they had never done in five long years since they had come into his care—he found himself wishing it could always be thus. And when he was in Bronwyn's arms...

Ah, when he was in Bronwyn's arms he forgot everything evil and ugly in his life. Here was light, and joy, and hope. She gave that to him. She gave that to all of them.

Dear God, if only life could always be this way. He had never known such contentment as he had these last days with Bronwyn and the girls. Had never known such love—

Love? The word swirled through him, but it did not make him recoil as he expected. No, it made him want to sink into it, into the realization that he loved the girls, and always had. And, more surprisingly, he loved Bronwyn.

He pulled back, and scoured Bronwyn's face, watching as her eyelids fluttered up, revealing eyes brimming with what appeared to be the same emotions coursing through him. Dear God, he loved her. He loved Bronwyn.

But she could not love him. If he did not think he was deserving of the love of his three wards, what made him think he deserved the love of someone as incredible and brilliant and giving as Bronwyn? And besides, soon he would leave her and the girls behind, and return to London. Just as he wanted.

As her lips curved in a smile that was full of promise, however, and she lowered her head once again to take his lips in a kiss, his last thought before passion overtook him was that perhaps that wasn't what he wanted at all. No, what he truly wanted was to stay in Bronwyn's arms, forever.

Chapter 17

S he was done.

Bronwyn leaned back in her chair and gazed down at the small packet on the library desk with equal parts relief and anxiety. She had not thought to ever complete her paper. Stolen moments could only get her so far, after all, and with the busyness of the past days with Ash and the girls, she had not managed to carve out the time she needed to finish her work.

But to her shock Ash had pulled her aside that morning and decreed that there was to be no outing that day, at least not for Bronwyn.

"I'll take the girls to the Elven Pools," he'd said as he'd gathered his wards together, a chattering, chaotic group, in the front hall, "so you might have the day to do as you like. You have not been to the meadow since the girls returned to Caulnedy, after all. Nor have you taken the time to work on your paper."

Then he had leaned in close, giving her a brief, tender kiss. "The world needs to see your work, Bronwyn," he'd murmured before herding the girls out the door.

She had been too stunned to speak. But once they had closed the door, and the quiet of the house had settled around her, she had been filled with an excitement about returning to her work that she had not experienced in too long. She had locked herself away in the library at once, barely taking the time to eat as she worked feverishly throughout the day to revise her paper.

But now it was done, and ready to send off to the Royal Society. She had poured her heart and soul into the piece, and it was her best work to date; surely they could not refuse to accept her findings.

But as she went to seal the packet up, she paused, suddenly fearful. She chewed her lip, gazing down at the neat pile of papers, all wrapped in brown paper, ready to be delivered. Her work was done; it was ridiculous to waste a moment more in uncertainty. After all, she had spent years readying herself for just such a moment. Every bit of research, every word written, every specimen mounted, every sketch perfected, had been leading to this very occasion. Why, then, was she faltering?

It was not her typical fear of failure, that she knew. No, that particular emotion was familiar, a dull ache in her gut. This was new, and sharp, a fear that seized her limbs and dug into her shoulders with fierce claws of doubt. As her thoughts turned over the past days, trying to understand where this new uncertainty was coming from, it became clear just what had prompted this new anxiety: whereas before she'd had to worry only about herself and her pride if she failed, now she might fail Ash and the girls as well.

Which was too paralyzing a thought to contemplate. She needed air. She planted her hands on the desk and pushed herself to standing, ignoring her shaking legs. She would take a quick walk and clear her head, and by the time she returned she would be right as rain and able to send off the packet with no qualms.

Not giving the parcel another glance, she strode from the room, making her way to the front hall. The house was still quiet, Ash not yet returned with the girls. She wondered what they were doing, how they were enjoying their outing. And, not for the first time, she marveled at the change in her husband, that he would willingly spend time with his wards. That was not the only change, for he was different with her as well, the night before proof of that.

A small smile curved her lips, her step slowing and body warming as she crossed the marble tile of the foyer. Something had shifted between them last night, a line redrawn in the sand when he had opened up to her about his mother. For a beautiful moment she had even forgotten this was all temporary.

But it *was* temporary, she tried to remind herself. In a mere four days he would be leaving. She had best remember that. Theirs was not a romantic interlude. There was no affection between them.

Yet she knew, even as she tried to remind herself of their original agreement, that it was a lie. She cared for Ash, truly cared for him. In fact, after seeing him open up to the girls, after his unflinching support of her work, after the tenderness he had showered her with, it was quite possible she might even love him.

She faltered at the front door, her hand on the latch. No, she could not love him. It had been the one rule between them. She had been so certain they could never love one another that she had laughed when he had admitted the day after their wedding night that he worried she would develop feelings for him. Could she have truly been so foolish as to break that promise to him? But, even worse, could she have truly broken the promise she had made to herself all those years ago? No matter the time that passed, she would never forget her heartbreak when Lord Owens had betrayed her affections. Nor would she forget how it felt to be reminded that she could never be loved for who she was.

It did not take even a moment, however, to realize she had been that foolish. She loved Ash, and she wanted their marriage to be a real one.

She sucked in a sharp breath. The temptation to make a life with Ash and the girls, to have a family that accepted her for who she was, curled through her. It was a foolish desire—and one she had not realized she carried in her heart until this moment. Her entire life had been spent not fitting in, never being accepted for who she was. And feeling shame that she would never conform to the prescribed mold her parents insisted was her place in the world. She had come to terms with it, and had told herself if she was not happy, at least she was content.

Now here were people who wanted her to succeed. Could they—even Ash—come to love her as well?

So shocked was she at the unexpected longing that

coursed through her, she did not immediately see the
carriage in the front drive when she flung open the front
door—or the people alighting from it.

Damnation, her parents were here? She froze, her
hand still on the latch, remembering their last visit to
Caulnedy, and she wanted nothing more than to turn
and disappear back into the house to hide. She could
have the butler inform them she was out for a walk.
Or that she was indisposed. And would be for the next
twenty years.

Before she could do just that, however, her mother
spied her.

"Bronwyn, darling," she exclaimed, rushing forward.
"My dear girl. My wonderful daughter. When we heard
you were once more entertaining guests we could not
fail to return. But how well you look."

She embraced Bronwyn, enveloping her in her
plump arms before stepping back then, looking her up
and down. "Though still as thin as ever," she clucked.
"Mr. Pickering, look how thin our daughter is."

"She is at that," her father declared, coming forward
and pinching her cheek. "Best put some meat on those
bones, Poppet, else Buckley shall not be able to do his
duty in planting the next duke in your belly."

He laughed uproariously, his wife along with him.
Bronwyn, for her part, could only stare numbly at them.
It was not anything she had not heard before. Though
in the past their comments on her curves, or lack
thereof, had never touched on her ability to get with
child. This newest addition to their critique made it so
much worse.

"But come and see," he continued, oblivious to her distress. "We have brought you a surprise all the way from London."

Through her numbness, a fatalistic dread swept over Bronwyn, an intuition that something horrible was about to occur. What in the world could her parents have sent for all the way from London?

Or, rather, who, she thought as an elderly woman stepped down from the carriage, followed by a light-haired man who was all too familiar. And whom Bronwyn had prayed she would never have to see again.

"Lord Owens," she breathed. "And Lady Brindle."

The dowager marchioness and her grandson looked at her with the same disdain they had shown her when she had last seen them in London. It was a memory she had done her best to forget over the past six years, that moment when her dreams had come crashing down around her head, even as her family had been forced to flee the city lest Bronwyn's heartbreak be made public.

But why had her parents brought them here? A foolish question, she soon realized. The elder Pickerings had been embarrassed and furious over the entire situation in London. Since then, this duo had been the reason her parents had been so determined in the following years that Bronwyn marry a lofty title. They had been certain that, should they have a daughter who was of equal footing or a higher position than the marchioness, the woman would be forced to concede she had made a mistake in forcing them from London.

"Doesn't married life suit our daughter?" her mother simpered. "We did not want to lose Bronwyn for anything; we love her so very much. But how could we separate two people so in love? I daresay dear Buckley could have been a pauper, and we could not have refused her." She tittered. "How lucky for us he was not a pauper at all, but a *duke*."

Bronwyn blanched, not only for the fact that her mother had referred to Ash as *dear Buckley* and was flaunting his title, but also that she had stated the marriage was a love match. It should not distress her; the woman had already told anyone who would listen that the duke had fallen head over heels in love with her at first sight. Her mother did not believe a word of it; rather, she said it to give herself more importance in the eyes of her audience. Especially now, as she rubbed Ash's title in Lady Brindle and Lord Owens's faces in the most embarrassingly obvious way possible.

Yet now that Bronwyn knew for certain she had fallen in love with her husband, it was like a vicious blow. Ash, she knew, did not—could not—feel the same.

Lady Brindle dipped into a curtsy, though it was rudely shallow. "Your Grace," she said, eyes narrowed as she took Bronwyn in from her mop of chaotic curls to the tips of her half-boots. "I wish you joy on your marriage."

"Yes," Lord Owens said in his smooth way, bowing even as his gaze held her own with a disturbing degree of intimacy, as if they shared a special joke between just the two of them. "Please do accept our felicitations. Forgive us for not attending your wedding, but we could not make it out of London in time. You understand."

"Of course," she managed, even as her skin crawled.

How could she have ever thought this man handsome and kind? How could she have ever believed herself to be in love with him?

But they were all looking at her in expectation. Flushing, she said, "Won't you come in?"

"How kind of you to offer," Lady Brindle drawled with a curl of her lips so slight Bronwyn nearly missed it.

Bronwyn led the group into the house, giving quick instructions to the butler before showing her guests to the drawing room. All the while she felt everyone's eyes on her, watching her as if she were an animal in a menagerie. For more than a week she had forgotten what this was like, the constant feeling of disappointing everyone around her, the expectation for her to do something and her not having an idea what that thing was.

But she was a duchess, Bronwyn told herself as her mother went into raptures over the house and Lady Brindle looked about her as if she were in a beggar's hovel. Surely she could handle one disapproving marchioness and her heartless grandson.

* * *

Ash had thought he would be much too busy to miss Bronwyn. He had never before taken the three girls on an outing, after all, and had not known what to expect. No doubt it would be a stressful, chaotic endeavor.

But though he had been in a constant state of alert, making certain Nelly did not slip on the rocks surrounding the pools, breaking up quarrels, and answering all manner of questions, Bronwyn was never far from his thoughts. In those rare moments of quiet, he could not help but think of her in this very spot when last they'd been here, the feel of her above and around him. Nor could he forget last night, the way his heart had opened up to her and he had realized his love for her. It was something he had never experienced with anyone. And it still had the power to shake him. All day long he had looked forward to returning to her so he might hold her again.

But she needed time to herself to complete her work. And so he had kept the girls out as late as he was able. When the shadows began to grow long and the food in their basket was gone, he finally turned back for Caulnedy. Anticipation sizzling through his veins as they came up to the rear of the house and he sent the girls to their rooms to clean up before dinner. Perhaps, he thought as he hurried to the library, he might be able to steal a moment with Bronwyn while the girls were busy elsewhere. But she was not there as he had expected. Just as he was exiting the room to continue his search of her, however, Mr. Hugo approached, Mrs. Wheeler trailing behind him, looking for all the world like an avenging angel.

"Her Grace is currently in the drawing room," the butler said in his monotone way.

"With those parents of hers," Mrs. Wheeler interjected, pushing past the butler. "As well as some fancy nobles from London." She glared up at Ash. "Your wife looks as miserable as anyone I've ever seen. You'd best go and join her, before I go in there myself."

Ash, who had never seen the mild-mannered house-keeper looking so furious, didn't pause before he was hurrying for the drawing room. He didn't know what the devil was going on, why her parents were here—again—or who these people were that the Pickerings had brought. But he wasn't going to waste time asking questions.

He never expected, however, just who their noble guests might be.

Though *guest* was not a word he would have applied to Lord Owens. Or *noble*, really. The man was a snake, having tried to ruin Brimstone's reputation on more than one occasion with claims of rigged tables. All in an effort to distract from the fact that he had lost a small fortune—and several pieces of property and family jewelry as well—to Brimstone's coffers.

"Ah, and here is our dear son-in-law," Mrs. Pickering exclaimed, clasping her hands to her bosom and looking at Ash with adoring eyes. "Dearest Buckley, do come and meet our friends, come all the way from London to wish you and our Bronwyn their felicitations."

"Oh, but Buckley and I are old friends, aren't we?" Owens said with a wide smile and narrowed eyes. He laughed, an oily sound that sent shivers of disgust up Ash's spine as he stood and held out a hand for Ash to shake. "What a small world, given my special friendship with Bronwyn—oh, but it is *Her Grace* now, isn't it. How lucky for you, Buckley, to have snapped up such a prize."

Ash saw red. The implication was clear: Owens wanted him to think there had been something intimate between him and Bronwyn. He recalled what she had told him of the man who had broken her heart. Was it Owens, then? Was he the bastard who had purposely pursued her only to humiliate and hurt her?

A quick glance at Bronwyn, at her tightly pressed lips and the pallor of her cheeks, and he knew the answer to that was yes.

But as much as he wanted to plant his fist in the man's smirking face, with an urge he had not felt since beating his father nearly to death, he would not give him the satisfaction. That's what Owens wanted: to enrage him, to cause chaos.

Instead, Ash grinned a feral grin and stepped forward, grasping the man's hand tightly. Very tightly. He was rewarded when Owens winced, the evil mischief in his eyes falling away to reveal a hatred so intense Ash was surprised it did not incinerate him on the spot.

Little did the man know Ash had been baptized in the fires of hell by growing up under his father's cruel hand. Such an expression did not affect him, not in the least.

"Oh, I assure you," he said in a low, dangerous voice, "I know very well the prize I have in Bronwyn."

"Why, this is splendid," Mr. Pickering said, puffing up his chest with his perceived importance, oblivious of the tension that filled the room. "Owens, I had no idea you knew Buckley. This reunion calls for something a bit more significant than a mere afternoon social call. You all must come to our home in Knighthead Crescent tomorrow evening; we shall serve a dinner in honor of this occasion."

"What a wonderful idea, Mr. Pickering," his wife

effused. "Mayhap we might persuade Lady Tesh and the Duke and Duchess of Dane to attend as well. What an evening that shall be."

"Oh, but I am afraid that is impossible, my dear Mrs. Pickering," Lady Brindle said, her disgust for the woman clear in her flared nostrils and curled lip. "Owens and I are just passing through, you see. We are on the way to our ancestral estates in Durham, and shall be leaving Synne in the morning."

"Such a shame," her grandson stated, taking his seat once more—one that was far too close to Bronwyn for Ash's comfort. He looked at her with interest, eyelids heavy and lips curved in what he no doubt thought of as a seductive smile. "I would so like to renew my acquaintance with Her Grace. It has been too long."

Bronwyn, for her part, looked faintly ill. "Perhaps it is for the best," she said, shifting ever so slightly in her seat to put distance between her and Owens. "I would hate to leave His Grace's wards while we are all still settling into Caulnedy."

When it appeared as if Owens would pursue Bronwyn across the sofa, Ash decided he'd had enough. "You don't mind if I sit beside my wife, do you?" he asked. "We are newlyweds, after all." Without waiting for an answer, he inserted himself between the two, nearly sending Owens to the ground.

"My apologies," he said, without an ounce of sincerity, watching as the man, shooting daggers his way, dusted himself off, as if he had touched something polluted, and made his way to a chair beside his grandmother.

"Think nothing of it," Owens gritted.

"But how refreshing to see a Duke of Buckley so besotted with his wife," Lady Brindle said. "Your father was not one for the softer emotions, if I recall."

Ash, in the process of receiving a cup of tea from Bronwyn, froze, his insides turning to ice.

"Did you know the previous Duke of Buckley then, my lady?" Mrs. Pickering asked.

"Indeed, I did." The woman pursed her lips as she looked at Ash. "I knew him quite well, in fact. You resemble your father, Your Grace, with that dark hair and those unusual eyes." She smirked. "Though I'm certain that is not the only resemblance you have to him."

Ash's vision went dark at the edges. It was not the first time his father's cruelties had been brought up in his presence, usually when a lord had just lost his fortune and was lashing out at Ash in fear and fury.

He had been ready for them then, always aware of just whose son he was, welcoming the reminder. He had never wanted to be complacent, to forget where he came from and what sins had been committed beneath his very nose. To do so would be more horrible than the sins themselves.

But while he had never forgotten his lineage, since arriving on Synne and marrying Bronwyn, he had forgotten how the world saw him as part of that lineage— something he had to shield the girls from. Though they had all been cushioned here in this paradise, this was not the real world. No, the real world was cruel, and cold, and would not fail to crush the girls' spirits with the same devastating shame under which Ash himself suffered. For a short time, he had forgotten what he had to protect them from.

And it was not just the Isle that had caused him to be complacent. Over the past week and a half Bronwyn had worked her way under his skin and into his heart. For the first time in his life he had been able to shed the yoke of his past, to embrace the possibility of a happy future, to let love into his heart...

He saw now that had been a fool's dream. He would never be able to escape who he was or where he came from.

Then Lady Brindle went in for the kill.

"But you mentioned His Grace's wards, did you not? Three young girls, if I've heard correctly. Where are the dear things?"

"Indisposed," was Ash's curt answer.

"Such a pity," she replied. "I had so hoped to meet them. It is so very generous of His Grace to take on their care. It is not often someone of his station takes children not related to him into his own home to care for them."

Ash's blood turned to ice in his veins. She could not know. It was obvious from the contemplative look in her eyes that she was grasping at straws.

Yet gossip and speculation did not require verified proof, did they? And, left to their devices, they spread like wildfire.

Dammit, he was a fool, a bloody fool. He should have hidden the girls, set them up in a quiet little cottage far away from him. It would have been better for them, after all, if they had never known him.

But in his selfishness he had kept them close, that last link to his mother and all she had tried to do to right those wrongs she had not had the power to stop.

"My mother's childhood nurse was very dear to my family; it is the least I could do to watch over her grandchildren now that she is gone. Any person worth their salt would do the same. Now," he continued, standing abruptly, "I'm sure you will want to get your rest before continuing your journey. It was so kind of you to make the time to visit us while you were on Synne."

Mrs. Pickering appeared dismayed. "Oh, I am certain they could stay for a bit longer. Isn't that so, Lady Brindle?"

That woman did not bother giving Bronwyn's mother even a glance. She rose, her eyes narrowed on Ash. "How kind of you to consider us, Your Grace. I do so look forward to seeing you and your dear wife when next we visit London." Smiling, dipping into a curtsy, she sailed out of the room. The Pickerings, dragging Bronwyn with them, followed her. Leaving Ash alone with Owens.

He turned to the man, all effort to remain even remotely civil having disappeared once Bronwyn was safely out of the room.

"If I ever see you near my wife or wards again, I shall not hesitate to make you regret it."

But the man appeared unfazed. If anything, he looked as if what Ash had said pleased him greatly.

"Oh, you've no worry on that score. I had my chance with your wife and found she wasn't to my taste. And a good thing I did, too, as she made such a spectacle of herself when I ended things. We were kind enough to keep it quiet at the time, but it can be so difficult to subdue unsavory tales." His smile widened. "I shall see you at Brimstone, Buckley."

"You were banned from Brimstone," Ash ground out.

The man, in the process of heading for the door, turned and laughed. "Oh, I'm certain you shall reconsider such an ill-advised decision."

With that he sauntered from the room. Ash, glaring after him in impotent rage, found he could only blame himself. He had wanted too much, and had forgotten that the walls he had built up about himself had been built for a very good reason.

He thought back to the night before, how desperately he had wanted to stay with Bronwyn, his realization that he had come to love her. And his foolish hopes that she might care for him in return and they might have a marriage in truth. How could he have ever even dreamed he could claim that blessing for himself?

He stalked from the room, doing his best to ignore the sounds of the Pickerings as they said their farewells to their daughter, making his way out a side door and heading for the stables. Yes, he had been a fool, he told himself brutally as he saddled a horse for a punishing ride, needing to put some distance between himself and Caulnedy. But he would be a fool no longer.

Chapter 18

$\mathcal{B}$ronwyn tried to pretend that nothing was wrong, that her parents forcing Lord Owens and Lady Brindle on her had not changed anything, that life could continue as it had been for the past week and a half.

Yet everything had changed. How had she forgotten the horrible lesson that Lord Owens had taught her? And how could she have ever believed that she was anything but that same odd, awkward girl who had spent a lifetime trying and failing to fit in? Especially as Ash's attitude since their unexpected visitors' departure was back to the cold distance from before.

No, she told herself, that was not true. It was not back to what it had been before. It was so much worse. At least then there had been a consideration about him. Now there was none at all. Instead, there were solemn glances before his eyes fell away altogether, monotone replies to increasingly hesitant attempts to draw him into conversation, and a distance she could see no way across. All the while the girls looked on with troubled eyes, proof that whatever was happening with Ash, it was not just in her head.

By the time Ash followed her into her room after an unimaginably tense evening, Bronwyn felt she would shatter from the strain between them.

"Bronwyn," he murmured as he closed the door behind him, "we need to discuss our situation."

Why did those words sound like a death knell? Though her insides were churning, she schooled her features to the same neutral unconcern she used to wear like armor.

"Of course. But before we begin, allow me to apologize. By now you will have guessed that Lord Owens was the man I told you of, the one who led me to believe he was courting me."

For the first time that evening she saw a crack in the distant look in his eyes. There was almost tenderness in his expression. "You've no need to apologize," he murmured. "I know how Owens manipulates people. Whatever happened with him is in the past."

Ah, God, why did she feel the sudden urge to cry? "Nevertheless," she said briskly to stave off the tears that threatened, "I know it must have been distressing to you. And I am sorry you were subject to that."

"Like I said," he murmured gently, "your past is your past."

His words should have brought her relief. But all she felt was a horrible hollowness. What had she expected would happen after her apology? Had she truly believed that Ash had been so obsessed with Lord Owens being the former object of her affections that he had been consumed by jealousy? Had she thought her apology would magically fix everything? Foolish woman.

As expected, what she had said did not change a thing between them. "But their presence here did remind me that I am needed back in London. We have been in a bit of a bubble here at Caulnedy, and I had begun to forget this was all temporary."

As had I. Bronwyn swallowed hard, feeling as if she were standing before a firing squad, waiting for the killing shot.

"But the girls have responded to you beautifully," he continued. "Really, it was a genius idea to bring me in and help to ease your way. It worked better than I ever imagined it would. Even Regina has opened up to you."

He fell silent.

"However," she prompted, the one word sounding strangled.

He pressed his lips tight and nodded. "Right. However, I think we can both agree that it is time I remove myself from the situation. I leave in a matter of days, and it wouldn't do to have the girls become too attached."

Or for you to become too attached. He did not say the words, but the implication was there in the way his gaze skimmed over her, as if he could see to her very heart and was embarrassed for her. Her cheeks burned with her humiliation, for once more she had given her heart where it was not wanted.

"Of course," she replied through numb lips. Feeling

unmoored, her eyes dropped from his and jerked about the room, searching for something solid to grasp onto in the swirling maelstrom of her emotions. Suddenly her gaze anchored on her bed. The bed that had seen so many of their intimate moments, that had witnessed her body awakening to sensation and her heart to love.

"And what of our nights?" she found herself whispering. She looked back to him. "Are those to end as well?"

The amber of his eyes deepened, and he looked as if he were burning from the inside out. She expected him to agree then that yes, it would be for the best.

Instead he strode toward her, catching her up in his arms. His mouth found hers, hungry and insistent, an almost desperate quality to his kiss that awakened something equally frenzied in her. She clung to him, her hands diving into his hair, her body pressing up into his, beseeching him. In a corner of her brain she realized this felt like a farewell, and it frightened her. For a moment she felt the mad urge to declare herself, to beg him to stay.

But if she opened herself up and allowed her raw emotions out, only to have him still leave, it would destroy her. And so she kissed him harder, forcing the words back down. Letting him know with each frantic caress, each desperate press of her lips, what she could not say.

The heat between them became an inferno, swift and utterly undeniable. There was no time for undressing, no time to even find the bed. He lifted her off her feet and pressed her to the wall. She wrapped her legs

about his hips, her skirts bunching about her waist, his
hands frantic on her thighs and beneath her bare bottom.
Their harsh breaths filled the room, even as his hand
came between their bodies to free his manhood from his
breeches. And then he was sinking inside her.

She tore her mouth free, her head pressing back
against the wall as he filled her to the hilt, his deep
groan mingling with her gasp of pleasure until she could
not tell the sounds apart. But there was no reveling in
the sensation of him being inside her. No, their need for
one another was too great. He began to move, seemingly
helpless to do anything else, his hips slamming into
hers. And she welcomed each thrust inside her, the wall
giving no quarter behind her.

In mere minutes her body exploded around his, so
violent in its release she cried out. Suddenly his mouth
was on hers, swallowing her cry, even as his own
shout filled her up, making her climax that much more
powerful. And in that exquisite moment in time, as she
floated among the stars beside him, she was able to
forget the pain, the heartache, the uncertainty. And she
was happy.

* * *

That happiness, however, was as fleeting as it was cruel.

But she would not think of Ash carrying her to her
bed, of his tender undressing of her or of him climbing
in beside her to hold her against him. Nor would she
think of how she had fought sleep with everything in her,
knowing that if she were to drift off, he would leave.

No, today she would recall how it felt to wake to an empty bed. To feel the cold sheets beside her and drift her fingers over the faint dip in the pillow where he had rested his head as he'd curled around her. She had known there was something different in the loneliness today. Though there were still three days before their agreement came to an end and he left for London, she knew deep in her battered heart she had already lost him.

But pain was good, she told herself as she went through her morning routine. It reminded a person that they should not be complacent and trusting, and that life was not a fairy tale.

And she fed it, brutally. He would no longer be joining her for breakfast as he used to, she thought as she ate that lonely meal. And he would no longer be accompanying her and the girls for luncheon and outings, she reminded herself as she attempted to guide his wards through the new day. This was how life would be from now on; they had best get used to it.

And, somehow, she had managed it. The day passed, with Nelly and Eliza asking only a dozen times or so where Ash was. And if Regina appeared slightly more subdued than usual, Bronwyn would chalk it up to the girl adjusting to their new normal.

When Bronwyn woke the next day, she was certain it must be easier, now that she knew what to expect. No matter her sleepless night—Ash had come to her, but like the evening before their lovemaking had been swift, and desperate, and he had left the moment her head had hit the pillow—she was determined to pretend everything was well. And besides, she did have one thing to look forward to: the Oddments were set to meet in the afternoon. She had not been to their meetings in weeks, and could not wait to see her dear friends.

Just as she was readying herself to leave, however, there came a knock at her bedroom door.

Her heart leapt in her chest. Had Ash come? In the next instant, however, she quickly stifled the burst of hope. Foolish woman. Of course he had not changed his mind. She had best get it through her head that whatever interlude she'd had with him was over.

"Come in," she called out.

The door opened hesitantly to reveal Regina.

"Do you have time to talk before you go?"

Bronwyn blinked, wholly unused to this new, more open side of the girl. Attempting a smile, she motioned Regina in.

"Of course. Let's move to the chairs by the hearth and we can talk as long as you like."

The girl nodded and moved inside readily enough. But once they were settled she remained silent, staring at the empty hearth seemingly without seeing, her fingers nervously picking at the seam in her trousers, an article of clothing she had taken to wearing daily.

Bronwyn, not knowing quite what to do in this situation—the girl was obviously troubled about something—bit her lip. Finally, when it seemed Regina would not proceed without encouragement, she cleared her throat and said, "You wanted to talk about something?"

The girl started, looking at Bronwyn as if just realizing where she was. "Yes. That is—" She frowned, looking down once more, rubbing her palms up and down her thighs. "Ash is done with us, isn't he?"

Bronwyn's heart twisted in her chest. Ah, God, she should have realized the girl was affected by Ash's sudden absence. "I would not say he is done with us," she replied carefully. "He is readying himself for his return to London, is all."

The look Regina shot her was frustrated and angry and pained all at once. "You needn't pretend all is well," she said, her voice thick. "I am not stupid, you know. And neither are my sisters. We can see that Ash has changed toward us, that he is done playing the doting guardian. But I would hear it from you, so I might be better prepared to help my sisters through it."

Damn you, Ash. Her heart broke as she beheld the grief and fear in Regina's eyes. But no, she had no one to blame but herself. She had been the one to force Ash and the girls together, hoping to heal things between them and give them a semblance of a relationship. This here was proof positive that she didn't know a blasted thing about dealing with people. If she had just minded her own business, Regina, and no doubt the other girls as well, would not now be hurting.

Swallowing down hot tears, she replied, "We all knew he would be leaving at the end of the fortnight."

The girl fairly exploded from her chair. "I know he said as much," she cried. "But I did not think he would—"

She bit her lip, cutting off the words. Bronwyn, however, heard them all the same, for they echoed what was in her own heart. *But I did not think he would truly leave us.*

But she could not think of her own grief. She had the girls to consider.

She rose and made her way to where Regina stood near the window. The girl held herself ramrod straight, her gaze pointedly focused on something outside. Yet Bronwyn saw, by the way her arms hugged her middle and a muscle ticked in her jaw, that she was holding herself together by the thinnest thread.

Regina would not listen to platitudes. There was too much anger and pain in her, and pride as well. Bronwyn could tell her Ash loved them all until she was blue in the face, but that would mean less than nothing to this girl, who had been hurt far more than anyone her age should have been.

Instead she said, quietly, gently, "I have realized over the course of my life that we cannot control what other people do; rather, we can only control our own reactions to them. Easier said than done, I know," she continued with a wry quirk of her lips when Regina looked bleakly her way. "I am still learning that lesson. It is not an easy one to learn. And it still hurts, dreadfully." She reached out and placed a comforting hand on Regina's arm. "But I think it's made a bit easier to bear if you have friends by your side. And I shall always be by your side. I will be here for you whenever you need me."

She did not know what to expect. Whatever it might have been, however, it certainly wasn't Regina's quivering lip, or the tears that pooled in her dark eyes, or the sob that ripped from her throat as she threw herself in

Bronwyn's arms. As the girl cried out her pain, Bronwyn found herself crying right along with her. Ah, God, but it was like looking back in time to the vulnerable girl she had been. She had been seventeen, not much older than Regina was now, when she'd had her heart broken so brutally by Lord Owens. A betrayal that had taught her nothing so much as that she could not be loved for herself. That who she truly was invited ridicule and disdain.

It had been years before she had found those friends who had saved her. Years of pain and fumbling and uncertainty and self-hatred.

She would be damned if she would allow Regina to suffer as she had.

As Regina's sobs quieted, Bronwyn pulled back, taking a handkerchief out of her pocket and gently dabbing at the girl's cheeks.

"Would you like to go with me to meet with my friends at the Quayside? And perhaps afterward, we might visit the Gadfelds, and you might see Coralie again."

The hope that sputtered in Regina's eyes was nearly enough to make Bronwyn go off crying again.

"Do you think they would mind?" she asked in a small voice.

Bronwyn smiled at her. "I'm certain they wouldn't mind at all."

Chapter 19

The days since Owens's visit, reminding Ash who he was and why he had to remain distant from Bronwyn and the girls, had been misery. He had been desperate to rectify his mistake, keeping as busy as possible, filling the time with all manner of business. From scouring the local employment agency for governesses and music instructors and whoever else Bronwyn and the girls might need in the coming years, to making certain modistes and milliners—and even a tailor, so Regina might have all the trousers she required—were at the ready, to meetings with a local solicitor, there had not been a minute spent idle. He had even traveled to nearby Whitby on the mainland for anything Synne did not provide.

No matter how busy he had kept himself, however, he could not stop from thinking of Bronwyn or the girls. And no matter how many times he told himself that he would not visit Bronwyn's bed, he found himself slipping through their adjoining door each night and taking her in his arms and losing himself in her sweet body—all the while burying her deeper into his heart.

Now, a day before he was to leave for London—a day that was coming both much too quickly and could not come quickly enough—it was taking everything in him to stay away from them all. The moment the sun had risen he had fled the house, filling each minute with business and work and errands until he was nigh exhausted. When the time came to return to Caulnedy, he had to do battle with himself to keep from hurrying home to them.

He started. *Home*? A strange word, indeed, to associate with Caulnedy. When he had first arrived after tracking down Eliza and Nelly, he had done everything he could to stay outside those walls. The place had given him too much pain, reminding him of his mother, and how he had failed her, and how in his selfishness he had remained blind to the suffering of so many others.

Now, however, it had become a place of happiness, where he had begun to develop something of a relationship with his wards, where he had learned to love. All the result of a slight, stern, pixie of a woman in spectacles.

Bronwyn. Ah, God, he did not want to leave her. But leave her, leave all of them, he must. All his life he had lived under the shadow of his father, the shame at having that man's blood in his veins fairly eating him up inside until he hated himself almost as much as he had hated who had sired him. He could not let that happen to the girls, could not allow such degradation to crush their spirits, especially not after all they had already been through. And he could not allow Bronwyn to be tainted by it either. For while their life together thus far had been idyllic, there would be no holding back the ugliness of the world forever. Owens and Lady Brindle had been proof of that.

But no amount of reasoning would soothe the longing in his soul that he might stay with them all forever.

Sighing, weary down to his bones, he nevertheless straightened his shoulders and urged his mount on. The sun was setting, the forest that surrounded the long drive growing shadowed. He would have one last dinner with them all, say his farewells, and retire so he might prepare for his departure. And then in the morning, before dawn broke, he would be gone, and they would finally be able to live lives free of him and his father's stain.

What he did not expect as he neared the manor house, however, was a lone rider coming toward him. But even if he had not recognized the woman, the parrot on her shoulder would have given her away: Miss Seraphina Athwart, proprietress of the Quayside Circulating Library. The one who had threatened him with that cryptic *the Oddments are watching* on the day of his and Bronwyn's wedding.

Surely they could acknowledge one another and be on their way. But as he went to pass her, she pulled her horse up, blocking his path, and all hope for a quick leave-taking from her disappeared like a puff of smoke.

"Miss Athwart," he murmured. "I hope you are doing well."

She glared at him, her opinion of him plain on her face. "I am, in fact, not doing well, Your Grace," she said, her words clipped and furious. "And can you guess why I am not doing well?"

Frustration surged, and all manner of sarcastic answers flew through his mind. In the end, however, he remained silent. There was no use in adding fuel to the already blazing fire of her anger.

"Please do correct me if I am wrong," she continued, "but I believe I did warn you on your wedding day not to break Bronwyn's heart." She straightened in her saddle. "And now, sir, you have done just that. And I will not stand for it."

Why, he wondered desperately, did her words only awaken a faint hope that Bronwyn might truly have come to care for him? But no, he thought wildly, trampling that hope as surely as an elephant tramples the grasses at its feet, that was an impossibility.

He scowled at Miss Athwart, praying it hid the turmoil within him. "I assure you, I have not broken Bronwyn's heart. In fact, I have done everything in my power to make certain she would not be affected."

She scoffed, a rude sound that echoed through the trees. Her parrot repeated the sound—and no wonder, for it was one he must have heard daily from this Fury of a woman.

"Then you do not know my friend at all. For she is in pain." She gave a low growl of frustration, one that made her mount dance. "If I were a man, I would call you out," she spat.

He had no doubt she would at that. But Miss Athwart's

anger was his least concern. Was Bronwyn in pain, as she said? Ah, God, he truly was a bastard, as selfish and unworthy of love as he had always known, for the idea made that sputtering hope in his chest flare brighter. If her heart was breaking, it meant she had fallen in love with him, just as he had with her.

No, he told himself furiously, desperately, he did not want Bronwyn to have fallen in love with him.

"You are wrong," he managed, his voice hoarse.

"I am not wrong," she replied. "And you shall make it right."

"How the devil am I to make this right?"

"You forced her into this sham of a marriage," she snapped. "You have trapped her, as surely as if she were held in a locked cell." For a moment her expression transformed to one of deep pain. In the next minute, however, the fury was back in place, burning brighter than before. "You made a vow to her, Your Grace."

"And I am trying to keep that vow," he gritted.

"You are not," she spat. "Else you would stay with her. But no, you are thinking of only yourself."

"I am trying, for once in my miserable life, to not be selfish!" he cried, the words bursting from him before he could hold them back. "Everything I am doing is for her. If I was thinking only of myself, I would stay and make a life with her. But Bronwyn deserves so much better than me."

Miss Athwart gaped, as if seeing him for the first time. "My God," she whispered. "You have fallen in love with her."

His hands tightened in shock, his horse shifting in agitation beneath him. He hardly noticed for the roaring in his ears. "No," he replied, shaking his head violently. "Of course not."

"You have," she insisted. Her brows drew together, confusion plain in her face. "Why, then, are you leaving her?"

Ah, God, this woman saw to the heart of him. She did not even know him, and she could recognize what he was trying so desperately to hide. He had to escape her presence before he gave even more of himself away.

Drawing upon every ounce of self-control he had left, he straightened and stared down at her. Once more he was the dangerous gaming hell owner, and she recognized it if the alarm in her eyes was any indication.

Yet instead of bringing him comfort that he was finally returning to himself, he felt as if he had slipped into clothes that no longer fit.

"You are wrong, madam," he said with as much darkness as he could muster. "And I would appreciate you not to involve yourself in my marriage. Bronwyn and I have an understanding, and I expect you to respect that. Good day."

With that he urged his mount on, passing her without another glance. He could do this, he told himself as he rounded a bend in the road and the lights of Caulnedy shone through the deepening gloom. He would get through the evening, and would not visit Bronwyn's bed, and tomorrow before dawn he would finally be through with this place and all the heartache it gave him.

As he spied Bronwyn's outline in one of the windows

backlit by candles, however, and his heart surged with longing for her, he knew it would not be so easy.

* * *

Just as he had feared, the evening had been pure torture.

Dinner had been silent, each person mired in their own thoughts. It was so very different from those occasions when Bronwyn had brought them all together after a day of activities and outings. Then, Eliza and Nelly had been boisterous and joyful, talking of their day. Even Regina had chimed in on occasion. And Bronwyn... Ah, God, she had seemed happy, the closed-off look in her eyes replaced by something that was almost contentment.

She was not content now. No, she appeared strained, her skin ashen. More than once the thought whispered through Ash that Miss Athwart had been right— Bronwyn was in pain. Had she come to love him?

No, it was merely wishful thinking on his part, that selfish side of him that would insist on being heard though he tried with all his might to silence it. There was nothing to love in him.

He did not bother to sit with them after dinner in the drawing room. The meal itself had been horrible enough; he would not subject them further. Finally, however, it came time to retire for the night, and time to say his farewells. Leaving his study, he climbed the stairs to the nursery. Eliza and Nelly were there, quiet and subdued, so different from the boisterous girls he'd been forced to chase halfway across the country. He ached to apologize for leaving, to tell them how much he cared for them and would miss them.

But it would be better for them if he did not. His whole reason for leaving them here with Bronwyn, a safe place far from him, was so they might grow up healthy and happy and away from that shame that followed him about like an albatross.

"Eliza, Nelly," he said. "I've come to say goodbye."

"Goodbye," Eliza replied without looking at him, her voice acidic as she busily straightened a pile of books.

Nelly, cradling a doll in her arms, looked up at him, her large eyes welling with tears. Ash ached to take her in his arms, to tell her all would be well. Before he could say anything, however, her sister grabbed her by the arm and dragged her away into the adjoining room. Ash watched them go, his heart fracturing.

But he was not done with his farewells.

Regina did not immediately answer her door when he knocked. He listened for a moment, his heart sinking. Was she hiding somewhere in the house, perhaps in an effort to avoid him? Truly, he would not blame her if she did. Just as he was about to go searching for her, there were footsteps on the other side of the door. And then it was thrown wide, and Regina was there. Dressed in trousers and a loose shirt, her hair in a thick sable plait down her back, she looked as angry and disdainful as she used to before Bronwyn had come into their lives.

She glared at him. "You needn't have bothered to say goodbye, you know."

Though he knew she was simply lashing out at him,

her words were like barbs. He had not realized until this
moment how dear their new closeness had become.

"Of course I was going to say goodbye," he replied
quietly. "I don't know when I will see you again."

"And how different is that from the last five years
while we lived in your London house?" she shot back.

He pressed his lips tight, fighting the urge to respond
in kind. She was merely acting on her anger, he told
himself. That realization only managed to add to his
guilt, a guilt that had returned tenfold since Owens's
cursed appearance.

But at least there was one thing he was doing right
in his damnable life; he was making certain the girls'
futures, and Bronwyn's future as well, would be brighter
than he could ever provide for them.

"Be that as it may," he replied evenly, "there is something I wished to discuss with you before I go."

Her eyes narrowed dangerously. He thought she
would slam the door in his face. Instead she moved
aside, allowing him to enter.

He could not recall stepping foot in Regina's room
before. Or, at least, not since she was a child, just arrived
under his care. Then, her possessions had been few: a
quilt that had been stitched up by her Gran, a handful of
books, and a few articles of clothing.

Now, however, the space could not be any more
different. The quilt was still there, of course, carefully
draped over the foot of the bed. But now it had plenty
to keep it company. Not only had all of her belongings
from London been brought, but the treasures she had
amassed in the past weeks as well, fossils and piles of

books and rocks and plant samples and all manner of jars containing God knew what covering every surface available.

She stood amid it all, her arms crossed over her chest, feet planted wide, as if preparing for a blow.

"Say what you have to say," she bit out. "I need to prepare for bed."

He flinched, then frowned. She was right, of course. It was best to do this quickly. The faster he could have this over and done with, the sooner he could take his leave of Bronwyn and ready himself to quit this place.

"You are sixteen now," he began. "Nearly a woman grown. Soon you'll be entering society, finding a husband, having a family of your own."

He had hoped to continue, touching on what would be her part in helping her sisters find good matches and see they were settled well. Regina, however, had other ideas.

"Who is to say I shall marry?"

He blinked in surprise. "I had assumed—"

"You assumed wrong. I don't wish to marry. Not now, not ever."

He frowned, his head spinning. "I know it may seem incomprehensible now—"

"No, you are not listening," she bit out. "This has nothing to do with me being too young. I know what I want for my future, and that does not include marriage. If the Oddments don't need husbands, I don't either."

His frown deepened. *The Oddments*? Bronwyn's friends? He thought back to Miss Athwart, so furious as she faced him, ready to go to battle for her friend.

But what did she, or any of the others, have to do with anything?

Before he could question her on it, however, she was hustling him toward the door. "Now I'm sure you must prepare for your journey on the morrow," she said, her voice dripping disdain. "Do give my regards to Mr. Beecher."

In the next instant he was in the hallway, the door slammed in his face. What the devil had that been about?

He didn't have long to wonder, however, for suddenly Bronwyn was at his side.

"You mustn't be cross with her," she said softly, pulling him away from the door. "She's merely upset at your leaving and is lashing out."

Which he knew. Ah, God, he knew. But with guilt piling on guilt from Miss Athwart's attack, the unexpectedness of Regina's declarations, and the grief he'd been so desperately trying to bury, when he looked down into Bronwyn's face and realized this was the last time he would see her in God knew how long, if ever again, something broke in him.

"What the hell was she going on about? What was that about the Oddments and her decision to not ever marry?"

Bronwyn, her features already unnaturally wan, paled further. "I . . . I don't know what you're talking about."

"Regina," he snapped. "She declares she will not ever marry. She claims your friends are proof she does not need a husband."

Confusion was palpable on Bronwyn's face. It was

obvious she didn't have a clue what he was talking about. But his fear and anxiety and self-hatred and grief would not be silenced, drowning out all common sense.

"Dammit, Bronwyn, I cannot have the girls influenced in such a way. They need to prepare to take their proper places in the world, a world that will not be kind to them if—"

If the truth was ever found out about their parentage. But the words lodged in his throat, pain lancing through him until he could hardly breathe.

Bronwyn blanched. Then she flushed with fury, her body going rigid, hands forming into white-knuckled fists at her side. *"If they remain unmarried.* Isn't that what you were going to say?"

He gaped at her, horrified that she would assume such a thing. "No, of course not—"

But Bronwyn was beyond hearing him. "Because heaven forbid a woman does not conform to what society deems appropriate. No matter what we may wish to do with our lives, what dreams and aspirations we may have, we are merely women, after all. How lucky for you to find someone so desperate she could not possibly refuse you. What a laugh you must have had."

"I never laughed at you, Bronwyn," he tried, reaching for her hand.

She snapped it out of his reach. "It matters naught," she said, her voice acidic. "I shall have a better time of it than most, I suppose. I secured as much freedom as I was able to before submitting. I can only hope the girls are so *lucky.*"

With that, she spun about and marched down the hall

to her room, slamming the door behind her. The sound echoed through the great gaping emptiness in his chest. He came close to rushing after her, taking her in his arms, confessing how dearly he loved her and the girls and that she was everything to him.

But in the end he garnered enough willpower to head for his own room. And, for good measure, he immediately made his way to the door connecting his room to Bronwyn's and viciously turned the key. He would not visit her tonight, or ever again. If he did, there was no doubt in his mind he would break down and confess his heart to her. And he refused to be so selfish. Yes, she was angry, and hurting. But better that she hurt a bit now than suffer at his side for the rest of her life. And no matter how much she might come to hate him, it could never come close to how deeply he hated himself.

Chapter 20

*I*n the five days since Ash's departure from Caulnedy, Bronwyn had done everything in her power to keep herself and the girls busy. They hardly spent a moment inside the manor house, instead filling their time by exploring every corner of Synne they could manage.

All save for the Elven Pools, of course. No, she would not be able to return to that place for a long while.

Even as she filled the girls' days with activities and outings, all in an effort to heal their hearts from the beatings they had taken upon Ash's leaving, she had nevertheless known it would not be so easy for her. While she was as exhausted as the girls each night when they finally retired to their beds, there was no effortless slipping off to sleep for Bronwyn. Though her body ached and her eyes burned from exhaustion, her mind spun, whirling like a hurricane in her head, each moment she'd spent with Ash as clear as day. And with the memories came hot tears that tracked down her face and fell to her pillow. Damn him. Damn him for getting past her carefully built defenses and making her love him.

But no, she had to remind herself time and time again, he had not made her do anything. She had no one to blame but herself. She had been the one to insist he remain on Synne for a fortnight, and that they should live as man and wife for that time. If she had just swallowed her pride and braved the talk his desertion would have caused, allowing him to return to London immediately as he'd wanted, she would not now be pining to have him back in her arms. And she would have gone on, blithely unaware of how wonderful a person he truly was, though he tried his damnedest to hide it from the world.

Most importantly, she would not have forgotten that she would never be loved for who she was. No, she would have remained alone for the rest of her life had she not befriended two young girls by chance. A horrible fate, as far as society was concerned, and unfortunately an opinion held by Ash as well. Hadn't he let her know the night before he left, after all, that the world would not look kindly on his wards if they did not marry? It was the one thing expected of a woman, after all, and something he expected for his wards as well.

It should not have pained her that he felt that way. Didn't most people? She and her friends were in the minority. It was why they had formed the Oddments. Even so, it stung to know he expected a woman to marry, though that woman may want a different future. No doubt his enthusiasm for her chosen profession was merely because of her already having married him, and therefore there could be no harm in it.

But these thoughts were getting her nowhere. Shaking her head, she grabbed up her reticule and made her way from her room. The Oddments were meeting this morning, and she and Regina had planned on attending together. The girl had fairly blossomed at the meeting the week before, and Bronwyn had recognized her expression well. It was full of the same emotions that had taken her over when she had attended her first meeting with her friends, a recognition that she had finally found people who could understand her.

When she knocked on Regina's door, however, she found the room empty. Was the girl already waiting below? But no, she was not there, either. A quick search of the house, and she was finally located. Though it was in the last place Bronwyn ever expected to find her.

All three girls were on the floor in the nursery, a small orange kitten playing in the circle they had made with their legs. As she watched, Regina held a piece of string above the kitten. It batted at it, quickly losing its balance and tumbling backward. The girls laughed, their faces alighting with their joy.

"Do you think we can keep him?" Nelly breathed, hopeful eyes wide on her elder sister.

"I will ask Bronwyn," Regina replied with a smile.

"Oh, she'll say yes," Eliza declared happily, tickling the soft pink pads on the kitten's feet.

"What shall we name it?" Nelly asked.

"Whatever you wish," Regina said.

The look the younger girl gave the eldest was enough to make tears spring to Bronwyn's eyes. She had seen a slow shift in their relationship over the past days since Ash's departure. Whereas before Eliza and Nelly had shown a thinly veiled disdain for their eldest sister, lately they had begun to converse with her, asking her opinion on matters and making sure she was included in what they did.

This, however, was something altogether different. There was genuine affection as Nelly giggled and grabbed Regina's hand when the kitten performed a clumsy tumble, and something like admiration as Eliza asked her elder sister a question.

She should slip out. This moment among the three was too special to interrupt.

Regina, however, spied her before she could close the door.

"Oh! I'm sorry, Bronwyn. Is it time to leave?"

Cheeks flushing hot that she had been seen, Bronwyn reluctantly moved back into the room. "It is," she replied. "But you all seem to be having such a lovely time. Would you rather stay?"

"Oh, please stay," Nelly wheedled, grasping Regina's arm.

"Yes, please do," Eliza joined in. "We have to name the kitten. If," she corrected with a pleading look Bronwyn's way, "we can keep it, that is?"

Bronwyn smiled. "Of course you can keep it."

A general cheer went up. Regina, eyes glowing, looked up at Bronwyn.

"I do think I would like to stay, actually."

"Of course," Bronwyn answered.

The girl grinned at her before she turned back to her sisters. They fell to talking and laughing, the joyful sound following Bronwyn as she moved into the hall, closing the door behind her.

She was glad, so very glad the girls were forming strong relationships with one another. It was the way it should be. It showed they were healing, and would continue to heal.

And she would not think how it made her feel more alone than ever.

* * *

The interior of the Quayside Circulating Library was pleasantly cool as Bronwyn hurried through. It was nearly August, and Synne was at its warmest, drawing people from all across England to summer at its shores. Blessedly, however, it was still early in the day; those on holiday were not yet about, and it was easy to move through the library as she made her way to the blue brocade curtain at the back.

As expected, the rest of the Oddments were already seated within the small office. They called out a greeting as she ducked inside and hung up her reticule.

"Bronwyn, I am so very glad you're here," Adelaide said as Bronwyn extricated herself from Mouse's energetic greeting and settled herself into a chair. She held out a plate with two separate piles of pastries on it. "I am trying to decide which recipe is best for a new flavor of cake to serve at the Beakhead, and so far there are equal votes for each. Which do you prefer, the rose hips or the damson plum?"

"We would have come to a consensus if Katrina could decide," Honoria said as Bronwyn did as she was bid, taking one cake from each pile.

Katrina gave Honoria a wounded look. "I cannot help it; they are both so delicious."

"Yes," Honoria replied with exaggerated patience. "But that does not mean you cannot choose the one you prefer."

"I prefer them both," Katrina declared. "I cannot choose; it wouldn't be fair."

"To what, the cakes?" Honoria laughed. "They haven't any feelings, I assure you. And if they did, they are in your stomach now, and so it doesn't matter."

"Not the cakes," Katrina shot back. "It is not fair to Adelaide. She has worked so hard on them both."

"Oh, I won't be affected in the least, I assure you," Adelaide blithely stated. "It is just business, after all. The better the cake, the more I sell, and the more money I make." She laughed.

Bronwyn, her mouth full of cake, watched the back-and-forth with relief. Perhaps now she could forget her heartache, and the memories she tried so damned hard to forget, and the long, lonely nights she dreaded.

Well, for a short time, at least. Until she returned to Caulnedy and had to remember all over again.

No, she would not allow herself to wallow in her grief, especially not here, in the one place where she was accepted for who she was.

"Katrina is right," she interrupted, determined to

focus on the here and now. "They are both exceptional. But I do believe the damson plum is the one I prefer."

"There, you see?" Honoria said, sending a smirk Katrina's way. "Was that so difficult?"

"The damson plum it is," Adelaide said with a satisfied nod.

They all fell to talking once more, busy chatter that filled the small room with happy sounds. So determined was Bronwyn to take it all in, she did not immediately realize that Seraphina had not said a word.

Frowning, she looked her friend's way. To her surprise, Seraphina was peering at her with a disturbing intensity.

"Is something wrong?" she asked.

Seraphina started and flushed. "What? Oh, no. Sorry. My mind wandered, is all."

Which really wasn't like Seraphina. Bronwyn opened her mouth, intending to ask her if anything was amiss, when Honoria spoke.

"I see Regina has not accompanied you. Is she not joining us today?"

"No, she wished to remain behind with her sisters."

"You should bring them all over to the vicarage," Honoria said with a smile. "I know Coralie would love to see Regina again. Better yet, let us all head to Caulnedy. We can make an evening of it. And if you have not yet sent your work to the Royal Society, you can show us what new illustrations you have created."

Bronwyn started. The Royal Society. Damnation, how had she forgotten the packet she had readied to send off to them?

Before the question had time to take shape in her mind, she knew the answer: she had been so focused on distracting herself after Ash's departure that she had forgotten all about her work.

Well, no more. When she returned, she would send the packet off and immediately begin working again. She had all the time in the world now. A fact that brought a disturbing amount of sorrow.

The next hour was filled with all manner of talk, from S. L. Keys's latest installment in the *Gaia Review and Repository* to Lady Tesh's plans for a folly to the new miniaturist who had opened up a business two shops down. All too soon, however, it was time to leave. Bronwyn said her goodbyes, then quietly made her way out of the circulating library. As she exited the Quayside and stepped out onto Admiralty Row, she had a sudden flash of that day not long ago—had it truly been just five weeks?—when the Juniper boy had knocked her bag from her shoulder, leading to her first meeting with Ash. For a breathless moment she paused on the pavement just outside the door, looking up and down the street, as if she would spy Ash's familiar magnetic presence among the milling people. But no, he was not there. Nor would he be ever again. He had his life in London, and she had hers here. She had best get used to that fact.

Just as she was about to start for her carriage, however, a hand on her arm stopped her. She turned to see Seraphina standing beside her, with that same intent look from before.

"Do you have time to talk?"

Concern flooded Bronwyn. Her friend appeared hesitant, nervous even, so very different from her typical bold certainty. "Seraphina," she murmured, "you haven't been yourself all day. Is something wrong?"

"No...That is, yes...That is..." She gave Bronwyn a helpless look. "I really am no good at this kind of thing."

Bronwyn blinked. "What kind of thing?"

"You know," her friend said impatiently, waving her hand in the air. Phineas fluttered his wings, an agitated reaction to his mistress's frustration. "Relationships. Emotions. *Feelings.*" She made a face.

Still, Bronwyn was at a complete loss. "Whose feelings?"

"Yours. Or, rather, yours and your husband's."

Bronwyn's breath rushed from her lungs. "Ash?"

Seraphina growled low. "Just come upstairs, will you?" she fairly begged. "And do it quick, before I come to my senses and forget the whole thing."

She turned about and stalked inside the Quayside, making her way back to the blue brocade curtain, where there was not only the small office they used for their meetings but also stairs that led to the rooms Seraphina and her sisters shared above the circulating library. Suddenly shaking, though she couldn't comprehend why, Bronwyn followed. Soon they found themselves closed inside the Athwarts' small private upstairs parlor.

"Sit," her friend ordered, though she did not follow suit as Bronwyn perched on the edge of the worn settee. Instead, she walked to an iron perch in the corner, depositing Phineas on it before starting up an agitated pacing across the faded rose-patterned rug.

Alarm shot through Bronwyn. She had never in her life seen her friend in such a state. "Seraphina?"

Her friend held up a hand. "Wait, let me think." She continued her pacing, each step faster than the one before, her skirts snapping about her ankles. Bronwyn, watching it all with a kind of fatalistic dread, felt she would scream from the suspense.

Finally Seraphina stopped, pinching the bridge of her nose and closing her eyes. "I was not sure if I should say anything. After all, it could be nothing. I have been known to misread people." She let loose a harsh laugh. "Which is an understatement if there ever was one."

Before Bronwyn could question her, however, her friend threw her hands wide and strode to the seat next to Bronwyn.

"I really don't know how to broach this particular subject, but you seem so very sad, and I cannot say nothing."

Bronwyn blinked, though this time it was not in shock. No, this time it was to stave off the tears that threatened. "I don't know what you're talking about," she managed. "I am not sad. In fact, I have never been happier."

The look Seraphina gave her was pure incredulousness.

"I may be rubbish at understanding emotion, but I can see quite clearly when one of my nearest and dearest friends has had her heart broken."

Bronwyn really had nothing to say to that. And

even if she did, she doubted she could have given voice to it, for her throat closed up with the most unwelcome tears.

"And the crux of it all is, I do believe the man loves you just as much as you love him."

Rearing back, Bronwyn gaped at her friend. "What are you talking about? Ash does not love me."

Seraphina shook a finger in her face, making Bronwyn fall back even farther until she was nearly supine against the cushions. "I knew you would say that. And I know the reason why as well. You think you cannot be loved for who you are, when nothing could be further from the truth. I love you as you are. And I know the other Oddments do as well."

The tears did come then, tracking down her cheek at her friend's gruff admission. It was something that Katrina or Adelaide or even Honoria would have said with ease. Yet she never expected it from Seraphina, who held her emotions so very close to her chest, who was more often than not abrasive and stern and almost painfully serious.

"Ugh," Seraphina groaned when she spied Bronwyn's face. "Don't cry. I swear, I cannot abide tears." Even so, she sniffled loudly as she fumbled in her bodice and extracted a handkerchief, which she thrust into Bronwyn's hands. "Let's have no more of that now. We are getting off track. The fact of the matter is, I have reason to believe your husband cares for you much more than he ever let on."

"Whatever gave you such an idea in the first place?" Bronwyn mumbled thickly, removing her spectacles so she might dab at her eyes. "It is not as if you have ever been in conversation with the man."

To her surprise, however, Seraphina suddenly looked highly uncomfortable. "Actually—"

Bronwyn frowned. "Yes?"

Her friend heaved a sigh, rolling her eyes. "Fine, I admit I *may* have stopped him on the road to Caulnedy the evening before his departure after I visited with you."

A night she recalled too well. Not only was it the last time she saw Ash, but it was also the same night she had been slapped with the realization that he thought just as everyone else in society did, that a woman's sole value depended on whether she married.

"And I may have told him that I didn't appreciate him breaking your heart. And that he'd better make it right."

"Seraphina." Bronwyn groaned. "You didn't."

"What did you expect me to do?" her friend demanded, even as guilt flushed her cheeks with color. "You were miserable, more miserable than I've ever seen you. He had to be made aware of what he had done."

Bronwyn, however, was beyond mortification. She dropped her face in her hands. "But now he will think I've fallen in love with him."

"But you have!" her friend cried.

Bronwyn looked up at her friend in disbelief. "I don't want *him* knowing that! Can you imagine how much he will pity me? The strange, socially inept woman he took for his wife, a woman he wanted only to mind his wards, falling in love with him? It is horribly pathetic."

"You are not pathetic," her friend said fiercely, taking Bronwyn's hand in hers and giving it a little squeeze. "You are brilliant, and brave, and resilient. Any man would be lucky to have your affections." Her lips twisted. "Not that any man could ever *deserve* them."

"Oh, Seraphina," Bronwyn managed, giving a watery chuckle as she pressed the sodden handkerchief to her eyes once more. "I am so lucky to have you as my friend."

"Of course you are," Seraphina declared, even as she blinked furiously to hold back the tears that shone in her own eyes. "But I digress. The fact of the matter is, the duke looked every bit as miserable as you. And then he said something completely unexpected, something that made me believe his heart was well and truly entangled."

She should not ask. Bronwyn knew that as well as she knew her own face in the mirror. She did not want to hear her friend's ridiculous reasoning as to why she thought Ash might love her. If it gave her any kind of hope, it would crush her.

Even so, she found herself whispering, "What did he say?"

"He said the reason he had to leave was because he was thinking only of you."

Bronwyn's heart sank, the small bit of hope that had managed to come to the surface pulled once more beneath the waters of despair that had been her constant companion for nearly a week. "That means nothing," she rasped. "He was merely referring to our bargain that he leave after a fortnight."

But her friend was not deterred. "No," she said, her frustration palpable. "You're not understanding. Damn, maybe I'm not remembering right. Let me think." She closed her eyes tight, pressing her fingers to her temples.

But Bronwyn had heard enough. "I have to go," she managed, standing and making her way to the door.

"Wait!" Seraphina cried. "I remember now. He said that he was trying for once in his life to not be selfish, that everything he is doing is for you, that if he was thinking only of himself, he would stay with you and make a life with you. He said you deserve so much better than him."

The hope returned, so powerful she stumbled. *It doesn't mean a thing*. They were mere words, said in the heat of the moment. He was just defending himself from Seraphina.

And yet...

"Bronwyn?"

Her friend's voice, hesitant and uncertain, reached her. Dragging in a deep breath, knowing that if she turned around and looked her in the eye she would break down, she said as firmly as she could manage, "You misread the situation, Seraphina. Now, I really must get back to the girls."

Before her friend could respond, she was out the door and down the stairs as fast as she could manage. But no matter how quickly she ran, she could never escape the pain that small spark of hope had brought to life.

Chapter 21

*T*here was one thing, and one thing only, that Bronwyn could comprehend on the drive back to Caulnedy: she had to forget everything Seraphina had said to her about Ash. If she did not, it would destroy her.

Of course, the one thing that had always comforted her when she was in distress had been her research. She would throw herself into her work. There were enough insects on Synne to keep her busy for the remainder of her life. First and foremost, however, she was determined to finally send her paper off to the Royal Society, to have that chapter of her life over and done with, to move forward onto something new that was not remotely connected to Ash in any way.

Which is what she would have done as soon as she arrived home and made her way to the library and the desk where her packet lay—if she had not spied a

carefully folded letter atop the packet. Her name was
scrawled across the front in sharp, angular writing. And
though she had never had cause to see his correspon-
dence before, she knew in a moment who had left it
there for her to find.

Ash.

Hands shaking, she reached for the letter, carefully
breaking the wax seal and unfolding the parchment. The
letter was short, and simple. But it had that small spark
of hope from earlier transforming into a flame.

> *My dearest Bronwyn,*
>
> *I know you have been reluctant to send this paper
> in to the Royal Society. But please do not squander
> your talents. They are much too important to re-
> main hidden. You are gifted, and the world cannot
> fail to appreciate your contributions to science.*
>
> *Yrs,*
> *Ash*

And below, in a hesitant scrawl: *If you have need
of anything at all, please let me know. I am here for
you. Always.*

She stared at the letter for what felt hours, reading
the carefully penned lines over and over until her eyes
blurred and the words jumbled together. She had forgotten how his support of her had made her feel, the
deep sense of acceptance it had given her. He had never

failed to show her, in word and deed, that he believed in her. Even after their fight, even after he had left them, he had still made certain to encourage her and show his belief in her by leaving her this letter.

Once more Seraphina's words came back to her: *I have reason to believe your husband cares for you much more than he ever let on.*

Ah, God, what if he truly did love her as much as she loved him?

In the next moment she was striding out of the room as if she could outrun the optimistic cadence that was singing through her. Even if he somehow did care for her, it didn't matter. If he had wanted to make this marriage real, he would have stayed. And he had not. He had adhered to their original agreement, leaving when the fortnight was over. And he would not be coming back.

So focused was she on beating reason into her head, she did not immediately see where she had wandered to. When she finally did look up, she saw she was in the portrait gallery.

She had not been here since that first day, when Mrs. Wheeler had given her a tour of Caulnedy. Then she had been a new bride, uncertain of her place. Now, married not even three weeks, it nevertheless felt as if it were a lifetime ago, and that she was a completely different person from the one she had been then.

Heaving a sigh, she started down the long room. When she had last been here, she had been too over-whelmed to truly take in the scope of the portraits about her. Now, however, she studied every one, seeing Ash in each of them. This one had his dark hair; that one had his strong jaw; yet another had his build. Finally she reached that one portrait that held the most interest for her: Ash's mother.

She stared morosely at the girl in the painting. A memory surfaced, of the last truly intimate moment she and Ash had shared, that night in her bed after the trip to the beach. He had told her of his mother, and how wonderful she had been, and how he had brought her here to die.

She frowned. But from all accounts, the duke had not died until several years after his wife. Why, then, had a young Ash spirited his mother away from the man to spend her final days here?

And why did all her questions about her husband keep coming back to the tragic passing of his mother?

Bronwyn didn't know how long she had been standing there, staring at that girl, when Regina's voice sounded in her ear, snapping her back to the present.

"There you are, Bronwyn. We had wondered where you had gone off to."

Blinking blearily, Bronwyn glanced about. The shadows had grown longer. It must be nearing time to ready for dinner. Damnation, how long had she been here?

"I'm sorry, Regina," she managed, giving the girl a wan smile. "I must have lost track of the time. Were you searching for me for long?"

"Not long, no. Your parents have arrived and asked to see you. When we couldn't locate you, Mrs. Wheeler and I made it a game with the girls to search for you."

Bronwyn nearly groaned. Her parents? They were the

last people she wished to see in that moment, considering the fragile state of her mind.

"I am sorry for worrying you all," she said. "I'll be there right away. I just need a few moments to prepare myself."

Instead of moving off, however, the girl stayed where she was. But her gaze was no longer on Bronwyn. No, it had snagged on the portrait of Ash's mother. And she looked quite literally as if she had seen a ghost.

"Bronwyn, who is that woman?"

Bronwyn blinked, looking at the portrait of the late duchess. "That is Ash's mother when she was just a girl." She frowned. "Why?"

Regina could not seem to take her eyes from the oil painting. "That is the late duchess? But...I've seen her before," she rasped.

Bronwyn's frown deepened, a tingling starting up at the base of her skull. "What do you mean, you've seen her before? Do you mean because she resembles Ash?"

"No, because I've seen *her* before. The woman herself. Or," she continued, scanning the portrait in frustration, "a woman who looked much like her, though much older. And not nearly as happy or healthy-looking as this girl."

It could be a mistake on Regina's part, a faulty memory. Yet Bronwyn found herself asking, "When did you see her?"

"I was six years old. No," she corrected herself, her gaze going distant with memory, "five. She brought a young woman named Morgan to Gran's cottage. Morgan was heavy with child, and very frightened. She was always crying. And after she birthed Nelly she left, and we never saw her again."

Tension threaded through Bronwyn like veins through marble. "The late duchess brought Nelly's mother to your gran to birth her child? Are you certain?"

"Very certain." Regina tilted her head as she studied Ash's mother. A small smile lifted her lips. "She was kind. Though she appeared unwell, she nevertheless spoke so softly to Eliza and me, and gave us sweets and dolls. I remember thinking she looked like a princess."

As Regina continued to gaze at the portrait, Bronwyn's mind was whirling. She had been told the old nurse was the girls' grandmother. If so, why had the late duchess brought Nelly's mother to that cottage to birth her child? Regina had said that she and her sisters all had different mothers. Was it possible the late duchess had brought them all to her old nurse's home? And why?

As she looked at Regina's profile, however, she suddenly saw something she hadn't before: her strong jaw with that slight cleft in the chin. So similar to Ash's that it took her breath away.

Dear God, was it possible the girl was related to him? Not only related, but perhaps... his sister?

In an instant the truth of the matter became clear, as if she had just swiped her hand across a foggy window and could see the depth and breadth of the landscape beyond. Regina was his half sister. And, quite possibly, Eliza and Nelly were as well. The old duke, a man Ash despised, was their father. And Ash's mother had protected the girls her husband had impregnated, securing a safe place for them to birth their children.

It seemed outrageous, implausible. Yet the more she thought on it, the more she recalled small things that Ash had said or done that gave more credence to the idea until it was so obvious, she was surprised—and ashamed— she hadn't realized the truth before now. The girls were his half sisters. And Ash loved them and wanted the best for them. And, somehow, he thought that included keeping himself as far from them as possible.

He said you deserve so much better than him.

The absolute idiot.

Before she could begin to comprehend what this meant or what she should do about it, however, her parents stormed into the room, Lady Tesh and Katrina— and Freya—following. Mrs. Wheeler trailed anxiously after them all, and Eliza and Nelly pulled up the rear. Like a chaotic parade that absolutely no one looked forward to.

"Bronwyn," her father admonished, striding up to her, his face red, "how could you have kept us waiting so long? Not only have you insulted Lady Tesh, but your mother is also beside herself. You have added onto her anxiety by keeping us waiting an abominably long time. You must apologize at once."

She did not need this right now. Not when everything she thought she had known about Ash and the girls and possibly her future with them all had been tossed up in the air. But if she did not see to calming her parents, there was no telling how much worse this situation would become.

Drawing upon every ounce of patience she possessed, she said in as calm a voice as she could manage,

"I am sorry for keeping you all waiting. Why are you upset, Mother?"

Her mother resembled nothing more than a performer in a dramatic play as she clutched her hands to her bosom and leveled an outraged stare on Bronwyn. "As if you did not know. Your father and I thought you had finally done your duty by us in marrying, and marrying well. Now we learn that not only has Buckley, your new husband, left you behind so he might return to London, but you have no intention of joining him? Oh, Mr. Pickering," she wailed into her handkerchief. "Once more we are made a laughingstock by our ungrateful daughter."

Bronwyn sighed. It had only been a matter of time. But she had hoped—nay, even prayed—that her parents might remain blissfully unaware for months, perhaps years to come, that their daughter's husband had for all intents and purposes abandoned her. It had been an impossibility, of course. But she had not expected them to learn the truth less than a sennight after Ash's departure.

"Well?" her father demanded. "What do you have to say for yourself, young lady?"

"What do you wish me to say?" she asked wearily, painfully aware of their rapt audience.

"That it is not at all true, of course," her mother exclaimed, glaring at Bronwyn from eyes that were curiously devoid of tears despite her wailing. "You shall quiet these rumors, and travel to London to join Buckley."

Bronwyn gaped at them. "You cannot be serious."

"We are," her father growled. "And to make certain

you do not embarrass us, your mother and I shall accompany you. We shall stay with you both in Buckley's London town house, and will assist you in hosting a ball to show all of the *ton* that you and your husband are not estranged. It is no matter that it is not the season; he is a duke, and anyone who is worth their salt will attend. These rumors will be put to rest immediately. We shall not allow gossip to be made about you and your marriage."

At the thought of being forced to drag her parents to London to prove to society that her marriage to Ash was not over, all while throwing herself on the mercy of a man who had never wanted a true marriage with her, something in Bronwyn snapped.

"You mean you do not want anyone talking about *you*, don't you? I know you do not care about the state of my marriage."

Her mother gasped. "Bronwyn!"

But Bronwyn was done placating her parents at the expense of her own happiness. "Tell me you have ever had a true consideration as to what I might want," she demanded. "Up until now, your only hope was that I should marry a title, preferably one of a higher status than that of Lady Brindle, so you might prove that you are not the imposters that she thinks you are. You were so desperate that I do so, you stole all of my research, all of my equipment, then lied and told me you destroyed it so I would focus more on finding a husband. And when *that* failed, you threatened to remove me from my friends and my research and the only place I have ever been happy."

They all gaped at her in silence. She should probably stop, but her hurt and her fury were too great to take heed.

"Is it any wonder," she continued wildly, "that I was willing to marry a stranger, one who wanted nothing more than a marriage of convenience? I jumped at the chance of a loveless union to escape a horrible future. Only now—" Her voice broke, and she tried again, needing to get this out, as if she were lancing an infection. "Only now I am more unhappy than ever. And all you care about, all you ever cared about, is how *you* look to society." A sob ripped free from her chest, and she covered her mouth with her hands.

"Oh, my dear," Katrina rasped mournfully.

The tears in her mother's eyes were real now. Though they were not for her daughter. No, Mrs. Pickering was too wrapped up in herself and her own cares. She gazed at Bronwyn, looking for all the world like a wounded puppy. "Is this what you truly think of us? Do you believe us to be these monsters?"

Four and twenty years of habit had Bronwyn wanting to soothe her mother and give in to what she wanted.

But now that she had finally stood up for herself, she refused to back down.

"I do not believe you are monsters, no," she replied. "You are my parents, and I love you both. However," she continued sternly, "I am a person in my own right, not a puppet for you to use at will. And now that I am a married woman, you have no right to dictate what I do with my life. You need to respect me, and my choices, and trust that I am making the best decisions for me."

She waited with bated breath, not certain how her parents would respond. They simply stared at her for a long moment, equal parts confusion and outrage and hurt on their faces. Finally her mother spoke, her voice forlorn.

"I never understood you. All these years, and you still remain an enigma to me."

"You don't have to understand me, Mama," Bronwyn replied quietly. "You just have to love me and trust me."

Her mother searched her face before, with a tight-lipped nod, she turned and walked out of the room. Her father, with a hurt glance her way, followed his wife. Bronwyn stared after them, sad, yet lighter than she had been in years. She did not know what the future might hold for her and her parents. It would no doubt take them time to get over their hurt, if they ever managed to do so. But she had finally drawn a necessary line in the sand, and she would never regret that.

But in her upset, she had forgotten she was not alone. Until Lady Tesh spoke up.

"I must say, Your Grace," she murmured thoughtfully. "That was an impressive sight indeed."

Bronwyn blanched, realizing in horror that she had just reprimanded her parents in front of the woman they had been trying for years to impress. "I'm sorry you had to witness such a display, my lady," she choked out.

"I'm not," Lady Tesh declared bluntly.

"My lady," Katrina tried, casting a concerned glance at Bronwyn and the girls, "perhaps it would be best if we were to leave—"

"Your Grace," the dowager viscountess said in a

carrying voice, cutting off her companion, "is it true then that this entire thing between you and Buckley was a mere farce?"

Bronwyn felt all the fight leave her at that bold question. Yes, it was beyond the pale to question someone on their marriage in such a way. Yet with Lady Tesh, it was not a surprise. The woman was as ever plainspoken and direct, a fact that Bronwyn had admired more often than not. At least she did not hide behind a false smile and placating words, all the while spitting venom behind a person's back, like so many other members of society did.

And what use was there in denying it? The truth would come out eventually; she may as well do it on her own terms.

"Yes, my lady," she replied, looking the woman in the eyes, showing her she was not cowed or ashamed. "The duke and I had every intention of living apart from day one."

The look in the old woman's eyes could only be called approving. "It is a common condition in many high-society marriages," she replied. She narrowed her eyes in thought. "Though I admit, I am surprised such is the case with you and Buckley. Especially considering how deeply you seem to care for one another."

Bronwyn sucked in her breath. "I assure you," she managed, "you have misread our relationship. I have none of the softer feelings for His Grace." But the declaration sounded false even to her own ears.

"No," Lady Tesh murmured, "I don't think I have. But there are others who are more qualified in making such a statement." Suddenly she turned to the three girls, who were unusually quiet, standing together off to the side and watching the exchange with rapt interest. "What say you, my dears? Have you detected an emotional connection between the duke and duchess?"

Bronwyn fully expected them to take her side in this matter. She and the girls had become close, after all, and she thought for certain they would stand as a united front with her. Instead, to her consternation, they all nodded emphatically.

Nelly bounced on her toes, her eyes bright. "Oh, yes, my lady," she gushed. "They would always look at each other in the most romantic way."

"We most certainly have not," Bronwyn declared, aghast.

"Of course you have," Eliza declared with a customary roll of her eyes. "Though I wouldn't call it romantic. More like nauseating."

"It was not nauseating," Nelly declared hotly, before she was once more in raptures, sighing dreamily and clasping her hands to her narrow chest. "When I grow old, I hope to have just such a marriage."

The dowager, Bronwyn noticed, was looking much too smug. "M-my lady," she stuttered, feeling her face heat, "you must have seen that the girls have active imaginations. They were seeing things that weren't there." She turned to Regina, certain she would find common sense in the girl. "Isn't that right, Regina?"

"Actually," the eldest sister began ruefully.

Bronwyn gaped at her, feeling betrayed. "You, too?"

Regina shrugged in apology. "You were happy with him, Bronwyn. And since he left, you haven't been."

"I have been happy," she grumbled mutinously.

But as she looked about the small circle, it was obvious not one person—not Lady Tesh, or the girls, or Katrina, or Mrs. Wheeler, or even the blasted dog—believed her. Hell, if she had been in their position, she wouldn't have believed her either.

She sighed in defeat, her shoulders slumping. "Fine, you're right. I have not been happy."

Lady Tesh beamed. "There, was that so hard? The only question now is," she mused, eyeing Bronwyn with interest, "what will you do about it?"

It was on the tip of Bronwyn's tongue to tell this woman that there was nothing she *could* do about it. If Ash had wanted to make their marriage a real one, he would have returned for her. But after all she had learned from Seraphina, after discovering Ash's letter regarding her research, after unearthing the incredible information that the girls were very likely his half sisters and he was staying away from them for their benefit, she knew she was just making excuses.

Her gaze wandered to the portrait of his mother once more. Whatever had happened in the past, Ash did not feel he was worthy of being in his sisters' lives. Or in her life. It was up to her to let him know that he was.

Fear and anticipation coursing through her, she turned back to the dowager. "I rather think," she replied slowly, her heart pounding in her chest, "that I'll be setting off for London first thing in the morning. Or, rather," she corrected, looking to the girls, who were gazing back at her in wide-eyed hope, "we all are. Together."

Chapter 22

"**D**ammit, Buckley," Beecher growled from Ash's office door. "You look like hell. When was the last time you got some sleep?"

Ash hadn't slept well since leaving Bronwyn and the girls a week and a half ago. But he sure as hell wasn't going to tell his partner that.

"My bed is unmade," he muttered, not looking up from the ledgers he was carefully poring over. "Proof that I have spent the required time there. You may check yourself, if you must."

Instead of leaving him the hell alone, as Ash's tone invited, however, Beecher entered the room and approached Ash's desk. "A mussed bed does not prove that one has spent their time there sleeping." He gave a rough laugh. "God knows I have rumpled many a sheet *not sleeping*."

Ash merely grunted, hoping the other man would

take the hint that he wished to be left alone. Beecher, however, was either incredibly dense or frustratingly stubborn—or both—for he propped one hip on Ash's desk and folded his massive arms across his chest, proof that he had no intention of leaving. The desk, though sturdy and massive itself, groaned under his weight.

"Are you truly going to brood for the remainder of your days?" The man picked up a letter opener, twirling it expertly among his fingers, the sharp blade flashing in the air. "Because I don't mind telling you that it's become tedious as hell."

Ash glared up at the man. "Is that so?"

"It is."

"And what, do you propose, should I do to rectify the situation?" he asked through tightly clenched teeth.

Beecher gave him a superior look. "Oh, I think you know the answer to that, my friend."

Praying for patience, Ash leaned back in his seat and pinched the bridge of his nose. "If I knew," he managed, "I would not be asking you."

"And they call me stupid," Beecher muttered, heaving a world-weary sigh. "I believe the only thing that will soothe your considerable temper and keep you from working yourself down to nothing is to return to the Isle of Synne and your wards. As well as that wife of yours."

Bronwyn. Pain sliced through him, more potent for the fact that over the past week and a half Ash had done everything in his considerable power *not* to think of her. Something he had failed miserably at, but that was neither here nor there.

"I don't know what the devil you're talking about," he grumbled, hunching back over the piles of books stacked on his desk. "I have already told you that my marriage is one in name only. My wards will remain on Synne with my wife, as was decided before we married, and as the girls wished. Now, as you can see, I've fallen behind in my work and have a considerable amount of catching up to do. Don't let the door hit your arse on the way out."

The man simply remained where he was, fiddling, like a bored child, with anything on Ash's desk he could reach. Ash did his best to ignore him, but his concentration, such as it had been since his return to London, was well and truly lost. No matter how hard he stared at the columns of numbers before him, he could not recall a single figure once his gaze skimmed over it.

Finally, exhausted beyond bearing, he threw down his quill. It clattered across the ledger, leaving a spatter of ink. Ash didn't care. Beecher was right, he had not been sleeping.

He'd tried. God knew he'd tried, forcing himself to rest, laying his head down on his pillow and resolutely closing his eyes, willing himself to drift off into dreamless sleep.

But time and time again it had eluded him. Or, when he finally did manage to fall under Somnus's spell, he was plagued with dreams of Bronwyn, of losing himself in her arms and never letting her go.

Those occasions, when he could no longer fight against the pull of her, were by far the most painful of his already torturous days and nights. He woke from them in a sweat, his body aching for her, his heart crying out for her.

He'd thought, given time and distance, that he would forget about her, that he would finally cease loving her and he could get on with his life, such as it was. Now, however, it seemed he loved her more each day. And he knew, no matter how many years passed, he would continue to love her.

He must have stayed silent too long. Beecher let out an exasperated breath and pushed to standing. For a moment Ash thought the man had finally come to his senses and would leave him alone. But no, he only began striding back and forth across the thick rug.

"You have been back in London for a total of six days," he grumbled as he paced, his thick brows drawn together in frustration. "How do I know it has been six days? Because I have counted them, hoping each day would be the day you came to your senses and realized you were not meant to be alone, that you need those girls and your wife in your life. And each day you seem to grow worse, more determined to wallow in self-pity and despair."

"I cannot return to them, Beecher."

"And why the hell not?" the man demanded. "Because you're a prideful arse and you feel you don't deserve them? I've no doubt that's true. I cannot imagine anyone who would want to deal with you for any length of time, much less three—no, four now that you are married—young women. But that does not mean you cannot aim to deserve whatever happiness you can claim with them."

"Who's to say I was happy?" he rasped.

Beecher's bark of laughter was rough. "The only time a man is this bloody miserable is when he's denied what he wants the most. Though knowing you, you're not being denied it so much as you're denying yourself. You always were a damned masochist when it came to emotions."

Ash threw his hands up in the air. "And what am I supposed to do about Brimstone while I'm hying back to Synne?" he demanded, ignoring the ache in his chest at the thought of doing just that.

"D'you think Brimstone will languish without your moody arse here? Sell your portion for all I care. There are plenty who would love part ownership in the place, you needn't worry on that score."

"I don't know why the hell I put up with you," Ash growled.

"For my delicate manners and sparkling wit, I suppose." Another rough laugh, and finally the man headed for the door. When he reached it, however, he turned back, and his expression was more serious than Ash had ever seen it.

"Just think about returning to them," he murmured. "For your own sake."

Before Ash could think how to respond to that, Beecher was out the door.

For a long moment Ash stared after him, allowing, even welcoming, his outrage to take control of him at his partner's interference. How dare the man deign to speak of what he needed or wanted? How dare he speak of Bronwyn or the girls at all?

But his anger did not last even a minute. He knew that, despite his gruffness and bluster, this was Beecher's way of showing he was worried about him, that he cared for him.

Sighing heavily, he pressed the heels of his hands into his aching eyes. The last week and a half had been hell on earth. When it had just been him and the girls, and they had lived but a short distance away, life had been difficult enough. He'd had clear ideas of his place in their lives, and had known that in keeping his distance from them, he could protect them from the truth of their parentage and the shame of having the blood of such a person flowing through their veins. There was no battle within himself to get close to them. The last thing they needed to be burdened with was to know their true origins.

Once Bronwyn had come into their lives, however, the certainty that he could remain distant and unaffected had been destroyed; slowly and bit by bit, but destroyed all the same. She had touched his heart in ways he had not thought possible. He wanted things he had never allowed himself to want before, though he knew all too well that he did not deserve a single one of them. And though he knew he was a selfish bastard for wanting it, he would give everything he owned to have her arms wrapped about him again.

An impossibility. And the sooner he got that undeniable fact through his thick skull, the better off he would be.

But knowing what he had to believe, and actually believing it, were two very different things. He let loose a low curse. Before Bronwyn, he had never forgotten whose son he was. He had been painfully aware, every second of every day, that he was his father's son, and that if he had not been so damn selfish he might have been able to stop the bastard from destroying so many lives, much less that one person who had meant the world to Ash. And his mother might still be alive.

Without thinking, he yanked open the desk drawer and pulled out that familiar green journal. He had brought it with him to Synne, having felt compelled to keep it near him while he was at Caulnedy; he supposed having his mother's words near him in the place that had meant so much to her had been like having her there with him as well. Upon his return to London, however, it had only reminded him of all he had lost. He had considered relegating the blasted thing to the trunk in the town house where it belonged. There were no curious children running amok there any longer, no sticky fingers to steal it from its hiding place. He could replace it and close everything up once more nice and tight, with an extra lock for good measure.

But he never had. No, he had shut it up in the drawer at his side, as physically close to him as possible without actually keeping it in his breast pocket. He stared down at the tarnished gold lettering embossed on the front. Mayhap Beecher was right. Mayhap he truly was emotionally masochistic. He had been loath to part with this book, which not only reminded him of his mother, but also now of the girls and even Bronwyn. If Eliza had never nicked it from that trunk, if she had never read the stories within, if she and Nelly had not been so enamored of his mother's descriptions of Synne, they never would have run away. He never would have gone after them, or met Bronwyn, or married her. And he certainly never would have learned what it was to become close to those girls...or to fall in love with his own wife.

Sighing, he opened the cover and listlessly flipped through the pages, his mother's familiar delicate, looping words like salt in a wound. Perhaps it would have been better to have burned the thing years ago. It had never given him anything but pain since her death, anyway. And now the pain was so heavy, so deep, he thought he might drown in it.

But he knew that, even if he had the chance to travel back in time and do away with the cursed thing, he never would. There was nothing in heaven or on earth that could make him do away with the one thing that had inadvertently brought Bronwyn into his life.

But enough of torturing himself. It was time to put the thing away and return to his day-to-day drudgery. And tonight, before half of society descended on Brimstone for its nightly bacchanalian revelries, he would bring the blasted thing to the town house and lock it away for good.

Just as he was about to shut the cover, however, something strange caught his eye, an awkward, peculiar writing he didn't recognize. Frowning, he peered closer at it.

And he lost his breath entirely. This writing was childish, and fresh, the entry dated during their time on Synne, Nelly's name written in careful script beneath it.

She must have stolen the journal from his trunks during

his stay at Caulnedy, just as Eliza had stolen it from his trunks at the Mayfair town house. He should be furious, of course. She had altered something that was precious to him, one of the few things he had left that was his mother's, seeing as his father had destroyed nearly everything else in his rage after Ash had spirited her away.

Yet he wasn't remotely angry. Instead, he felt gratitude that he had this memento of her.

Dragging in a shaky breath, he skimmed Nelly's writing. Soon, however, he began to read it closer, for it became quickly obvious to him that this was no mere scrawl, but something with a purpose, a retelling of her time on Synne. It was as if she had picked up where his mother had left off.

No, not where she had left off. Rather each entry began with *Dear Miss Mary*, as if Nelly were writing letters to his mother, each of her passages detailing the adventures she and her sisters and Bronwyn had shared. And to his shock, he had played an important part in each one. It was not until he reached the end of the passage telling of their trip to the beach and the fairy coins, however, that he realized how important.

Ash was wonderful at finding fairy coins. I did not tell him, but I made a wish on each coin we found that he might stay with us, that we were a real family. Maybe, if I wish on enough fairy coins, it might come true.

Ash had not understood until that very moment that one could feel equal parts joy and despair, that one could simultaneously be broken by grief yet buoyed by happiness. *Family*. She wanted them to become a family. Little did she know...

He should put the journal aside. This was too much for him to handle. Yet no matter that his mind knew better, he purposely ignored it, allowing his heart to take the lead for the first time in over a decade. And his heart wanted to continue reading Nelly's entries, though they could quite possibly destroy him.

But there was only one more, and the tone of it was so different he could hardly believe it was written by the same person.

> *Miss Mary, Ash is leaving. Maybe I wished on the fairy stones wrong. I must have done something wrong to make him not want us any longer.*

If Ash looked down to see that Nelly had reached out from the page and taken his heart in her hands and crushed it, he would not have been surprised. She thought he didn't want them and it was her fault he had left?

But the passage was not done, not by far.

> *Eliza pretends she does not care. But I hear her crying at night when she thinks I am asleep. Regina is back to being angry. And Bronwyn is so sad. I wish I knew what I did wrong so they did not hurt anymore.*

He gripped the book so tightly his knuckles turned white. He had thought that by staying away from them, he was protecting them. The dukedom was a cursed thing, after all. The farther the girls were from anything it touched, himself included, the happier they would surely be. And they would forever remain oblivious about who their father truly was and what that man had done to their mothers, never having to know the shame and pain Ash carried around every minute of every day from such knowledge.

But he had been wrong, and in holding himself back he had unintentionally hurt those he cared for in an entirely different manner. Nelly's passages, a young girl's heart poured out on the page to a woman long dead, was proof of that. Worse, she thought it was something she had done, when it could not be further from the truth. Now they were hurting. They had lost so much in their short lives. He could not allow them to lose anything more. Somehow he had to let Nelly and Eliza and Regina know that it was not their fault, that he loved them and wanted them though he did not deserve them. And Bronwyn—

His breath hitched in his chest. Ah, God, he loved her, so damn much. More than anything he wanted to be with her, to make a life with her. If he returned to Synne and saw her, he would never be able to leave again. He would not have the strength.

He stilled, an image taking shape in his head, of spending his life with Bronwyn, of making a home for the girls, one where they would never have to question whether they were worthy of love again. It was so powerful, he could not breathe for wanting it.

Was it really so simple? Could he truly claim a life

with them all, to end this purgatory of an existence? He still had no qualms that he was undeserving of whatever love he might receive from any of them. But maybe, just maybe, Beecher was right and he could aim to deserve it.

Excitement and anticipation thrummed through him as he recalled those halcyon days he had spent on Synne with them all. They could have that every day. The girls never needed to know their origins, and what he truly was to them. No matter how people might talk, he could keep that secret to himself for the remainder of his life. The girls would never need to know their devastating heritage. No, all they needed to know was that they were loved and wanted.

And he could be with Bronwyn.

She might, of course, refuse to accept him back. He had been an unmitigated arse, after all, and had hurt her terribly.

But if there was even the slightest chance she might agree, even the possibility that she might come to love him even a fraction of how deeply he loved her, then wasn't it worth it?

He was across the room before he knew what he was about. Beecher would, of course, gloat. But Ash didn't give a damn. All he cared about was packing his things as quickly as possible so he might start the journey back to Synne. So focused was he on what needed to be done, that when he threw open his office door he nearly bowled over the slight figure standing on the other side.

He stumbled to a stunned halt. "Bronwyn."

Her name escaped his lips like a benediction. He must

be hallucinating. That was the only possible way she could be here. It was some fever-crazed dream brought on by his need to see her again. Or he was asleep. Yes, that was it. He was exhausted, after all. No doubt he was not standing here with her before him but instead was still at his desk, and had somehow nodded off. And so, dragging in a deep breath, he took the sensitive skin of his wrist between his fingers and pinched, hard.

But no matter the pain, she remained, a veritable vision standing before him. And then she spoke.

"Hello, Ash."

Chapter 23

*O*ver the past four days, Bronwyn had kept herself fed on a steady diet of determination and
pure nerve. Throughout the tedious trip to London
with the girls she had not faltered once in her plan:
she would seek Ash out, and immediately tell him that
they all loved him dearly and wanted to be a family
with him.

Now that she was here in front of him, however…

She gazed up at him, her inane words still ringing in
her ears. *Hello, Ash*? That was the first thing she decided
to say to him after all these days apart?

He must have been equally stunned by the idiocy of
such a greeting, for he continued to stare at her as if
he were seeing a ghost. Which could be either positive
or negative, depending on how one felt about the ghost
in question.

She cleared her throat, losing nerve by the second,

painfully aware of the massive gentleman standing behind her, watching their every move. "Er, Mr. Beecher insisted on showing me to your office," she explained lamely.

Finally, Ash seemed to notice his partner. He glanced up, his eyes narrowing. "Beecher?"

Though Bronwyn was not facing the behemoth of a man, she nevertheless heard the grin in his voice when he spoke.

"I vow, Buckley, I did not ever think I was going to have the good luck to meet this saint of a woman who agreed to marry you."

Bronwyn flushed, glancing at him. "I assure you, sir, I am no saint."

A rough bark of laughter escaped Mr. Beecher. "You would have to be to marry this bast—er, fellow. But this is wonderful, Buckley. Now you don't have to go to her; she has come to you."

Bronwyn gasped, her gaze flying back to Ash, pathetic hope surging in her. "You were going to return to us?"

She would not have been surprised if he vehemently denied it. After all, while she was achingly aware of how desperately she loved him, she didn't have a clue what his affections toward her might be, no matter Seraphina's assurance that he felt the same. It was an uncertainty she had tried with all her might to ignore over the past days. If she thought on it too much, panic and doubt would set in and she would never make it to London and Ash.

Instead of denying that he had any plans to return to

Synne, however, he stared at her as if he were a man parched. His eyes roved over her face, skimming her features with a tenderness she had not expected. For the first time since leaving Synne, she truly began to believe they might have a chance together.

"Mr. Beecher," Bronwyn said breathlessly, not taking her eyes from Ash, "would you mind giving my husband and I a bit of privacy?"

"Of course," the man said magnanimously, waiting for her to step inside before closing the door behind her. Just on the other side of the panel his bellowing voice could be heard. "Don't disturb Buckley. He's got his wife in there."

Ash winced. "I'm sorry about that," he managed. "Beecher is not the most fine-mannered person." Suddenly his voice thickened, his expression turning tortured. "But more than that, I'm sorry, more sorry than you can ever know, for what I put you through those last days on Synne. And that last fight especially, making you believe I looked down on you for remaining unmarried for as long as you did."

"It does not signify," Bronwyn replied, the words a mere whisper, even as her heart beat out a healing cadence in her chest, his heartfelt apology like a salve to her soul.

"But it does signify," he insisted fervently. "No matter it was not my intent, you should have never been made to feel unworthy. You, who are braver and stronger than anyone I have ever known. And I would be proud if Regina, or indeed any of the girls, took after you. It matters not what they decide to do with their lives; the only thing that matters to me is that they are happy."

Tears burned her eyes. "Oh, Ash. Don't you know, the one thing that can make them happy is to have you back in their lives?" She swallowed hard, her nerves tying her tongue in knots. Then, taking a deep breath, she forced out the words that needed to be said. "They need their brother in their lives."

Ash's face paled. "What did you say?" he rasped.

His reaction was all the verification she needed that her suspicions were true. She took his hand in hers. "Ash, I know what the girls are to you."

"Do they know?"

"No."

He swayed on his feet, his relief was so great. Alarmed, she took his arm and guided him to a chair. Once he was safely seated, she continued.

"No, they do not know. I wanted you to tell them."

He looked at her as if she had lost her mind. "I'm not going to tell them. They cannot know."

She was not shocked, not in the least. She had come to an eye-opening conclusion in the past days, being confined to a carriage with three lively girls: Ash had kept the truth from them not because he was ashamed that they were related, but rather because he was trying, in some inane, roundabout way, to protect them. She didn't know why. But after what Seraphina had told her, she had no doubt it was true.

She had seen enough of his interactions with the girls to know he cared for them, deeply. They were the most important people in his life, and he would go to any lengths to see they were safe and cared for. Why else would he marry a complete stranger to provide a steady home life for them?

Therefore, it was not a stretch at all to assume he would deny himself the comfort of their love in order to make certain they were protected. The maddening, amazing, wonderful man.

Kneeling down before him, she looked him straight in the eye. "Those girls are stronger than you think they are," she said clearly and distinctly. "And the one thing they want, the one thing they have wanted in the five years since they have been in your care, is to have your love. I guarantee, if they can have that, the comfort of it will be enough to soften the blow of whatever truth you have to share with them."

The look he gave her was miserable. "You cannot know that." He dragged in a shuddering breath. "If you knew the whole history, you would understand."

She took his hand in hers. "So tell me."

For a moment she thought she had gone too far. Whatever wound he was nursing, it was an old one, something he had picked at time and time again, never allowing it to heal. And here she was, someone who had come into his life a mere month and a half ago, expecting him to reveal all to her.

Just when she was about to move away and give him his space, however, he spoke, his voice low and strained.

"To tell you, I have to start at the beginning. Which is not a pleasant story to hear."

In answer she settled on the floor at his feet, leaning

her body against his legs, letting him know she wasn't going anywhere.

He sighed, though whether it was from weariness or relief she couldn't tell. "I've told you my father was a bastard," he started. "But you cannot begin to guess how horrible life was with him. The Dukes of Buckley were known for their cruelties, and my father was no different from the generations of men before him. He was angry and discontent, using his words and his fists to assert his dominance over everyone in his sphere that he deemed beneath him. I, of course, was a common magnet for his rages. My father, while far from perfect himself, demanded perfection from everyone he lorded over. That was especially true for his son." His mouth quirked humorlessly. "It was not a pleasant household to grow up in."

Bronwyn bit her lip to keep from crying. While her father had been ridiculous and demanding, he had never once been physical with her. She could not imagine the damage such a thing could do to a child.

But he was not through. Not by far.

"In my concern for my own well-being, I was blind to the suffering he inflicted on others in our household. And while I reveled in being sent away to school, for all it allowed me to escape his wrath, I never once thought where else my father's rages might be directed."

He stopped, closing his eyes against a memory he could not free himself from, swallowing hard. Bronwyn, her heart in tatters, blinked back her tears and squeezed his hand, a silent show of support for whatever he had to say next.

When he finally continued, his voice was hoarse. "I was not supposed to be sent home early from term. But the other boys never failed to remind me whose son I was, you see, and I felt the need to defend myself. Although I suppose it is a blessing they bullied me so unmercifully, for if they had not, I would never have seen my mother again. As it was, I was too late to save her—"

His voice broke, but he quickly shook himself and continued.

"She had been hiding the truth of his beatings for years. This time, however, was so much more brutal. I will not soil your ears with the full extent of what my father did that caused my mother's death. Suffice to say, she stepped in to protect someone from my father's wrath, and received that wrath on her own fragile head instead. The moment I returned home and saw what my father had done, I spirited her away. If only I had done so sooner, before there had been a need to, she might still be alive."

"Oh, Ash," Bronwyn whispered brokenly.

He dragged in a deep breath and looked in her eyes. "I brought her to Caulnedy, where she had grown up, the place she had loved and told me tales of and where she had been happy. And I think she was happy again, or at least content, for what little time we had there. But the damage my father had done was too great. Mere days after we arrived, she died in my arms."

Unable to speak, Bronwyn brought his hand to her lips and kissed it. So much pain and heartbreak at such a young age. It was no wonder he had wanted to spend as much time out of Caulnedy as possible, for all the painful memories it must have dredged up in him.

"I returned to my father, determined to kill the man who had killed my mother," he continued. "And I nearly did. I beat him, Bronwyn, nearly to death. But as much as I wanted to, I could not end his life. For if I did, I would be no better than he was. Even so, it damaged him, leaving him a mere shell of the man he had been. A more fitting punishment, perhaps, than ending his misery. I broke ties with him, went to London, and met Beecher. We built Brimstone, and I made my fortune, and though my guilt never left me over what my mother had suffered, I believed I had finally succeeded in putting it all behind me. Until my mother's old nurse showed up on my door, and I learned that my father had been even more cruel, even more evil, than I had ever conceived."

He rubbed a hand over his face, as if trying to erase the memories trapped in his head. "It was not just my mother who suffered. Young women who worked in his household were victimized. My mother, who had no power and was more often than not a victim herself, nevertheless did everything she could to prevent such attacks on others. When she failed, she found a safe place for them to birth their children, gave those women new lives. Her old nurse became grandmother to those children. And here that woman was on my doorstep, sick and dying, and begging me to take care of those girls."

He opened his eyes, and the amber depths were bottomless pools of misery. "And so you see why I cannot tell them of the truth of their births. I cannot place that burden on them, of not only knowing what kind of man sired them, but how he brutalized and raped their mothers. I have shouldered the shame and guilt of being the son of such a man, and will not allow them to suffer as I have."

Ah, God, so much heartache he had been saddled with. "But perhaps it will lessen the burden for all of you, if you know you have each other to lean on," she tried gently.

But he was already shaking his head. "I will not be selfish again, Bronwyn," he rasped. "It is my fault, after all, that my father went on unchecked for so many years. If I had been any less selfish I might have saved their mothers from his cruelties."

"Ash," she cried, lurching up on her knees, taking his face in her hands. "You are not to blame for what your father did. He was an evil man and was responsible for his own actions. And you were a mere boy, just trying to survive."

But he was shaking his head. "I should have known, should have been there. Instead, I blinded myself to it to save my own skin. All I cared about was how *I* was affected. I never once considered that others must have been suffering as well."

"And what could you have done?" she demanded.

"I don't know. Something. Anything but what I actually did, which was absolutely nothing."

Ah, God. His guilt was so deep, so fathomless, she did not know how to find him at the bottom of this well.

She stilled. But maybe she was not the one he needed to save him.

"Ash," she said gently, "you have to see, now more than ever, that you need to tell the girls they are your sisters."

He shook his head, shock and hurt saturating his features. "Did you hear nothing of what I said? I cannot burden them with such a horrible history. It is better they wonder for the rest of their days who their parents were than to know what their mothers suffered at my father's hand, and that they share the blood of someone so evil."

"I may be rubbish when it comes to people," she answered softly. "But if there is one thing I know, it is that love and acceptance can heal just about any wound." She paused. "And I know this because that is how it has been for me since you all came into my life."

He sucked in a sharp breath, his hurt replaced with tenderness as he gazed at her. It was on the tip of her tongue to tell him that she loved him. It was what she had come here to do, after all.

But now was not the time. No, now he had to heal the breach between him and his sisters.

She took his hand in hers. "Do you trust me?"

He did not hesitate. "With my life."

Her chest expanded with emotion. Later, she promised herself. She would take the memory of those three words out, and pore over them, and how they made her heart sing.

Now, however, she had more important things to do, such as giving Ash the family that he had purposely denied himself for so long, and all over a wrongly held guilt that he was responsible for the sins of his father.

"They are stronger than you think, and they deserve to know the truth. Secrets won't do anything but widen the divide between you." She rose to her feet, holding her hand out to him. "And they need you." *Nearly as much as you need them.*

She waited for what felt like hours, her breath trapped in her chest, her hand trembling as she held it suspended in the air like a marionette's. Finally, his breath leaving him in a rush, he took her hand and rose.

"Very well," he rasped. "I'll tell them."

"*We* will tell them," she said with a small smile. "Together."

* * *

Ash could not recall a time in his life when he had been more frightened. Not even when his mother had died had he felt such fear as he did standing before the front door of his town house and preparing himself to tell three young girls the devastating truth of their parentage.

He wanted to run, to flee the country if need be. His body fairly shook with it. Just when he thought he would snap from the pressure, Bronwyn tucked her hand in his. The effect of that contact, so simple and yet so powerful, loosened the constricting band about his chest. He dragged in a shaky breath and looked down at her.

She smiled up at him, her turquoise eyes sure and steady behind the lenses of her spectacles.

His heart swelled. She had asked if he trusted her, and he had not been lying when he said he did. But he had not been able to voice the rest of it. The truth of the matter was, he trusted her as he never had anyone in his life before. He had not realized how very much until she asked him. He had been a fool, a damn fool, for wasting so much time when he could have claimed happiness and love with her from the very beginning.

Well, he would not waste a moment longer. Dragging in a deep breath, he opened the door.

"Ash!" Nelly came tearing across the hall, her small body colliding with his, thin arms going about his waist. "You've come."

"I told you Bronwyn would do it," Eliza announced with self-importance, striding forward. When she looked his way, however, there were tears in her eyes, determinedly sniffed back. And then her arms were around him, too, and she pressed her face into his waistcoat, hiding her expression from his view.

But not quickly enough. Ash saw, in that heartbeat of a moment, her features twist in a silent sob. Fighting back tears of his own, he wrapped his arms about them both. Then, glancing around to see if that third beloved face was there, he finally spied her: Regina, in a loose-fitting shirt and breeches, her feet on the last stair tread and her fingers wrapped about the banister.

"Hello, Regina," he said.

She didn't say a word, merely pressed her lips tight and nodded. Then her eyes drifted to Bronwyn, as if to seek reassurance.

Bronwyn smiled comfortingly at her. Drawing in a shaky breath, Regina released the banister and stepped down to the marble tiled floor.

"Bronwyn says you may have something to tell us?"

He swallowed hard, his arms tightening on the two younger girls. He found himself glancing at Bronwyn as well. Her steady gaze gave him strength, and he turned back to his half sister. "I do," he said thickly. "Shall we go to the sitting room?"

They all filed in, Nelly and Eliza keeping close to his side, as if they feared he might disappear in a puff of smoke if he ventured too far from them. But once they were all settled within, he found he could not sit. He stood before them, like a prisoner before a judge and jury, prepared to confess all and see what his punishment might be.

The three girls waited, staring at him with wide eyes, a mix of fear and uncertainty and adoration on their faces. Bronwyn sat off to the side, a small, encouraging smile on her face, though her eyes were tight with strain. When he caught her gaze, she stood and moved to his side.

He immediately grasped her hand, welcoming the comfort she gave him, knowing he could do anything as long as he had her by his side. Then, taking a deep breath, he faced the girls.

"First, I want to tell you all that my leaving was not your fault. Nor was it your fault that your mothers left you, or that Gran was forced to leave you. You are not to blame for any of that. Sometimes things happen that are beyond our control. And sometimes adults make idiotic decisions that affect others in ways they never intended. But what others decide, or are forced to do, is no reflection on you."

He paused, praying his words sank in, before continuing.

"Secondly, I want to say how sorry I am for keeping a specific piece of information from you for so long. Though I had hoped to protect you, that is no excuse for leaving you in the dark. Bronwyn is right; I should have trusted you."

They all looked at him in silence, surprise and confusion and alarm flooding their features. Before he lost the nerve, he blurted, "I am your brother."

Ash braced himself for all kinds of reactions to his hasty words. What he did not expect, however, were the whoops of joy from Nelly and Eliza. And then he was bracing himself for an entirely different reason, for they rushed him, their small bodies crashing into him, nearly knocking him off his feet.

"We have a brother!" Nelly cried.

"Oh, this is fabulous," Eliza exclaimed. "I have always wanted a brother."

Ash frowned. "You don't understand," he tried. "The old duke is your father."

But they didn't seem to hear him. Confused, he found himself once more looking over their heads to Regina. She would understand just what that meant.

And she did. He saw it in her dark eyes, that comprehension of the truth. And the pain and grief there shattered his heart. She rose from her seat, making her way toward him. He tensed; she would take the younger girls away from him now and would insist they have nothing to do with him.

Instead, she did the very last thing he expected her

to do: she reached over her sisters, wrapping her arms about his neck, pressing her wet cheek to his. And then her watery voice sounded in his ear.

"I don't care who my father was," she whispered brokenly. "I am only glad I have you for a brother."

No words could have torn through him with such devastation and hope. It felt as if his heart were a forest quickly ravaged by fire, and then just as quickly doused with a healing rain. Over their heads, he caught a glimpse of Bronwyn's face. Tears poured down her cheeks, even as happiness shone from her brilliant, beautiful turquoise eyes, a perfect mirror of what was in his own soul. He continued to look at her, his own guardian angel, until tears blurred his vision.

* * *

Bronwyn was happy for Ash and the girls. Truly, she was. She wanted nothing more than for them to heal and form a close relationship with one another, to become a true and loving family.

But one thing had dampened her joy: every time one of the girls asked Ash what was in store for the future and if they would all live together as a family, Ash's smile would falter, and his gaze would drift to her before slipping away, and he would quickly change the subject. And Bronwyn was reminded in the most painful way that nothing had truly changed between her and him. There had been no declarations of love, no decision to put their original agreement aside, no vow to turn their marriage of convenience into a marriage in truth. What, she couldn't help but wonder, was her purpose in this family, now that Ash no longer needed her to care for his sisters?

But Bronwyn was not the same person she had been before leaving Synne. Yes, she was as odd and awkward as ever. Now, however, she saw that regardless of that, she deserved happiness, and no one was going to hand it to her on a silver platter; no, she had to reach out and take it for herself. And so, when the girls retired and she and Ash made their way to their rooms, she did not disappear inside her own to wait and hope he joined her, as she had on Synne. It was time to take the proverbial bull by the horns.

Before he could bid her a good night, she took hold of his hand and pushed into his room, dragging him in behind her, shutting and locking the door for good measure.

"I know the past hours must have taken an emotional toll on you," she said, speaking fast lest she lose her nerve. "But there is still more to discuss. And I would appreciate it very much if you would remain silent so I might tell you what I traveled all the way from Synne to London to say."

She saw the questions in his eyes, but he did as she asked, pressing his lips tight, waiting for her to continue.

She nodded, suddenly unaccountably nervous. "Right," she said, clenching her hands in her skirts. Then, taking a fortifying breath, she straightened and looked him in the eye.

"I know you only wanted a marriage of convenience,

and you have no use for it, now that you and your sisters have reconciled. I am once more of no use."

Pain flashed in his eyes, and he opened his mouth to speak. She held up a hand, a warning to remain silent. Blessedly he listened, his jaw closing with a snap, though he didn't look pleased in the least to do so.

"I am no longer of use to you or the girls now that you have each other," she continued, her voice growing stronger. "But I wish very much for our marriage to be a true marriage, and to be part of your family. If you'll have me."

He gaped at her. "If I'll have you?" he rasped.

Once more she held up her hand. "It is not because I don't wish to return to my parents. Though," she admitted ruefully, "I of course don't wish that. But it has no bearing on my wish to remain with you and your sisters. As you may have guessed, I have fallen in love with the girls. They are amazing and brilliant; how could I not? And—"

Here she faltered. Once the words were said, she could not take them back.

But she recalled Seraphina's certainty that he loved her, and the hope she'd tried so valiantly to fight back took root once more. She looked him in the eyes.

"And I love you," she whispered. Then, stronger, "I love you, and I want to be your wife. I want to spend my life with you, and—"

Whatever she had been about to say next—truly she hadn't a clue, for she was just spouting whatever came to her in the heat of the moment by then—was lost as he strode to her and took her in his arms. His mouth crashed down on hers, swallowing her gasp.

The kiss did not last long, however. His head rose, just a fraction, and he gazed down into her eyes. And the tenderness there made her heart sing.

"You think we have no use for you?" he said, his voice hoarse with emotion. "You think you are not of value? Well, listen to me now, my wonderful, incredible wife. To me, you are priceless. To my sisters, you are priceless. You are a part of this family, the glue that holds us all together."

He smiled, and Bronwyn's heart, which was already full with unbelievable happiness, overflowed.

"And I love you," he rasped, his gaze caressing her, as if she were indeed a priceless treasure. "I have loved you for weeks now, and perhaps even before that. You are brilliant, and strong, and giving. And I am so damn lucky that you tumbled into my path that day."

His hand cupped her cheek, his thumb wiping away a trail of wetness. Only then did Bronwyn realize she had begun to cry.

"I know my first proposal was a pathetic thing, and we had agreed this was to be a marriage of convenience. But you deserve so much better, Bronwyn. And so, though I'm sadly lacking a ring, I think a new proposal would be just the thing."

Then, before she could react, he released her and dropped to one knee.

"Bronwyn," he said thickly, his hands grasping hers tightly, "I love you. I want to spend my days making you happy, showing you how cherished you are, helping you

to chase your dreams. And I want to spend my nights
with you in my arms. I want to have a family with you,
create a home with you. More importantly, I want to tell
you, every second of every day, that you are my heart
and soul. You are my life, Bronwyn. Will you be my
wife in truth?"

"Yes," she choked. And then she was in his arms.

She didn't know how they managed to undress, they
fumbled so with clasps and buttons and tapes. Finally,
however, there was nothing more between them. But it
was not just their clothing they had managed to toss
aside. No, with each kiss, each caress, each whispered
word of love, she felt as if she were breaking free from
a constricting chrysalis. And when Ash gazed down at
her as their bodies joined, his beautiful amber eyes free
of the uncertainty and pain that had seemed his constant
companion for as long as she had known him, Bronwyn
felt as if her heart took wing, soaring up into the skies,
with him by her side.

Hours later, as they lay sated in one another's arms,
the barest blush of dawn caressed their tangled bodies.
They had not closed their eyes once during that long
night, and though exhaustion pulled down on Bronwyn,
she was loath to drift into slumber. She did not want
this night to end, wanted to remember every second of
this beginning of their lives together. Even so, a yawn
escaped her lips, betraying her need for rest.

Ash chuckled, drifting his fingers over her bare arm.
"Perhaps it's best if we sleep," he murmured, kissing the
crown of her head.

"I don't need sleep," she declared mutinously, even

as another yawn broke free. "Very well," she muttered as his laugh rumbled under her ear, "perhaps I do. But I don't wish to. I'm aching to tell the girls that we are all to live together as a family. It was the one thing they wanted to know yesterday that you would not tell them."

He hugged her tighter to his side. "I wasn't certain how you felt about me then," he admitted thickly. "And I feared getting their hopes up. No, that's not quite right. I feared getting *our* hopes up, for I wanted it even more than they did." He let loose a heavy sigh. "I did not think I would ever be able to tell them the truth, that I was their brother. I thought for certain they would hate me for what our father did."

Bronwyn rose up on one elbow to gaze down at him. His hair was mussed, the beginnings of a beard shadowing his jaw, dark circles from a lack of sleep cradling his eyes. Yet his amber eyes were free of the haunting pain that had lurked in their depths since she had met him.

"They could never hate you," she murmured. "They loved you all along. You were just so busy protecting them you could not see it."

"I was a fool," he rasped. "Not only did I nearly lose you in my blindness, but I also caused Nelly to believe she was at fault for me keeping my distance."

"A bit of irony, that, for you were doing the very same thing, blaming yourself for the actions of another." She smoothed back a stray lock of hair from his forehead, gazing at him with tenderness. "Would that there had been someone to comfort you and tell you the truth, that you were never to blame for the atrocities your father committed."

He grasped her hand, kissing the palm. "And would that there had been someone to tell you that you are a treasure beyond compare," he said thickly.

Tears burned her eyes, even as she smiled down at him. "How lucky we are to have each other then."

"How lucky, indeed," he murmured as he pulled her down for a kiss.

Epilogue

*B*ronwyn dipped her quill in the ink, scratching out the last bit of her latest work, before placing the quill aside and sitting back with a contented sigh. It was done. Tomorrow she would send it off to her publisher in London. And the moment it was out of her hands she would get to work on her next book.

But for now...

Standing, she stretched her aching muscles and smiled wide. For now, she was eager to seek out a certain duke.

Ash, however, was not in his study. Nor was he in his rooms. Frowning, she headed to the gardens. Perhaps the girls might know where he had gone off to.

She heard them before she saw them. Boisterous laughter and busy chattering rang through the warm summer air, Eliza's strident voice—a tone the girl had learned from Lady Tesh, much to Ash's open lamenting

but secret joy—carrying above it all. Bronwyn rounded
the hedge and spied the sprawling group. Young women
and girls from all walks of life were gathered, as they
did several times a week at Caulnedy, the manor house
having become a sort of haven for all manner of learning.
When the group spied her, a cheerful greeting rose up.

"I'm sorry to disturb your meeting," she said with a
smile. "I was looking for Ash. Do you know where he
has gone off to?"

Regina, who was hunched over a collection of fossils
and in close conversation with several other young
women, looked up. "He said to tell you to meet him
where the azure damselfly lives," she said, her dark eyes
glinting with humor.

"Oh, are you going to the Pools?" Nelly piped up,
her brush poised above the fanciful watercolor she was
working on.

"You cannot go with her, you ninny," Eliza responded,
passing what appeared to be a small plant to the girl
next to her. "They are meeting to be *alone*."

Before Bronwyn could think to respond to that
frightfully loaded comment, the girl turned lively eyes
her way. "Are you done with the newest book then,
Bronwyn?"

Bronwyn's smile widened. "I am, actually."

"How exciting," one of the young women beside
Regina exclaimed, fairly bouncing in her seat. "Could
you tell us about it during our next meeting?"

"Oh yes, please do," another girl added.

Bronwyn, unable to speak for a moment because of
the emotions pouring through her, looked out over the

sea of eager faces as they waited for her answer. She had thought for so very long that she was alone, that no one could ever understand her. Even after she had found the Oddments, that feeling had persisted, making her feel like an outcast, though they had shown her nothing but support.

Until Ash and his sisters had come into her life, making her realize that she did not have to fit into society's mold to be loved. With them behind her every step of the way, she had put her work out into the world. And though it had not all been smooth sailing, though the Royal Society had refused her work and turned her away from membership, all because of her sex, she had not given up. She couldn't have, not with her family behind her, their belief in her work bolstering her on even the hardest of days. And out of the ashes of her first dream, so many more had risen, like brilliant phoenixes. Without that first heartache, she never would have pushed herself to pursue new avenues as, inspired by the nights she spent huddled with Ash's sisters, teaching them about entomology, she had begun writing scientific works specifically for young girls. Now, with her third such work done, and looking at these young women who had found acceptance in part by reading her books, she was filled with a gratitude so potent she thought she might cry.

Instead she smiled widely at them all. "I would love to," she managed.

A cheer went up. Her face hot, she said her farewells before hurrying out of the garden, her heart urging her on as she made her way toward Ash.

It did not take her long to reach the Elven Pools. In the two years since she had first walked here with Ash, she had been countless times, the place not only a favorite of her and her husband, but of the girls as well. Even so, she did not expect the sight that met her eyes when she reached the top of the rise and began the shale-stepped descent to the basin.

A bright blanket had been laid out beside the largest pool, exactly where they had picnicked in the days just after their marriage, a basket brimming with all manner of decadent food beside it, piles of flowers surrounding it all. And in the center of the blanket, sprawled on his back, was Ash. And he was...sleeping?

A bubble of laughter rose in her chest as a soft snore reached her, even as her heart melted at the sight of him. How long had he been waiting for her? The ridiculous, wonderful, amazing man. As quietly as she could, she made her way down the incline to where Ash lay, stepping onto the blanket, lowering herself to his side. And then, with infinite tenderness, she leaned down and kissed him.

She expected him to wake with a start. Instead, he groaned softly, his arms coming about her, dragging her flush to him, as if he had been waiting for just this. The next several minutes—or hours; truly she had lost all track of time—were spent blissfully exploring one another's lips before she raised her head to smile down at him.

"Thank you for the picnic. And the flowers. You must have scoured all of Synne for such a bounty."

"Flowers?" he asked. "What flowers? No, it wasn't

me. Must have been the elves." He grinned up at her. "Have you finished the book?"

The eagerness in his voice had her chuckling. "I have. I shall send it off first thing tomorrow."

He shook his head and cupped her cheek, his amber eyes filled with a wonder that had her heart knocking in her chest. "You are amazing. Did you know that? Absolutely amazing."

Tears burned her eyes as she gazed down at him. "I rather think you're the amazing one," she managed. "You gave up everything you knew, life in London, Brimstone, all for me and the girls."

"I didn't give up anything," he replied tenderly. "Instead I gained everything. And it's all because of you. Besides," he continued with a grin, "I rather think Beecher is more than happy that I'm not under his feet any longer."

Bronwyn gave a watery laugh as she brushed a stray lock of hair from his forehead. "I love you," she rasped.

"And I love you," he murmured, dragging her down for a kiss, not the first those ancient pools had seen from them. And certainly not the last.

Don't miss the next breathtaking novel from Christina Britton, coming Summer 2023

About the Author

Christina Britton developed a passion for writing romance novels shortly after buying her first at the impressionable age of thirteen. Though for several years she put brush instead of pen to paper, she has returned to her first love and is now writing full-time. She spends her days dreaming of corsets and cravats and noblemen with tortured souls.

She lives with her husband and two children in the San Francisco Bay Area.

You can learn more at:
    Website: ChristinaBritton.com
    Twitter @CBrittonAuthor
    Facebook.com/ChristinaBrittonAuthor
    Instagram @ChristinaBrittonAuthor

Get swept off your feet by charming dukes,
sharp-witted ladies, and scandalous balls in
Forever's historical romances!

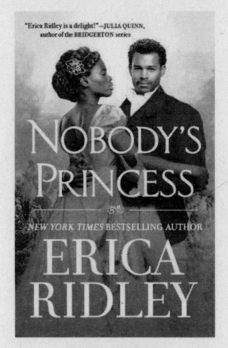

NOBODY'S PRINCESS
by Erica Ridley

When Graham Wynchester deciphers coded messages in the scandal sheets, he's convinced a royal is in need of rescue. But his quarry turns out to be not a princess at all... The captivating Kunigunde de Heusch is on a mission to become the first female royal guardswoman—*without* help from a man, not even a devilishly handsome one. But will she have to choose between achieving her dreams and following her heart?

Follow @ReadForeverPub on Twitter and join the conversation using #ReadForever

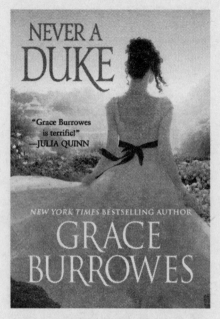

NEVER A DUKE
by Grace Burrowes

Polite society still whispers about Ned Wentworth's questionable past.
Precisely because of Ned's connections in low places, Lady Rosalind Kin-
wood approaches him to help her find a lady's maid who has disappeared.
As the investigation becomes more dangerous, Ned and Rosalind will have
to risk everything—including their hearts—if they are to share the happily
ever after that Mayfair's matchmakers have begrudged them both.

Discover bonus content and more on read-forever.com

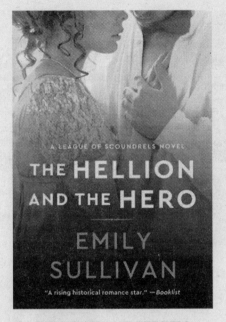

THE HELLION AND THE HERO
by Emily Sullivan

Lady Georgiana Arlington has always put family first—even marrying a man she didn't love to save her father. Now years after her husband's death, a mysterious enemy jeopardizes her livelihood. She must go to the one person she can trust: the man she left heartbroken years ago. Now a decorated naval hero, Captain Henry Harris could have his choice of women. But no other woman has Georgie's allure, nor her tenacity. Will he choose to assist her at the risk of his life and his heart?

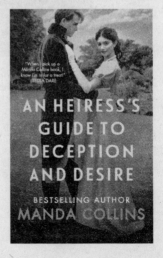